"A turbo-charged thriller by an author who knows his territory intimately. Clark develops a larger-than-life plot by bringing the reader up close to the nitty-gritty details of covert operations...theirs and ours. Satisfaction guaranteed. Don't miss this one!"
  - **Mike Owens**, Author of four novels, including *The Threshold, The End of Free Will, Screwed and Daisy's Choice*

The Slow Dancer Affair

Cover Design by Clarkbooks, LLC

ISBN — 978-0-9600573-0-6

Published by:

Clarkbooks, LLC

Norfolk, VA

THE
SLOW DANCER
AFFAIR
A NOVEL

PATRICK
CLARK

CHAPTER ONE

The few occupants in the darkened nook in the corner of the combat information center spoke in hushed voices so not to interfere with the concentration of the technician on the scope. The chief of the watch wiped a bead of sweat off his forehead with the back of his hand and undid the top button of his sweater as he leaned over the petty officer's shoulder to view the display.

A darkened shape within hazy green bands on the sonar LED position indicator, identified as Russian submarine 222, faded along with the acoustic signal strength. The petty officer who had found and passively tracked the contact removed his headset and tossed it on the keyboard then crossed his arms over his chest. "We've lost her." He looked over his shoulder at Captain Thomas Mansfield. "It's this cold-water, sir. The thermocline is unpredictable."

Captain Mansfield gave an understanding nod then sidestepped around the chief of the watch and left the combat information center. He zipped up his brown leather bomber jacket and stepped outside onto the frigid, starboard side open-air bridge of the USS Samuel Adams, one of the United States Navy's newest guided missile destroyers. They had hunted the Russian contact for forty minutes and in the process, had been drawn dangerously near the Bjørnøyrenna glacier in the southwestern Barents Sea. "Crap," muttered Mansfield. He took off his cap, ran his hand over his bald head and closed his eyes as he inhaled the crisp, cold air. *This Russian captain knows these waters better than I do.*

"Captain?" asked the officer of the deck as he joined Mansfield outside. "There are small ice formations ahead of us. What would you like me to do?"

Mansfield opened his eyes. His gaze wandered toward several small icebergs as the Adams slowly floated past them in the glassy sea. The bergs, with jagged edges and phosphorescent blue colors, were no larger than a compact automobile on the surface. "Slow your speed and maintain bare steerageway," ordered Mansfield.

The tall, lanky, lieutenant nodded and replied, "Roger." He turned and relayed the order to the helmsman.

As the ship slowed, Mansfield watched an aquamarine-colored iceberg with a shape similar to a painter's easel slowly pass down the starboard side. Onboard was a large seal that lay flat on the berg. He barked, seemingly to protest their presence in his domain.

Mansfield scanned the horizon and squinted at the reflection of the bright sun off of the iced surface of the massive glacier ahead of them. "Lieutenant, this place is one of the wonders of the world." He put on a pair of green colored aviator sunglasses then waved his arm to show the expansive area. "Twenty years ago, this entire approach to the glacier was frozen."

The junior officer turned and looked back at the area the ship had traversed. He shivered and closed the button on the top of his heavy blue wool pea-coat then faced Mansfield.

When the ship reached a point approximately five kilometers from the edge of the glacier, Mansfield ordered, "Turn the ship to starboard and steer a course of zero-eight-zero and parallel the glacier. Maybe we can re-establish contact with this submarine."

"Roger, sir," replied the lieutenant.

As the ship turned, Mansfield, with the lieutenant close behind, stepped inside and observed the activity on the bridge. A junior enlisted sailor "drove" the large ship by rotating the go-cart-sized ship's wheel while he monitored the navigation and engineering displays of the integrated information system on the twenty-four-inch retinal display.

Mansfield sat in the captain's chair on the starboard side bridge wing, propped his legs on the railing and lifted a pair of binoculars to his eyes. He surveyed the sea in front and the ice-covered land mass adjacent to and beyond the glacier. *Unspoiled, pristine, so magnificent. It pains me to think that this won't be here for future generations. Instead, there will be oil platforms, filthy oil carriers and dirty little towns to support the oil business.* He scanned the horizon from left to right. *The only question is; will they be American or Russian platforms?*

Mansfield's brief respite was interrupted by a petty officer, first class. "Sir," he said as he stepped halfway out of the pilothouse to the bridge wing and spoke rapidly in an excited voice. "Combat reports two unidentified radar contacts. Aircraft at two-thousand feet and inbound at high speed."

Mansfield stood.

"There!" The officer of the deck pointed as two small dots appeared on the horizon astern of the ship. "Bogies at two-zero-zero relative!"

Mansfield raised his binoculars and looked in the direction of the bogies. "Have they been interrogated for friendly identification?" he asked the petty officer first class.

"They're not pinging, sir."

"Officer of the Deck, sound general quarters," ordered Mansfield.

He focused his binoculars. The two small dots began to take shape. *Definitely military aircraft and in these waters, it's a damn safe bet they will not be ours.* He placed his grey battle helmet on his head and fastened the chinstrap.

The distinctive pulsating general quarters-alarm squawked from speakers throughout the ship. Sailors scurried about and prepared for potential hostile action: watertight doors were slammed closed and secured, the crew donned battle helmets, and additional battle stations were manned.

Mansfield maintained his focus on the incoming aircraft as they rapidly approached. They were both in a gradual descent.

The officer of the deck placed a headset over his ears and established communication with the tactical action officer in the combat information center. "Combat reports the aircraft are inbound at five hundred knots!" he reported.

The two aircraft approached without a sound. "Those look like F-14s," the petty officer, first class, observed. "I didn't think anyone was still flying those."

Mansfield focused his binoculars and noted that the air inlets on the aircraft angled in and the two tailfins angled slightly which, made the jets distinctly identifiable. "No. They're Russian. MiG-29s," he stated. "Is there any indication they are locking radar on us?"

"Negative."

Probably just a harassment run but two can play that game. "Report weapons control status," ordered Mansfield.

Fitted with the most advanced AN-SPY-1 AEGIS Air and Missile Defense Radar, the U.S. destroyer sent out beams of electromagnetic energy in all directions simultaneously and was capable of searching and tracking hundreds of targets, as well as providing missile guidance to an acquired target.

"Aye, sir," the officer of the deck replied. "Weapons control reports targets acquired and tracking."

The two aircraft had descended to an altitude several hundred feet above the surface of the water. They closed to a range where binoculars were no longer needed, so Mansfield set them on the rail next to him. His heart raced, his hands perspired, and his mouth was parched.

"Have they locked on us with their targeting radar?" asked Mansfield.

"Negative. The contacts have not locked on," replied the lieutenant. He cupped his hands over his headset and added in a tremulous voice, "Sonar reports contact re-established with Russian submarine 222. The track indicates that the sub may be maneuvering for a target solution! Sonar recommends readying anti-torpedo decoys!"

"Damn it!" replied the captain. "Prepare to deploy decoys."

With a puff of black smoke from the jet on the right, the two aircraft split up. That bogie climbed in altitude and accelerated. The aircraft on the left descended.

"Prepare to deploy," bellowed the officer of the deck into his headset.

"Right full rudder, all ahead standard," shouted Mansfield. "Begin a rapid zig-zag course."

"What the hell are they doing?" asked the lieutenant as his gaze followed the aircraft.

"Lieutenant, right full rudder, all ahead standard," repeated the captain in a loud voice.

The officer of the deck cupped his hands over his headset. A moment later he raised his shoulders and furrowed his brow. "Combat reports fire control solution is locked in on bogies alpha and bravo! Sir, I think the tactical action officer is confused about what to deploy."

Wha-wha-wha. The vertical missile launch-door alarm blared, followed by a hydraulic moan then a metallic clunk as the door locked in the open position.

Mansfield ran to the front of the bridge-wing and peered over the rail toward the sixty-two launch cells on the forecastle. Two launch doors were open. "Negative!" shouted Mansfield as he turned to face the lieutenant. "Officer of the Deck, missile launch is not authorized!"

"Sir, shall I deploy the decoys?" asked the officer of the deck.

Within seconds, a loud boom confirmed that the first aircraft broke the sound barrier. A vapor cloud surrounded the jet as it flew directly adjacent to the Adams at an altitude of five hundred feet. Moments later the second jet's engines screamed as it passed the Adams no more than fifty feet above the surface of the water and within thirty feet of the ship's pilot house.

Mansfield forcefully placed his hand on the lieutenant's shoulder to get his attention. "Officer of the Deck, did you not hear me? Missile launch is not authorized!" he shouted.

Air pressure generated by the aircraft created a small wave on the water's surface. Mansfield raised his forearm to shield his eyes as sea foam was sucked off of the water's surface.

"Sonar reports Russian sub 222 is lost below the thermocline again," reported the lieutenant.

Orange balls of fire erupted from the second jet's engines as the afterburners fired. The jet went supersonic and rapidly climbed in altitude.

"Lieutenant!" shouted Mansfield.

Whoosh. Whoosh.

Smoke and fire rose up over the Adam's forecastle as two RIM-162 Sea Sparrow anti-aircraft missiles slowly ascended then rapidly went supersonic. Two white contrails pierced the clear blue sky.

"Son of a bitch! What have we done?" moaned Mansfield.

A fireball appeared on the horizon, followed, seconds later, by a sound . . . like thunder. Moments later a second fireball appeared. More thunder.

CHAPTER TWO

The tree-lined boulevard was busy. Well-dressed businessmen carried leather briefcases and strode past young mothers pushing children's strollers at a leisurely pace. Captain First Rank Pyotr Kulakov of the Russian navy was off duty and had dressed out of uniform in khaki slacks and a white, long-sleeved button-down shirt. He strolled along the boulevard, hands in his pockets until he reached his destination, and sat on a shaded park bench across from the Raiffeisen Bank on Novorinsiy Drive in the embassy district of Moscow. The bank was two blocks away from the United States Embassy at a location that would allow him to examine every vehicle that entered the small parking lot in front of the walk-up ATM at the bank.

Kulakov leaned against the back of the wrought iron bench and rested his arm along the top. He smiled at a young mother followed by a boy as he ran to catch up to her as she walked at a faster pace than the boy's short legs were capable of.

The afternoon sun drifted behind the tall buildings of the Lotte Plaza, which brought a welcome shade. Kulakov closed his eyes and drifted into a distant memory of a time, years earlier when he was on holiday at his Sochi villa. *"Papa, Mama, look!"* Six-year-old Nicolay *ran out of the blue water at the waterfront villa and pointed at a pod of dolphins. Oksana Kulakov wore a bright red bikini that revealed her toned, athletic physique. She wrapped her arms around Nicolay, lifted him in the air and twirled until they fell down in the shallow water, laughing. "Pyotr, come join us," pleaded Oksana. "The water is wonderful."*

The loud blare of car horns followed by men shouting startled Kulakov and he opened his eyes. Two men stood next to their dull looking Moskvich sedans, and after exchanging a short verbal volley, they each re-entered their vehicles and drove away.

A warm fall breeze caused an empty plastic water bottle to rumble past him on the concrete sidewalk. *Clack, clack, clack.*

***

Michael Hewlett stirred out from under the bedsheet and moved his legs over the side of the bed. His toes touched the cold linoleum floor.

Behind him, his Russian companion spoke in accented English and asked in a soft voice, "Must you go?"

Hewlett turned around. She lay on her stomach, naked except where the white silk bed-sheet covered her ankles. She raised up and leaned on one elbow. Her long strawberry-blond hair hung below her toned, ivory-colored shoulders and touched her breasts. She was pouting.

Hewlett reached over and stroked the side of her breast with the back of his hand. She fell back first on the bed and moaned softly. She shivered as he leaned closer and gently stroked lower, past her belly button.

He leaned over, kissed her soft lips and inhaled the shower fresh fragrance of her perfume. She placed her hand behind his neck and pulled him closer. He gazed into her striking, oval-shaped, hazel eyes. Reluctantly, he pulled back and said, "Veronika, this is killing me, but I really do have to go. I have a night shift, and I have to get back to the compound and change into more fitting attire."

Hewlett was a twenty-six-year-old foreign service officer on his sixth month of a two-year diplomatic assignment to the United States Embassy in Moscow. "One thing that my colleagues have stressed to me is that showing up late for work is an automatic invite to the *charge de affairs* to explain your whereabouts. I'd have to tell him where I was, and I don't think that he would approve of my relationship with you." He smiled at her then teased, "As beautiful as you are. He still wouldn't understand."

She sat up and put her arms around his neck. Her warm breasts pressed against his chest. "When will you come back?" she asked.

"Tomorrow morning. The same time that I did today." He slipped over the side of the bed and picked his clothes off a chair, pulled on his briefs, a pair of jeans, and a red golf shirt that he tucked in at the waist.

As he dressed, Veronika said, "I know this will be complicated but, I think I am falling in love with you."

Hewlett kissed her again and said, "Let's not worry about that now. Let's just live for the moment."

***

The shade from Moscow's skyscrapers continued to inch past him as the sun descended. "This arrogant Russian President," muttered Kulakov under his breath as he placed his hand on his forehead. *He acts like a Tzar. He and his henchmen, and the bureaucrats of the government have driven me to do this,* he thought. *They are dirty and foul. Bulls and geese!* He clenched a fist. "I must do this," he hissed.

As the afternoon rush hour approached, the vehicle traffic on Novorinsiy Drive increased. Being close to the embassy district, he keyed on the diplomatic license plates on several vehicles that stopped in the small lot of the bank, then departed. The plates were distinct. Red with white letters. The first three digits followed by the letter 'D' indicated the native country of the diplomat. Two digits to indicate the city of the registration followed a three-digit serial number. The three digits 004 were assigned to representatives of the United States. That was what he waited for. Forty minutes into his stakeout, a vehicle with plate number 004D023 47 pulled into the small lot and parked. He sat up straight and focused on the vehicle.

A tall man, brown hair, in his mid-twenties, stepped out of the silver Mercedes Benz A-class four-door sedan. He wore jeans and a red collared shirt tucked in at his narrow waist. He had broad shoulders and moved with the ease of an athlete toward the ATM.

Kulakov stood, crossed the street and walked toward the Mercedes. His head down, he gazed at the dirty white concrete in front of him. In his pocket was a sealed envelope. The note inside read; *I am Captain First Rank Pyotr Kulakov of the naval forces of the Russian Federation. I am Commander of the Baltic Fleet where I am responsible for the development of the Russian Arctic Naval Strategy. I have strategic information. I wish to defect. If this is of interest to you, contact me at this number 8.812.954.07.29 within seventy-two hours. State your name is Stanislov and that you knew my father.*

While the young man withdrew rubles from the ATM, Kulakov ambled past the Mercedes and removed the envelope then placed it in the narrow gap of the closed door. He then picked up the pace and walked toward the young man. They exchanged a friendly nod as the American returned to the vehicle and Kulakov continued toward Novorinsiy Drive. At a street-side bus station, he stopped and turned sideways. He stood and watched the American diplomat from the corner of his eye.

The young man reached the Mercedes and pulled the envelope out of the gap in the car door then stood with it in his hand and scanned the area. The man narrowed his eyes and tapped the envelope on the roof of the car a few times before he opened the door and stepped inside where he was hidden behind tinted glass.

The *pshuss* sound of compressed air brakes caused Kulakov to turn his gaze in the direction of the station. A red and white municipal bus stopped. Two gentlemen in suits and three young ladies with short skirts boarded it while carrying on an animated discussion. Kulakov walked east on Novorinsiy and stopped after fifty steps and looked back toward the diplomat's vehicle. The car door opened and the young man stepped half out of the car with his arm draped over the door and again scanned the area.

Kulakov smirked. *The message has been received.* He continued to walk on Novorinsiy Drive toward his Moscow home, where family and friends had gathered to pay their respect to the grieving parents of a soldier killed in action.

CHAPTER THREE

Journalists knelt in front of the bench, and camera shutters clicked incessantly to document a controversial meeting of the Senate Foreign Relations Committee. Michael Perry, United States Secretary of State, poured a glass of water from a pitcher and set it on the witness table where he was seated. He faced the elevated dais and the large seal of the United States Senate mounted on the wall behind it.

"Mr. Secretary, these are turbulent and dangerous times," declared Senator Mark Sanchez, Chairman of the Committee. "I applaud your blue-ribbon diplomacy with the Russian President. You skillfully avoided a full-scale retaliation which could have sent our two nations down a rabbit hole that might have launched a nuclear war. However, I can't help but wonder; can you explain how a U.S. Navy destroyer can mistakenly shoot down two Russian MIGs over international waters, without any provocation?"

"Senator," replied Perry, "I can only tell you what I have read in the *Post* and you, no doubt, have read this as well. That incident is still under investigation, but preliminary results show that it was caused by an inexperienced commanding officer and a breakdown in communication with key officers during a period when the commander was attempting to deal with several simultaneous, perceived threats. Beyond that, I will ask that you direct your questions about this incident to the Secretary of Defense. I do, however, hope that you recognize the most salient point to take away from *this* hearing is that without an aggressive Arctic strategy, I fear there will be more incidents like this that could bring us to the brink of war."

"This committee awaits your elucidation, sir." Sanchez sat back in his large chair, his thin lips pressed together.

Perry tapped his pen on the table for a moment, then explained, "Senator, the Arctic Ocean covers eight percent of the earth's surface. The data shows that it is warming twice as fast as the rest of the planet. In fact, ice is disappearing so fast that the Navy predicts the entire Arctic may be totally ice-free in summers by 2050, and that ships will be able to traverse between the Atlantic and Pacific Oceans via the Arctic. If we fail to address this now, other nations, particularly Russia, will gain a strategically dominant advantage in military and economic terms."

Sanchez dipped his head and his gaze peered over the top of his black-rimmed eyeglasses toward Perry. "Mr. Secretary, the Chair will acknowledge that ice is melting in the Arctic. Although I am skeptical of the doomsday reports of the rate that the ice is melting."

"Senator, the data is real." Perry set the pen on the table and clasped his hands in front of him. "The prediction is simply an extrapolation of that data."

"Even if I take your data at face value, I still fail to see why—other than the potential for coastal flooding in some areas—why does this administration consider this an evolving threat?" Sanchez turned and looked toward the other committee members on his left and then to his right, smiling smugly, his eyes narrowed to slits.

Perry ran his hand through his full head of grey hair then took a sip of water from the glass tumbler and replaced it on the table in front of him. "Senator, in the papers on your desk, you will see a U.S. Geological Survey. The report predicts that thirteen percent of all undiscovered oil on earth and thirty percent of all the natural gas lies above the Arctic circle. Most of it under the ice."

Perry scanned left and right to ensure that he had the attention of the committee members. "Already other nations are actively strategizing on the future of the high North, which includes tapping into those resources. The Russians, of note, are very aware that there is a treasure of resources beneath the Arctic waters and are actively planning for that contingency. Furthermore, as the ice melts and the Arctic Ocean becomes navigable, this will shorten the sailing distance between Asia and Europe by as much as thirty percent, thereby opening up a new trade route."

He pointed at a map that sat on an easel on the Senate floor. "The Russian President has already stated that he wants the Bering Strait between Alaska and Russia to become the next Suez Canal, and he is considering charging transit fees on cargo ships using the route."

Sanchez leaned back in his chair and crossed his arms. "Why should we be concerned if Russia charges transit fees in shipping?"

"Senator, with all due respect, you're missing the point." He frowned at those on the bench. "The Kremlin wants to put vast swaths of the Arctic region under Russian control, and they are already actively making plans. Just last month they conducted wide-ranging military maneuvers involving thousands of troops, over thirty ships and a hundred aircraft north of the Arctic Circle. They have begun restoring Soviet-era airfields and ports, eyeing control of the trade routes that are opening up as the Arctic Sea ice melts. And now Russian military planes have resumed the Cold War practice of patrolling dangerously close to U.S. airspace and buzzing ships off the Alaskan coast. Not only are these unprofessional and very dangerous maneuvers, as we have already seen, but they also are an indication of Russian intent to dominate that region."

Perry placed both elbows on the table and leaned forward. "Senators," he addressed the entire committee, "Arctic shipping, and the exploration of the natural resources there, will happen. Without our strong participation, it is likely to happen poorly, with negative consequences for American business, the environment, energy access, and security. Leaving Russia alone to shepherd shipping from the Arctic gives them dangerous leverage over global energy supplies. Gentlemen, this is a serious military and economic threat to our future, and it darn well needs to be taken seriously."

CHAPTER FOUR

The speed indicator on the head-up display projected a red beam against the windshield that read one hundred ten miles per hour as Cole Draper drove his silver Porsche GT3 near the end of one of the few straight stretches of track on the Virginia International Raceway. A bright morning sun peaked over the tops of the tree line directly ahead, just enough to cause a small amount of glare through the gold polarized windshield. Fence posts and track signs on both sides of Cole's periphery vision were a blur. Perspiration beaded on his brow and in the palms of his hands as he felt every slight movement of the vehicle.

Slow down now, the road turns sharp to the right, and sharp to the right again. He braked and downshifted, blipping the throttle between gears to speed up the engine and match tire speed so the wheels would not momentarily lock and cause the back end to get loose.

Ninety...eighty...seventy. Track guide recommended speed through the turn should be twenty-five? I'll take it at thirty-five. He focused his gaze toward the apex of the corner. The wide rear tires gripped firm all the way through, so he took the second turn at forty-five. Once he was through that turn, he accelerated quickly to seventy-five miles per hour and into sixth gear. Cole felt the grip of the rear tires increase when the rear spoiler automatically deployed at seventy. *Hard left ahead, then hard right, then hard left again.* He braked and downshifted again using the toe of his right foot to blip the gas and his heel to push the brake while working the clutch with his left foot.

This was Cole's first track run in his new GT3. He enjoyed driving high-performance autos to the edge of their envelope. He loved the adrenaline rush as he pushed the limit of his physical ability.

He eased down the front straight and pulled into the pit lane to finish his five laps right at twenty-four minutes and ten seconds. This was an average of forty-two miles per hour over the four-mile track. Not his best time ever, but since it was the first time he had driven this car on this track, he was satisfied with his time.

He pulled into the pit lane and up to the last in a line of three red fuel pumps to fill up for his next run. As he eased his lean, six-foot-two-inch frame out of the driver's-side door, the smell of fuel and internal combustion exhaust hung heavy in the air. He removed his white Bell sport helmet and black race gloves, placed the gloves inside the helmet and tossed them onto the passenger seat.

A VIR attendant, named Tristyn trotted out to meet him. She was twenty years old and a racing enthusiast. She wore her blond hair in a ponytail that protruded through the back of her red Ferrari ball cap. A white VIR racetrack-emblazoned polo shirt was tucked into her chino shorts that emphasized her long, tan legs.

"That was some pretty awesome driving, Cole!" She walked toward him, her finger tracing the curve of the smooth fender. "I watched you on the monitor. Your turns through eleven and twelve were really tight."

Based on his past experiences at the raceway, Cole expected Tristyn would flirt with him a little, and if he were about twenty years younger, he would gladly have flirted back, hoping it would lead somewhere.

"So how do you like your new ride?" she asked as she ambled over, close enough for him to smell her coconut-scented tanning lotion. Three new model Stingrays loudly accelerated down the main straightaway adjacent to the fuel pumps.

"Nice, very nice," he answered, raising his voice to account for the roar of the Stingrays. He walked toward the front of the car to the fuel cap with Tristyn in close tow. "I have to be honest though." He turned his head back to face her as he opened the fuel cap. "This is a better car than I am a driver."

"Maybe I could ride with you for a couple laps?" she asked coaxingly as she walked toward the back of the car, moving her hips like a runway model. She looked over her shoulder to confirm that he was watching.

Tristyn, I'll bet you are a heartbreaker. He watched her walk and admired her shapely figure.

Cole's ringtone, the theme from the old television series *Outer Limits*, sounded. He reached into his pocket, pulled out the iPhone. The call was from Diana Shelby, his part-time business partner, and full-time love interest. "I have to take this call Tristyn."

Cole had recently resigned from a secret government agency where he had been the lead agent of a joint anti-terrorism task force that included the CIA, Federal Bureau of Investigation, National Security Agency, and the Department of Defense. Cole's team had been responsible for locating and eliminating some of the highest profile terrorists and terrorism sponsors around the world. As an independent contractor, now he worked, from time to time, for various agencies of the government of the United States.

Diana had worked with Cole on the task force while she was a special agent with the National Security Agency. Recently divorced, she had moved from her apartment in Washington to a carriage house apartment in a neighborhood near Cole's home on a small peninsula on the Chesapeake Bay in the City of Norfolk, Virginia.

Diana knows I'm at the track. Why would she call me now? He tapped the face of his iPhone to accept the call and lifted the phone to his ear. "Hey, Sea Gal, what's up?"

"You're so funny," she replied, her voice rich, and silky. "I should never have told you that I was once a Seahawks cheerleader and damnit, give me a break, I only did it for one year!"

"I want to see some pictures."

"*That's* never gonna happen."

"But . . ."

"Never gonna happen," she replied in a sing-song voice

Cole chuckled.

"Are you between runs? Can you talk?" asked Diana.

Cole turned around. Tristyn had started walking back to her office, pouting just a little. "Just finished my first run in the GT3 and I'm lovin it." He gritted his teeth, suspecting that Diana was just making small talk before she dropped the hammer and revealed the real reason for her call, which undoubtedly would have something to do with work.

"Jeez, baby, you are one hell of an adrenaline junkie. If you're not jumping out of airplanes or repelling down steep cliffs, you're out driving sports cars at the speed of heat."

"It keeps me entertained." He turned around and admired Tristyn's backside one more time before she disappeared through the door to the attendant's office. "So, what's so important that it would make you want to interfere with my Speed Racer moment?"

"Your old friend, and former boss from the CIA, Todd Ramburt, stopped at your office a short time ago. He left a message. He'd like to meet with you as soon as possible in Washington. He said it's important. He wants you to call him when you get in town. And he said, bring your running shoes."

CHAPTER FIVE

Sochi, Russia
30th of October

The match was tied at one set each, and set score was five to four in Oksana Kulakov's favor. She studied her opponent as the tall blonde bounced the tennis ball in her pre-serve routine. The score was love-forty. This was Oksana's match point. Her opponent's eyes were focused on the center service line. *She will challenge my backhand.*

Oksana was a former professional tennis player, and though this was just a congenial match between friends, she still hated to lose. Perspiration dripped off of her wrist and formed a small puddle on the concrete surface in front of her. *It is always so damn humid here.*

Tasha Balkonskaya, her opponent and best friend since they were classmates at St. Petersburg State University, tossed the yellow ball high in the air and served it hard toward the center-line. Oksana took two steps to her left and crushed a powerful backhand over the net and out of Tasha's reach.

"Aagghh," growled Tasha. "You knew that I was going to serve to your backhand! Didn't you?"

"Yes, Tasha," Oksana strode toward the net with her hand extended in sportsmanship. She smiled. Her voice was soft and smoky as she continued, "Only a blind girl would have missed your cues."

"One of these days, Ana, I will beat you," vowed Tasha.

Oksana reached across the net and hugged her longtime friend then held her hand as they walked off of the court and took seats on a faded and cracked painted metal bench. Oksana reached into her red sport bag and removed two chilled bottles of mineral water and two damp towels. She handed one of each to Tasha.

"It is so hot today," groused Oksana. "This is so unusual for early fall in Sochi."

This was their last full vacation day in this resort city and former winter Olympic site located on the Russian coast of the Black Sea.

Oksana and Tasha had worked up a good sweat during their match and wiped their faces and necks with the cold towels. Oksana placed her towel on her lap and looked toward the site of the 2014 Winter Olympic village that was not far from where they were seated.

"The Olympic city looks like a ghost town," commented Oksana. "The government wasted billions of rubles, and now every building sits empty and not maintained."

"Yes, but those were a wonderful couple of weeks, weren't they?" Tasha replied.

Oksana was slightly perplexed by Tasha's answer. *Tasha, my good friend, you have always been so naïve about politics. Perhaps that is one of the reasons I am so fond of you. You're so carefree.* She turned towards her friend and placed her hand on Tasha's knee. "I miss you, Tasha," said Oksana. She sighed then continued. "You are my best friend. I wish that we could spend more time together than one short vacation every year."

Tasha remained silent as she reached over and placed her hand over Oksana's.

"Pyotr is gone so often and for such long periods," explained Oksana. "With Nicolay gone." A tear formed and she wiped it away with the back of her hand and turned toward Tasha. "Well, now I have three nice places to live, and without my husband or my son, each one is as lonely as the other." Oksana wiped away another tear, shook her head and said, "Nicolay didn't need to die."

Tasha tightened her grip on Oksana's hand and said, "I'm so sorry about Nicolay. I can't imagine the pain you must feel. He was a wonderful young man. You should be proud of him."

Oksana smiled and nodded.

They both remained still. It was an uncomfortable silence until Oksana broke it. "I'm disgusted, Tasha. I think that the President and the so-called oligarch's have been restoring the age-old and contemptable Russian tradition of excess by those in power and repression of the working class. Pyotr calls him a Tzar."

"Ana, stop. You are too political!" Tasha waged her finger at Oksana. "Honey, since our days in college I've admired your values, but sometimes you sound like you're embarrassed by your good fortune." Tasha zipped up her sports bag and looked away from Oksana. "You have nothing to be ashamed of. The world is full of those who have good fortune and those that do not. I prefer to be among those that have, and so should you."

"Tasha, dear." Oksana leaned forward with her elbows on her knees and anchored her attention on Tasha. "I'm not ashamed of anything. I just wish things could be different. I wish our government would do more for our people. I see it all the time. With all the new oil money, Russia has become a wealthy country again. And even though more goods are available in our markets, they are often still beyond the means of the average person."

Tasha's gaze strayed to something far in the distance, toward the decaying remains of the Olympic village. Oksana turned to see what Tasha was looking at and saw two large dogs scavenging through a dumpster.

She turned her gaze back to Tasha and moved closer, between her and the dumpster, forcing Tasha to maintain eye contact. "Tasha, there is a lot of oil money already coming into Russia. Pyotr is in the North right now, mapping shipping routes for new oil fields in the Arctic." Oksana raised her voice and continued, "I think that Russia will soon get even richer, and I'm afraid that all that new wealth will continue to go to only a small group of politically connected insiders and they will build useless buildings, like that village over there, and start stupid wars where young men like Nicolay die, simply to stroke the Tzar's ego."

"Ana, be careful. Those are powerful men that you are talking about, and I agree they may not always do what is best." Tasha's gaze averted downward. "But there is nothing we can do. Why concern yourself with these matters?"

Tasha's gaze returned to the two dogs.

My dearest Tasha, I wish that I could tell you that Pyotr and I have decided we will leave Russia and defect to America or Britain. You are the only person that I want to tell this to. You are the only friend whose opinion I would value. But, I cannot, and it makes me sad that I will never see you again. Oksana placed her hand on Tasha's knee. "I've upset you, haven't I?"

Tasha slowly turned back toward Oksana. She blinked, and her lips formed a closed lip smile.

Oksana returned the smile and said, "Let's not talk of this anymore." She regarded her long-time friend quietly for a moment. "I could use a martini. How about you?"

CHAPTER SIX

Almost a head taller in height than Ramburt, Cole ran at an easy pace along Turkey Run Loop Road, not far from the CIA Headquarters campus in Langley. The sky was overcast, and a slight mist kept their afternoon workout comfortable. Their pace through the tree-lined path allowed for casual conversation.

"We used to run a lot harder than this back in our glory days," said Cole as he paced his breathing with his steps.

"We had a coach and a dozen trainers then, Cole. And we were a lot younger and fitter," replied Todd Ramburt, Director of the Central Intelligence Agency. A former offensive lineman at the University of Virginia, Ramburt was stocky but very solid. He breathed heavily as he ran.

"Do you ever miss it?" Cole asked.

"The games? Hell yeah." He took a deep breath then continued. "I miss running onto the field on Saturdays with the crowd shouting U-V-A. But I don't miss the practices."

Cole's GPS-enabled fitness watch indicated they had passed mile two when Ramburt turned his head toward Cole and asked, "So, how is it going between you and Diana?"

"I hope you didn't ask me here to talk about that?" replied Cole.

"Humor me, will ya?"

Cole narrowed his eyes. "It's good. We've been having fun."

"Is it serious between you two?"

Cole stopped running. After a few steps, Ramburt stopped and turned to face him.

"What's this about?" asked Cole.

"I just want to know if the two of you are happy together?"

"And maybe it's none of your damn business. I can take care of myself." He placed his hands on his hips.

"C'mon Cole. Don't get defensive. I've known you since you kissed Bonnie Lisbon on the lips in the sixth grade, and I've known every girl or woman you've been with ever since. I like Diana, and I think you would be happy with her."

"Well, thanks for your input. I'll take it under consideration," replied Cole sarcastically.

"Jeez, Cole." Ramburt grimaced and shrugged his shoulders.

"Look, I'm not sure I'm ready to get too committed to anyone. Maybe I'm just not interested in that much responsibility, cuz it didn't work very well the first time."

Ramburt shook his head. "Cole, you fell head over heels and married the wrong person. She wanted you to be there for her all the time, and your job got in the way. That wasn't your fault."

"I wasn't home, so she cheated on me."

"So, you pounded the dude, got sued, lost your clearance and were forced to resign. Guess you showed her, huh?"

Cole raised his voice angrily. "What are you, my life counselor now?" He glared at Ramburt.

After a moment, Ramburt calmly replied, "Okay. That's fair Cole. "It's just — —"

Cole cut him off. "Stay the hell out of my love life."

"Alright. You've made your point. I'm sorry if you thought that I was trying to interfere, but you know that I love you like a brother. Since your divorce, I worry about you." Ramburt placed his hand on Cole's shoulder. "I want you to be happy."

Cole cocked his head and narrowed his eyes. "I know you do, but don't. I'm fine."

Their gazes locked, and they stood silently for a moment.

"Let's walk," said Ramburt as he scanned the area ahead and behind them on the path. After a few steps, he said, "So you're probably wondering about the real reason that I needed to see you."

"Figured you'd get around to that when you were ready, but I sure as hell wasn't expecting that last subject."

"You're probably also wondering why here, and not in my office."

Cole took a few steps back toward him then stopped. "This *is* a little unusual, but I'm listening."

Together they strolled at a comfortable pace. "An opportunity was dropped in our laps, and if we decide to go forward with it, it's going require us to conduct a little espionage against our friends the Russians." Ramburt stopped walking. "The President, in particular, wants to pursue this." Ramburt paused a moment and scratched his neck before he continued. "But we think it's best if we work this outside of official CIA channels."

Cole chuckled. "There are a lot of *but's* in that sentence, brother. You sure about this?"

Ramburt turned toward Cole and touched his elbow. "This is going to take some finesse and creativity to pull this off, Cole. That's why I thought of you."

Cole turned and replied, "I'm honored, and still listening."

As they continued to walk, Ramburt explained. "Six weeks ago, a senior officer in the Russian navy approached a foreign service officer at our embassy in Moscow. He indicated that he wanted to defect. Within a few days, one of our operatives contacted him. The Russian is a captain first rank, the equivalent to a rear admiral. He claimed that he was in charge of developing the Russian naval strategy for the Arctic. Which, if true, it could be a pretty substantial intelligence scoop because the Arctic has suddenly become a hot topic on the hill."

Ramburt glanced out of the corner of his eye towards Cole. "I know. The high North is melting fast, and there's a high-stakes scramble to see who can get the strategic advantage. I read the newspaper."

"Then you are also, no doubt, aware that we're late to the party. The Russians have made the Arctic a priority, and until recently, we haven't. So, naturally when this Russian said he had strategic information we were interested in what he had to say."

"Is he for real?" Cole asked. "It could be a trap."

"Nice to see that you haven't forgot your tradecraft." Ramburt turned around and scanned the path behind them to ensure they were still alone then continued. "We thought about the possibility that he could be a dangle, so we asked him to provide, on good faith, something that would prove that he was, in fact, in possession of valuable information and willing to share. Our operative met with him a week later. He picked up a thumb drive that contained the estimated naval force the Russians plan to position in the Arctic."

Cole stopped and turned to face Ramburt. "Holy shit!"

"Yeah, he was no dangle. I tossed that to the naval analysts. It confirmed the analysis they had already developed. In fact, the information he gave us filled in details that the analysts didn't have. So, our evaluation was that the intelligence was far too valuable to use as a trap."

"So, he's legit and wants to defect, and you obviously want to extract him," Cole replied.

"His name is Kulakov, and he's implied that he has some very specific terms for his defection. Not regarding what he will provide, rather in terms of how he will defect." Ramburt reached behind and rubbed the back of his neck again and scrunched up his face. "He won't meet with anyone from the embassy or any of our covert operatives. Under any circumstances. He said the Russian Federal Security Service, which is now known as the FSB, has become as oppressive as the KGB was at the height of their power."

"I'm familiar with the FSB," Cole replied sardonically.

"Yeah. Anyway, this Kulakov claimed that the FSB watch the movements of our embassy staff around the clock. Our new Russian friend has said he will not take any more chances and that we have been lucky not to have been detected already."

"You want me to meet with him?"

"Actually, I'd like you to do more than that."

"You want me to extricate him?" Cole asked, somewhat surprised.

"Extricate and hide him," replied Ramburt.

Cole chuckled. "Why me? Why not send an agency operative to do the job?"

"Because Kulakov insists that the FSB knows our people and our extraction methods and would interdict any attempt we make. I think the only way we can pull this off is for someone that cannot be easily traced back to the agency to attempt something bold and innovative."

Cole cocked his head and gazed at him.

"That's why I need you on this, Cole. I need you because you won't be recognizable to the FSB as an American operative. I need you because I know that you are clever and imaginative. I need you because you speak Russian."

"I speak many languages, my brother."

"Yeah, I know. I think the term is hyperpolyglot and you're a very rare person. But Cole, above all else, I need you because I know that I can trust you." Ramburt turned toward Cole. "What do you say? Will you at least go to Russia and see what his extraction terms are? I need to know if this is achievable."

Cole furrowed his brow and rubbed his neatly trimmed beard. He stood contemplatively for a moment then nodded and said, "Jeez brother, when you put it like that, I don't have much choice. Sure. I haven't been to Russia in a while. I'll give it a go. But there are a few details that need to be worked out before I can start."

"You already have started. I've had your clearance restored, and you'll be working under NOC, Non-Official Cover. It's important that you stay under the radar because we think there may be a mole in the office."

Cole suppressed a laugh then said, "When were you going to tell me that part?"

"I just did."

Ramburt extended his hand and Cole accepted it. "This could be big deal, Cole. I feel better already knowing that you're on it," said Ramburt. "You can set up ops at the safe house on Crab Creek. All the information we have on Captain Kulakov will be made available to you. Do your homework, and when you're ready, I'll sign the Operations Order."

"You knew I would agree, didn't you?"

Ramburt's smirk was his reply, then he said, "Thanks for stepping in, Cole. I have a feeling this is going to be a long and elegant project."

"Yeah, like a slow dance."

Ramburt snickered then said, "I couldn't have said it any better. Let's use that as the code-name. From now we'll call this Operation Slow Dancer. Never use Captain Kulakov's real name in any communication. Encrypted or not."

"Got it," Cole replied.

They stepped off together to continue their run, and Ramburt said, "Glad to have you on the team again, Cole. There were big holes to fill when you and Diana left the team."

CHAPTER SEVEN

Near Annapolis, Maryland
14th of November

Cole sat on the back porch of the safe house that sat on two acres of wooded property on Crab Creek in Maryland and gazed at the tranquil waters. Across the creek were two large estates. Cole had been informed that one was owned by a prominent politician, and the other by an influential aviation industry lobbyist. Trees lined the shores of the properties along Crab Creek and provided the owners with privacy from voyeurs and paparazzi.

A twelve-foot Chris-craft outboard sat halfway between the two shores. Cole resisted the urge to wave at the two agents dressed in sportsman gear with their lines in the water. He knew that each wore a nine-millimeter Glock handgun under their fishing vest and had access inside the boat to an array of automatic pistols and assault rifles. The boat was part of a rotating fleet that provided a permanent marine security presence for the safe house.

A fifty-foot boat dock with a covered lift was located at the shoreline, and the wet hull of an eighteen-foot Bayliner motorboat glistened in the sunlight as it dangled over the water.

Cole listened to a conversation as two agency technicians, dressed in blue overalls, discussed the weekly maintenance ride they had just finished in the Bayliner.

"That baby is tuned to perfection," said the younger technician as he pulled a rubber band out of his ponytail and his wavy brown hair fell to his shoulders.

"It's all yours, sir," said the older of the two who then smiled and handed the keys to Cole. "I hope you never need to use it fer anythin' but pleasure rides, but if you do, well, there ain't many boats 'round here that gonna catch you."

"Thank you, gentlemen," Cole replied. He stood and took possession of the keys.

"But feel free to take her fer a run anytime ya like," said the older technician. "Them boats need to be run, or the cooling systems gets clogged up."

Cole smiled as the technicians walked away. "I'll see what I can do," he replied.

He finished the cup of coffee and English muffin that he had been working on as he read an intelligence profile on Russian navy Captain First Rank Pyotr Kulakov that had been prepared for him and hand delivered by a Naval intelligence officer earlier.

He placed the cup on the table, gathered up all the pages of the intelligence report and went inside the house to a heavy metal door in the basement where he typed his six-digit passcode into the keyboard next to the door. He aligned his right eye with the light above the keypad to complete the retinal scan and the hydraulic rams unlocked with a clunk. The door slowly opened. He stepped into a fully outfitted, sensitive, compartmented, communication facility, where he could access and privately discuss secrets at the highest level of the United States government.

Cole sat at the classified computer and swiped his common access card which unlocked the computer, then typed in his secure password. At the ring of a bell, the computer came to life, providing Cole with access to top secret information.

This had been Cole's life for the preceding two weeks. Each day he spent eight to ten hours on the secret internet router network researching all of the information the U.S. intelligence services had on Captain Kulakov. He spoke frequently over the encrypted secure terminal equipment with the CIA operative whose cover was a low-level consular officer in the United States Consulate in St. Petersburg. His name was David Keenan, and Cole grilled him like an aggressive attorney would a suspected criminal. He needed to understand everything that was said during his meetings with Slow Dancer, and in what context.

At the end of his two weeks on Crab Creek, Cole had a sense that he knew Kulakov. A photograph and biography showed that he was forty-six years old, had blond hair cut short, blue eyes, was six-foot-one-inch tall and physically fit. He was a fourth-generation naval officer descended from Russian aristocracy, and the son of a respected admiral that died of natural causes at the young age of fifty-five. Married to an attractive retired tennis professional, together they had one son who served in the Russian army.

Cole assessed Kulakov was a consummate professional officer. He had numerous military awards for significant contributions in the reconstitution of the Russian navy after the fall of the Soviet Union. Most impressive though, was The Order of St. George awarded for his contribution to the development of the Russian naval doctrine in 2010, which highlighted the NATO alliance as a significant danger to Russian dominance in Eastern Europe. He was on a fast track for promotion and possibly destined to rise to the rank of commander in chief of the navy.

The profile that Cole developed on Kulakov was that he was a man with above average intelligence, highly ethical, professionally driven, forthright and pragmatic, and … he was a patriot. Cole leaned back in the black leather swivel chair. *So, what has driven him to a place in his mind where he has decided to defect?*

Cole used his smartphone that had been loaded with an NSA developed encryption app called Fishbowl to place a pre-arranged call to agent Keenan. It was answered on the second ring. Within seconds the Fishbowl-enabled phone was securely synchronized with agent Keenan's Omni terminal at the consulate in St. Petersburg.

They spoke for ten minutes. Keenan confirmed there had been no further communication with Slow Dancer and he provided an update on Slow Dancer's known activities.

"I haven't detected anything about his activities or demeanor that would indicate that he has changed his mind," reported Keenen. "But I haven't seen anything to confirm that he still plans to go ahead with it either. This guy is as cool as a block of ice."

"Understood," replied Cole. "This will probably be our last communication until I arrive in Russia, so I want to go over the protocol for contact and dead drops."

"Roger, sir. So, after you check in to the Four Season's Hotel, you will take a walk through the halls of the hotel and pretend that you are admiring the historic artwork they have hanging in the hallways. While you are doing that, you will be watched by one our assets to see if the FSB is monitoring you. On the third floor near the spa is a large painting of a nude woman wrapped in a red shawl. It's a painting by Boris Kustokov titled *Beauty in Red*. There, you will be approached by an elderly man that walks with a limp, and he will be wearing a beret. If the beret is red, you are to walk away. Return to your room and arrange to return to America as soon as you can. If the beret is blue. He will pass you a note. The note will explain the procedure for the first dead drop."

"Good," said Cole. "After that, each dead drop will include a note that describes how to notify each other of the need to meet or another drop."

"Yes, sir."

"Perfect. I think we're ready."

"Roger."

The door behind Cole opened, and Ramburt entered. He sat on a round stool and announced, "I just saw a report on CNN. A Russian destroyer and U.S. destroyer kissed bows during a 'Freedom of the Seas' demonstration in the Baltic. State Department has lodged a formal protest with the United Nations stating that the Russians were acting aggressively, interfering with freedom of navigation in international waters, and demonstrating poor seamanship. The Russian Foreign Minister has accused the American destroyer of operating in Russian territorial waters and has implied that they may enact sanctions against us. Couple this to the shoot down of their aircraft a few weeks ago, I expect the heat might get turned up on this mission."

Cole thanked Keenan for his help then disconnected the call. He spun around in his swivel chair. "That's not exactly good news."

"Took the words right out of my mouth, brother," replied Ramburt. "I know I sorta strong-armed you into doing this and I'd be lying if I said I wasn't concerned."

"You can stop right there. I'm still committed to this. Like you said earlier, it's important."

"And Diana is okay with this?" asked Ramburt.

"She's my partner," replied Cole. "In fact, since you brought it up, I want to bring her in all the way on this op. She's familiar with the way I operate, and she'll see right through me if I try to keep her in the dark on any of this."

"I don't see why not," replied Ramburt with a nod. "She still has her clearance so, bring her up to speed." He handed Cole a brown envelope. "Your arrangements and the details of your first meeting with Slow Dancer are described in the memo in the envelope. Memorize the blueprint then shred it."

Cole opened the envelope and removed the memo and a CIA-provided Canadian passport under the name Cole Madison, with an education visa as a tenured history professor interested in the study of Imperial Russia. Also included was a set of blue-colored contact lenses and a pair of rectangular-shaped wire-rimmed eyeglasses.

Cole perused the passport and mused, "Blue eyes instead of brown, eyeglasses, and it looks like I'll have to shave. I'll be a new man."

"You'll also have to dye your hair to get rid of that streak of grey."

Cole drummed his fingers. "History professor, huh. Wish I had paid more attention in sophomore history class."

"As I recall, all you were paying attention to during that class had long legs and wore short skirts."

"I think her name was Elizabeth," Cole replied with a grin.

Ramburt smirked, then said, "Here's a credit card on a bank account under the name Cole Madison, a fully tenured professor of history." Ramburt handed the small card to Cole. "Make the travel arrangements. I'll leave it up to you to bring Diana in on the operation as you see fit. She can accompany you as far as Toronto to help establish the alibi that the two of you are on holiday together." He stood and placed his hand on the door knob. "Your passport has been coordinated with the Canadian Security Intelligence Service. All the documents are in order at the University of Toronto in case anyone checks out your visa. The operation goes active on the eighteenth." With a nod, Ramburt added, "Good luck."

CHAPTER EIGHT

Toronto, Canada
18th of November

Cole and Diana flew from Norfolk, Virginia, to Pearson International Airport in Toronto, Canada, via John F. Kennedy International in New York. They breezed through customs and security then caught a taxi to the Ritz-Carlton Hotel near the convention center. Their deluxe room on the eighth floor featured a comfortable sofa, two chairs, and a king-size feather bed. Floor to ceiling balcony windows provided a view of the iconic Canadian National Tower with its towering radio spire and the three-hundred and sixty-degree revolving restaurant that sat twelve hundred feet above the ground.

"You realize that as a NOC you won't have a safety net if you get caught, right?" Diana asked as she unpacked her suitcase and placed items in the dresser. "No diplomatic immunity."

"That thought has not escaped me, dear." Cole sat on the sofa and kicked off his loafers. "I plan to be very deliberate. The thought of sitting in a Russian prison charged with espionage does not appeal to me."

Diana slammed a dresser drawer closed and turned toward Cole. "You can still change your mind."

Slightly perplexed, Cole replied, "No. I can't do that. I made a commitment."

"Yeah, well it pisses me off that Ramburt pressured you into doing this."

"Ramburt didn't pressure me. He explained the circumstances and I chose to do this. It's important. Look, baby, he has already given me the option to back out once, and I told him that I wouldn't do that."

Cole stood and walked over to Diana and embraced her from behind. He spoke over her shoulder. "This is important. The Russian President seems to be trying to rebuild the Soviet empire. I'd hate to see that happen."

Diana turned and faced him. "So would I, but do you have to be the one to save the world? You know I'll be worried sick while you're in Russia. Right?"

"Everything will be fine. I promise."

Diana stood with her hands on her hips. "This is probably not the best time to bring this up, but damnit, Cole, you decided to do this without even talking to me. That wasn't fair. It makes me wonder what kind of future we're going to have. Or, even if we going to have a future together?"

"You're right. This is not the best time."

"I love you, Cole. I want to have children . . . with you. I want to be a family"

"You know how I feel, Diana. Why are you acting this way?"

"Because I'm scared. That's why!"

"Don't be."

"Damn you, Cole. You tell me that you love me, but you make decisions that affect both of us without including me."

"Diana — —"

"And if you really love me, as the saying goes why don't you put a ring on it?"

"Diana!" Cole rubbed his hand through his hair then walked to the window where he craned his neck as he gazed up at the tower. After a moment, Cole calmly continued, "Not now, dear. I hope you understand that I have a lot on my mind right now. Let's not fight."

Diana took a deep breath then exhaled. "Well, I have a lot on my mind too, but have it your way. So, not now, but we have to have this conversation about our future soon. Okay?"

"Okay. Soon. I promise." Cole looked at his watch. "We have four hours to kill before I have to leave for the airport. Anything in particular that you want to do?"

Diana walked up behind him, put her arms around him and leaned her head on his back. "I love you. More than I can put into words." She reached down and unsnapped the button and pulled down the zipper on his jeans.

Cole turned to face her. "So, I guess you're not interested in a walk through High Park today. I hear the zoo there is magnificent," he teased before he kissed her. Her lips were soft and moist.

Diana leaned her head sideways against his chest and Cole lowered his gaze. She looked up at him with a grin and a twinkle in her eye. Cole undid the back zipper of her red-and-blue flowered tunic dress and helped her lift it off. While her hands were above her head, Cole gently kissed her shoulders then moved slowly down and kissed her breasts as he eased her backward onto the bed.

Cole undressed as she removed her black thong. He stood at the edge of the bed fully aroused and took in every detail; her tiny navel, the little brown birthmark on her abdomen just below the tan line, her ample breasts and curvy hips. *God, she is the definition of beautiful. Why don't I put a ring on it?*

Diana moved to the edge of the bed and lay back as Cole moved slowly toward her.

***

Two hours later they showered together. Cole shaved and dressed in an expensive Italian suit and shoes, placed the cosmetic contact lenses and non-prescription eyeglasses on his nose and transformed his appearance to match the Canadian passport and visa under the name Cole Madison.

"You look good without a beard," said Diana.

He lifted the room phone from its cradle and called down to the concierge to arrange a taxi to take him to the airport, then he turned to face Diana. She sat on one leg on the edge of the unmade bed. Her blonde hair was pulled back in a ponytail, and she wore a plush, white, Ritz-Carlton bathrobe.

"This will probably take about a week." Cole borrowed a famous line from the classic television series *Mission Impossible*. "Your job, should you decide to accept it, is to stay here and make it look like we're together the whole time. Put out some of my clothes for dry cleaning every other day and order room service for two. In case anybody from back home asks, the answer has to be that Cole Draper is on vacation in Canada with his beautiful lady friend."

"Right," Diana replied. She stood. As she did so, the robe opened part way and exposed a breast.

He stopped tightening his tie and fixed his gaze on her. "Do you know how beautiful you are right now?" he asked.

She stepped closer, hugged him and leaned her head on his chest. "I love you, Cole. Promise me you'll be careful."

Cole wrapped his arms around Diana and hugged her tight. "I love you too, and please don't worry. I'll be fine."

They kissed and held it for a long time before separating.

"I have to go."

Diana nodded and wiped a tear from her cheek with the back of her hand.

CHAPTER NINE

St. Petersburg, Russia
20th of November

The flights from Toronto to Pulkovo International airport in St. Petersburg, Russia, took a little more than thirteen hours. It required Cole to change planes in Frankfurt, Germany, from an Air Canada to a Lufthansa flight. He arrived in St. Petersburg at half-past twelve in the afternoon and followed other departing passengers through the modern and spacious Terminal Two. He located the baggage carousel for his flight in the retrieval hall, under four milky-white sculptures of angels with wings like an airplane, that hung from the ceiling with thin, almost invisible, cables. Cole smirked at the metaphoric illustration as he retrieved his nondescript black roller bag and then moved on to the customs queue designated for foreign nationals.

The line lumbered ahead for forty minutes before he passed through passport control where a woman with short, thick, brown hair, and a green border-service uniform greeted him with a stern look from behind a glass-enclosed booth. Cole handed her his completed migration card that had been provided during the flight, and smiled at her. She perused his passport and visa then stamped his passport and migration card. She removed half of the card and placed it in Cole's passport which she handed back to him, and then filed the other half in a drawer. She then waved him past, having never said a word.

Outside, Cole stepped up to the first of the red-and-black Mercedes Benz taxis lined up at the arrival terminal. The driver rolled down the window and Cole explained in Russian that he wanted to be taken to the Four Seasons Lion Palace Hotel on Admirateyskiy Prospeckt. After haggling over the price for a few minutes, the driver agreed to the sum and Cole stepped inside and buckled his seat-belt.

The hotel was situated in a repurposed nineteenth-century palace, just steps from world-famous landmarks; St. Isaac's Cathedral, the Hermitage Museum, Nevsky Prospeckt and the Mariinsky Theatre. Once the summer home of Prince Aleksey Lobanov-Rostovsky, the Lion Palace had also served for a period of time as the Ministry of War for the Russian Empire. Popular with tourists, the hotel had an international clientele. Two large marble Medici lions that appeared to be a favorite spot for selfie pictures guarded the columned entrance.

Cole registered at the large, red-marble reception desk and was assigned a comfortable room on the third floor. He tipped the porter 600 rubles, the equivalent of ten U.S. dollars, for escorting him there. Then he surveyed the room. A king-size bed with a half canopy was flanked on either side by matching paintings of child nymphs in a forest. Two chairs were placed in front of a faux fireplace, and the large mirror was mounted above the mantle. He opened the door of the small balcony and gazed at the tree-lined park on the Admiralty compound across the street and the Neva River beyond that.

Cole returned inside and unpacked. The porter had placed Cole's suitcase on a luggage rest with a violet-colored fabric top at the end of the king size bed. He placed his clothes in several small dressers situated around the room, which enabled him to casually search the room for hidden cameras or microphones. *All clear as far as I can tell.* He saw himself smirk at that thought in the reflection of the mirror. His attention then changed to his appearance. *Jeez bud, that was a long flight. You need a shave.*

He shaved and showered then dressed in jeans and a white button-down shirt. As previously arranged, he wandered through the halls and admired the authentic sculptures and interior decorations in every hallway and alcove of the hotel. On the third floor near the spa, Cole found the large painting of a nude woman wrapped in a red shawl. Alone in the hallway, he stood in front of the painting and gazed first to his left, then to his right. A short man, elderly and with a pronounced limp, approached Cole. He wore a blue beret. As he walked past without stopping, he handed Cole a sealed envelope.

Cole returned to his room and read the contents of the envelope. *Very specific*, he thought. *This Kulakov is a very cautious man that knows how to operate in the shadow world of espionage.*

He dined by himself at the Percoso, one of the three restaurants in the Four Season's Hotel. After dinner, following the instructions in the sealed envelope, he purchased a red ball cap with a Four Seasons logo, at the hotel gift shop. At dusk, he placed the cap on his head and walked through Admiralty Park, where he stopped near the equestrian statue of Peter the Great named The Bronze Horseman.

He circled the monument several times before a tall man with blond hair cut short, blue eyes and broad shoulders approached and stopped next to him. He appeared to study the monument.

"Peter looks pensive, would you agree?" the man asked in Russian, his voice, a smooth baritone.

Cole replied in the native language with the phrase he had memorized from the memo, "He was a man of many thoughts."

"You are Cole Draper. The American sent by the CIA," said the man.

Cole turned to face him and answered, "Yes."

"Do not face me. We cannot talk here. Meet me in two hours on the bank behind the Winter Palace. Be mindful that you are not followed." The stranger walked away.

Two hours to a location no more than a half mile away. He is very cautious. I'll assume this means he would like for me to take a slow, circuitous walk to root out any potential watchers.

***

Cole took a long, winding surveillance detection walk around town, designed to flush out any FSB agents that might be monitoring him. According to protocol, if he saw the same person in any more than one location, he would then avoid the rendezvous and re-schedule it. He entered a nearby subway, changed tracks at three stations, and exited back at the at the Admiralteyskaya station. A tour group following a man holding a small Swedish flag aloft passed toward their river cruise boat. Cole slipped into the crowd and after a few more turns around St. Isaac's Cathedral, having never seen the same person more than once, he was confident he had not been followed, so he headed to the meeting site near the Winter Palace.

After a few minutes, Kulakov arrived and walked alongside Cole.

"Follow me," he said, without stopping. He walked toward a small pier on the Palace Embankment nearby. "I trust you have not been followed."

"That is correct," Cole answered.

They stepped onto a small finger pier and Kulakov boarded a twenty-nine-foot polished wood motorboat made by Bavaria Boats in Germany. He picked up and cast off the stern line then said, "Get in and take hold of the bowline."

The deck of the motorboat was even with the pier, so Cole stepped onboard and moved forward as Kulakov started the two inboard Volvo Penta engines. Over the low rumble of the idling engines, Kulakov said, "Let go of the bowline."

Cole twisted the line off the cleat and tossed it on the pier as Kulakov backed the boat into the brown water of the Neva River. Cole then joined Kulakov in the open-air wheelhouse as the boat settled in at slow speed behind a grain barge traveling southwest. Cole gazed to his left as the boat slowly passed the well-lit yellow brick Admiralty building with its distinctive rows of white columns, numerous relief detail statues, and its gilded spire.

"St. Petersburg is beautiful at night, is it not?" said Kulakov switching to English with an oddly British accent.

Cole stood next to him. At equal height, they stood shoulder to shoulder. Cole turned sideways to face him. "Yes, it is. St. Petersburg is my favorite Russian city," Cole replied.

"Have you been to many Russian cities?"

"More than I am at liberty to say," Cole replied.

Kulakov turned his gaze to the river traffic ahead. "No doubt." After a few moments' he turned his gaze back toward Cole. "You will take my wife out first. She speaks very little English and will require tutoring."

Cole turned around and leaned his backside on the boat's control console. "Whoa. Slow down, comrade. I haven't agreed to take anybody out of your fatherland yet. If I decide to do this and something goes wrong, my ass could grow old in a Russian prison, and I'm not yet sure I want to risk that. So, you'll humor me by answering a few questions, right?"

"You Americans do love your colorful language."

"Yeah. But a few questions, if you don't mind?"

Kulakov remained facing forward as he monitored the traffic ahead.

Cole began, "I have done a lot of research on you, Captain."

He glanced sideways, and Cole met his gaze.

"You have checked all the right boxes. Your service record is distinguished. Everything I have read leads me to believe you are a Russian patriot. Your family has a military tradition that goes all the way back to imperial days, and you could be Admiral of the navy in a few years. So, before I agree to anything, I need to know why you're willing to throw all that away, and I need to be confident that you're all in and will not change your mind."

The muscles in Kulakov's jaw were taut. He drummed his fingers on the thick rubber helm for several moments then spoke with indignation and fury. "My great-grandfather was a very wealthy Count and, it is said, he was a compassionate landowner. His brother was a respected Admiral of the Imperial Navy. They and most of their immediate families were murdered by the Bolsheviks during the October Revolution. My grandfather was a small boy, so he was spared. He survived with very little and did what was necessary under very tough conditions. He was smart, and he was educated as a market socialist. So, as an adult, he rose through the communist ranks and became a district secretary. He married the daughter of a fisherman and had one son. They lived on an ungenerous salary and retired with an insufficient pension. But, with my grandfather's influence as a district secretariat, my father was able to secure an appointment to the Naval Academy, and he rose through the ranks. He was a respected admiral, and because of that, some of my families' properties were returned. I was proud to follow in his footsteps. My family status has been restored." He turned his head toward Cole and they made eye contact. "Mr. Draper, three months ago, my only son was killed by a sniper in the small Ukrainian town of Mykolaiv." There was anger in his glare.

"I'm sorry," Cole replied.

"The little Tzar lied to the world about Russia's involvement in the Ukraine. He lied to the people of Russia." He took a deep breath. "And he lied to *me*."

Kulakov slowed the boat to bare steerageway and stepped away from the wheel. He stood face to face with Cole. "Yes. Mr. Draper, I am angry about my son, and I am angry at our leaders. I do not trust them."

"I can understand," replied Cole.

"No, sir. You cannot understand. He and his circle of friends are dangerous. They are no better than common criminals. They have used the power of the state only to enrich themselves. The revolution came about because of the excesses of the Romanov Tzar and his nobility. This President and his cohorts are guilty of the same crimes against the people that resulted in the murder of my ancestors—and now the death of my only son."

Kulakov pounded his fist on the steering wheel. "There are tremendous resources in the Arctic, and I am afraid that the new strategic plan that we have developed for the Arctic could shift the balance of global power in favor of Russia and, more important, to the little Tzar." He clenched his fists. "I am afraid that in the long run, he will only continue to further enrich himself and those around him and actions, like the annexation of part of the Ukraine, seem to indicate that he has visions of restoring the Soviet empire, all under his supremacy. I cannot be a part of that. It will not be good for Russia. It will not be good for the rest of the world." He paused for a moment, then continued, "Mr. Draper, there are many reasons that I have become disillusioned, and they all start with the man that is President of Russia." Kulakov paused. "I am, as you say, all in."

He stepped sideways and stood behind the helm again. "Have I adequately answered your questions, Mr. Draper?"

Okay, Captain. You're convincing. I'll play along, but any inconsistency in your story—any sense that you're not being honest with me—I'm outta here. Cole nodded. "You've answered them."

"Good. Then about my wife. You will take her out first."

***

Kulakov clearly communicated what his terms were. He and his wife Oksana were to be extricated separately. She had to be taken out first, and when he was satisfied that the FSB was not searching for her, he would follow. "We want to disappear and never have to look behind in fear of being discovered," he demanded.

"It will be better if we extricate you and your wife together," Cole said.

"No. My wife must be safe. When I have confirmation of this, I will follow. I must know that she is safe before I will do that. These are my terms," Kulakov stated.

"I don't like it, and I don't understand it. Do the math, two trips are more difficult than one. Why are you so committed to this?" Cole asked.

Kulakov quietly maintained his gaze ahead on the river for a moment, then asked, "Are you married?"

"I was, but it didn't work."

"So, you are divorced."

"Yes, I am divorced."

"I am sorry."

"I'm sorry too but, I don't see what that has to do with my question."

"I think that everyone should have a special partner to share their life with."

"Look," Cole moved alongside Kukakov and forced eye contact between them. "If you're not going to answer my question, I can pack up my shit and leave today!"

"Mr. Draper," replied Kulakov in a calm voice, "I am answering your question."

Cole narrowed his eyes, and cocked his head.

"I love my wife. More than anything else." Kulakov turned sideways, and they stood toe to toe. "She has been treated badly by our government. Her brother died in a Lubyanka prison cell. Her promising career as a tennis professional was cut short because of concerns that she was becoming too 'westernized' and now our only son has been killed in an unnecessary aggression. A mother should not outlive her son." Kulakov puffed his lips and exhaled. "Oksana deserves to be happy, and I do not believe she will ever have that chance in Russia. She must be provided an opportunity to live the rest of her life the way she chooses."

"Okay, but I still don't see why — —"

Kulakov interrupted, "Because I am a high-ranking officer. My movements and actions are, quite naturally, monitored by our security forces and government news agencies just like your high officials are monitored by your FBI and news organizations. My wife is not subjected to that level of visibility. Simply put, Mr. Draper, the probability of successfully getting Oksana to America is higher if you take her alone. When I am certain that she is safely beyond the reach of the FSB, I will follow. With your help, I hope, or without, if necessary. In return for this, I will provide your CIA with electronic copies of the Russian Arctic strategy documents, including volumes of technical data such as locations that were chosen for navy development and the detailed topographical mapping of the ocean floor that is critical to the successful covert operation of submarines. Additionally, I will provide Arctic region hydrocarbon geological surveys that located oil and gas deposits, and I will provide blueprints and plans for the Arctic-class ice-resistant oil rig which will have the ability to function in freezing temperatures, which has never been done before. These are my terms."

Cole gazed at the river water for a few moments, then nodded. "I will relay your terms to my government."

"Good. I will look forward to their reply." Kulakov turned to face forward in the pilot station and eased the throttle up. "We should return to the embankment now."

Cole sat on the bench a few feet behind him.

"Mr. Draper."

Cole raised his gaze. Kulakov stood with his back to him as he piloted the boat.

"Will you ever marry again?" asked Kulkov.

CHAPTER TEN

St. Petersburg, Russia
21st of November

Cole woke early and took a morning run along the Neva River embankment, past Quai Robespierre to the ornately decorated, blue and white Smolny Cathedral. On his return run along the sparsely populated embankment, he used a lipstick applicator and marked a red X on the transparent glass bus stop enclosure on the south end of the Liteyniy Bridge. This would begin execution of the dead drop protocol. *Keenan from the consulate will see this on his morning walk and know to pick up a dead drop.*

After breakfast, Cole drafted a coded message that detailed all of the demands that had been made by Slow Dancer and asked for guidance from Ramburt. He placed the message in a discreet yellow envelope that he slipped into his rear pocket and checked his watch to ensure that he allowed sufficient time to walk to the pre-arranged dead drop location at the Russian National Library.

Cole left the hotel through the ornate lobby, and as he did so, he made a professorial show of his admiration of the polished marble inlaid floor and four marble columns set upon gold trimmed bases that rose to the painted ceiling mural. He stopped and spoke with the concierge and asked directions to the Russian National Library and expressed an interest in the collection of books and papers by the French philosopher and historian, Voltaire.

The concierge explained that the library that was founded in 1795 by Catherine the Great was a short two kilometers walk from the Four Seasons Hotel. "The National is the country's oldest publicly funded library, and it contains the most extensive personal book collection of Voltaire in the world," the concierge proudly proclaimed.

A cold front had come through while Cole was in his room. A chilly morning mist hung in the air, so he wore a light rain jacket and carried an umbrella as he strolled to the library. It took just over twenty minutes. When he arrived, he slowly walked along the outer wall of the large stone building, painted light blue with white stone trim. He gazed at the long wall of twenty tall columns that supported the roof. Next to each column stood a marble statue of some of histories' most famous philosophers. Voltaire, of course. Next to him, Homer, and Virgil and the Roman goddess of wisdom, Minerva, among others. He stopped in front of the main entrance and looked to his right, then to his left. *The architecture of this building, in fact, all of St. Petersburg, is impressive,* he mused.

Cole entered through an unpretentious redwood main door and stepped into the expansive grey marble hallway. He closed his umbrella and set it in a brass cylinder next to the door where other umbrellas had been placed, then followed discreet placards posted on the walls that guided him up a wide, white, marble staircase, to the location of the Voltaire collection on the second floor. The climate-controlled room had a large pink-colored marble column in the middle that rose to the ceiling. An ornate mural was painted on the ceiling that gave the illusion of four separate colorful arched domes. Along the walls were antique wooden bookshelves filled with the Voltaire collection.

A guard stood watch at the entrance. She was in her late-twenties with dark hair, and wore a grey uniform that looked to be tailored to emphasize her thin waist.

He perused the collection for about thirty minutes as the guard paced the room. Cole politely nodded as she passed him several times and she responded with a slight smile. He found the volume labeled Louis XIV exactly where the drop memo indicated it would be, on the shelf behind a life-size bronze statue of Voltaire. When the guard paced with her back to him, Cole pulled the envelope from his pocket and placed it inside the volume and returned the volume to the bookshelf.

As Cole left the Voltaire room, he stopped, and in Voltaire's native French language, he thanked the guard for her vigilant watch over the collection. "This collection is marvelous. Just marvelous."

The guard half smiled and nodded as he walked past her.

***

Cole exited the library after sixty minutes. The mist had cleared, and the sun was peeking through the clouds. He walked across the street to the small park at Catherine Square to await confirmation that the dead drop had been picked up. In the middle of the park stood a large marble monument of Catherine the Great. He read the plaque located at the base. *Dressed in her official gown. She holds a scepter in her right hand to signify the power of her sovereignty and an olive wreath of peace in her left hand.*

Ironic, thought Cole, given that he was conducting espionage against an enemy in a resurgent cold war. He sat on a park bench that faced the front of the monument and waited for the signal from a classified courier that would confirm that the envelope had been retrieved.

Just under an hour later, a man with wavy brown hair and the physical size of a jockey, stepped up to the front of the monument and removed his coat then draped it over his left arm. Cole started to count, and at the count of one hundred and thirty, the man put on his coat and walked away.

So, you must be Consular Officer David Keenan, Cole mused. He stood and walked casually, with his hands in his pockets, and returned to the Four Seasons Hotel.

CHAPTER ELEVEN

Washington, District of Columbia
22nd of November

Ramburt sat at the head of the ten-foot-long, boat-shaped, cherry-wood conference table in his office at Foggy Bottom. The room temperature was warmer than usual, so he loosened his blue tie and undid the top button on his white shirt. Two carafes were delivered by cafeteria staff and the smell of freshly brewed coffee hung in the air.

He held the decoded message that had been received from the St. Petersburg consulate in his right hand, his reading glasses in his left, as he addressed the Slow Dancer joint operation stakeholders. "You've all read the message from Draper." He faced his chief of staff who was seated to his left and asked, "How has operations assessed the risk?"

"High," replied the chief in a raspy life-long smoker's voice. "The coordination required to extricate one high-level customer is extensive, and the need for secrecy is paramount. Our analysis, based on Slow Dancer's status as a high-interest strategic asset is that there is a high probability that the FSB will monitor his movements closely. Thus, the potential for any casual slip of the tongue, or ill-advised action may alert Russian authorities that he is preparing to defect. If that happens, then our agent on the inside would be very vulnerable."

Ramburt leaned back in his chair and placed his hands behind his head.

"Our analysts advised me that risk goes up exponentially if we attempt to extricate Slow Dancer and his wife separately," the chief of staff continued. "In fact, the analysis was rated very high risk."

"I'm not exactly getting a warm, fuzzy feeling from you," replied Ramburt.

"Is there any way we can convince Slow Dancer to let us take him and his wife out together?" asked the chief of staff.

"You've read it. According to Draper's message, our customer was pretty clear that was not an option," Ramburt replied.

"Assuming that we are able to extricate Slow Dancer and his wife, what then?" asked the chief of staff. "The operations analysts that I ran this by all questioned whether we would be able to keep them hidden from Russian assassins. The newspapers have reported extensively on the Russian Presidents' ability to have someone surreptitiously slip poison in his dissident's drinks anywhere in the world. Our files have detailed many more incidents than what has been reported in the news."

"One step at a time," Ramburt replied. "Besides, if there is one thing that Draper excels at is creativity. They'll both be given defector status; new identities and the means to live comfortably. If there is anyone that can hide them, I would bet on Draper."

The Chief of Naval Intelligence spoke next. His voice was clear through the speakerphone on the table. "Well, for my money—let me just say this—The information that your Slow Dancer has offered, well hell, I don't think you could put a price tag on that. Let's just say, for example, if we knew the locations of the bases they plan to re-open or open through new construction, our strategy would jump ahead by several years. This is strategically significant information that he has offered."

Ramburt turned his gaze toward the CIA's chief of the international law legal team that sat to his right. "What say you, Bob? Is there any legal reason that I should not authorize this?"

"Sir, there is no legal precedent that would prohibit your man in Russia from helping a Russian officer defect. However, I'm obligated to tell you that, as a NOC, if he is caught, there is no legal recourse we can take to get him back. He's not there as an agent of the government, so diplomatic immunity does not apply. His release would have to be negotiated by the State Department," he replied. "And, I'll add, the information that Slow Dancer is prepared to provide, if he is caught, Slow Dancer will surely be executed."

"What about our guy?"

"Worst case scenario, it's a possibility." The lawyer raised his eyebrows and nodded.

Ramburt placed the message and his glasses on the table, then closed his eyes. A few moments passed as he stroked his chin, then he leaned forward over the table and asked, "Navy intel, what do you think?"

"I say go," he replied.

"Chief of staff?" Ramburt asked his second in command.

"Go. The intelligence is worth the high risk. But we need to be cautious and ready to pull the plug on short notice."

"Legal?" asked Ramburt.

After a thoughtful delay, he replied, "The risk is too high. Not one worth taking in the current environment."

Several people spoke at once. Ramburt raised his hands to quiet them. "Let's hear your logic."

"Sir, diplomacy between the Russians and us is toxic right now. We're still reeling from the shoot down of the MIGs, and there have been several close calls between other Navy ships and aircraft. State department is walking a high wire trying to prevent escalating rounds of sanctions. If we send someone into Russia to help one of their most senior officer's defect and they get caught, it could be just enough of a trigger for the Russians to break off almost all diplomatic channels. Channels that are needed to avoid further confrontations in the Middle East and the former East Bloc NATO countries that border Russia," replied the Chief of International Law.

"So, what would you propose?" asked the Chief of Naval Intelligence. "Should we put our heads in the sand and hope that the Russians will be kind to us after they place dominating forces in the Arctic?"

Ramburt leaned forward and propped his elbows on the table. "Okay gentlemen, thank you for your input." He drummed his fingers against the hardwood. "With apologies to legal counsel, I do think it is the best interest of the United States to pursue the extraction of Slow Dancer and his wife." He turned to his chief of staff and said, "Draft a message to the consulate in St. Petersburg for my release. The United States accepts Slow Dancer's terms and plan for extraction."

"Understood."

"Be very cryptic," added Ramburt.

***

Less than one hour later, a twenty-five-year-old junior agent sat at his desk in the communications center deep inside CIA headquarters as he encrypted the message he was given by Ramburt.

"Who is this Slow Dancer?" asked the junior agent. "There has been a lot of talk about him lately."

"That's above your paygrade, son. You're better off not knowing. Just code the message."

After tapping the SEND/RETURN key on his computer, he spun around in his chair and said, "Done, sir. Message encrypted and sent to the consulate in St. Petersburg."

Ramburt patted the agent on the shoulder and said, "Good job. Thank you."

CHAPTER TWELVE

St. Petersburg, Russia
23rd of November

Cole returned to the Four Seasons Hotel after a mid-day run along the embankment next to the Neva River and snatched a banana and a plastic cup of cucumber-and-lemon infused water from the concierge station. He consumed them as he sat in the lobby. He then returned to his room and found his phone message light blinking. He pressed the lighted button to retrieve it and listened to a message from a man named Alexandrinsky who said that the information he had requested concerning the works of Voltaire had been left with the concierge at the Renaissance Baltic Hotel next to St. Isaac's Cathedral and was ready for pickup under that name.

The return dead drop. That was faster than I expected.

He picked a hotel-sponsored tourist brochure from the end table and opened it to the city map in the back and found the location of the cathedral and traced the route he would take to get there. Cole decided that it was unnecessary to conduct a surveillance detection walk. *If someone from the FSB had listened to that phone message, they would already know that I'm going to pick up a package from the Renaissance Hotel. And even then, there's no reason to believe that the FSB would suspect the package contained secret guidance from the CIA.* Furthermore, he assumed that it was far more likely that the FSB would have followed the foreign service officer from the consulate and that he, or perhaps she, would have taken a thorough detection route and would not have dropped the package if there were any signs of surveillance. *This is covered in basic training at the CIA trade school*, he mused with a bit of sarcasm. *So, if I assume the foreign service officer did his job correctly, then I have nothing to worry about.* He leaned back in the desk chair, grimaced, and interlocked his fingers behind his head. "Aw, hell," he muttered. "I am, too, Captain Kulakov. I'm all in." He removed his running attire and took a hot shower.

* * *

The area around St. Isaac's Cathedral was crowded with day tourists from the many riverboat cruises that stop in St. Petersburg. There were three rows of tour buses, four to a row, parked on the street in front of the cathedral entrance. Cole wove his way through the crowds and past the cathedral and the museum where mostly middle-aged and elderly tourists stood in small groups, photographing the gold-plated dome and opulent sculptured façade with massive granite columns. *Not a single selfie-stick in this crowd,* he observed.

He crossed the wide road and gazed down the street of tall, nondescript buildings with canyon-like walls on both sides. Near the end of the second block on the left, he recognized the three glass-covered arches that were unique to the Renaissance Hotel entrance. He pulled a tourist brochure from his pocket that he had picked up from the Four Season's and compared the picture to confirm that he was in the right place, then turned and headed in that direction.

Cole entered the brightly lit and highly polished foyer. Three large crystal chandeliers and marble columns provided an elegant backdrop to the crowded lobby.

"Over five hundred lights," commented a passerby in English. "It's said that Catherine the Great herself commissioned those chandeliers."

Cole lowered his gaze from the ceiling then nodded and replied, "They're magnificent."

A queue of mostly businessmen in suits had formed in front of the hotel restaurant on the left. On the right side of the lobby was a long, wood-paneled reception desk. Cole approached one of three female clerks behind it. She wore a red hotel emblazoned-jacket and had blonde hair worn off the shoulders and large, inviting brown eyes. She smiled as Cole approached then asked, "May I help you?"

"Yes. Thank you," replied Cole. "I am here to pick up a package that was left for me by Mr. Alexandrinsky."

"Yes," she replied. "You must be Mr. Madison?"

Cole nodded.

The pretty young clerk turned and spoke to a second clerk who looked a few years older but was also quite attractive with her long auburn hair pinned up. The second clerk approached Cole, and in English, asked, "Can I please see some identification Mr. Madison?"

"Of course." Cole reached into his back pocket and pulled out the forged Canadian passport with the name Cole Madison.

The clerk quickly perused his passport. As she reached under the long reception desk to retrieve the package she said, "Mr. Alexandrinsky asked me to pass on his regrets that he was unable to meet with you in person. As you know his stay at our hotel was very short in duration." She handed the brown manila envelope to Cole. "Mr. Alexandrinsky also asked me to tell you that he hopes you have a safe return flight to Canada and that he looks forward to working with you again in the future." The clerk blinked her eyes and smiled.

Cole controlled his urge to laugh out loud. *I don't believe it. She's a CIA operative.* Cole smiled, nodded, and accepted the package.

He casually sauntered through the tourist crowds back to his room at the Four Seasons Hotel. After he locked the doors and closed the heavy curtains on his room windows, he opened the envelope and read the message:

Terms for SD and his partner approved . . . break . . . Contact SD and communicate decision . . . break . . . Conduct initial plans and return asap.

Short n' sweet. Cole ripped up the message into small pieces. When night came, he took a walk along the Palace Embankment on the river and slowly dropped the small pieces of the ripped-up message into the Neva River.

***

The next day, he holed up in his hotel room and developed a rough outline of an extraction plan for Slow Dancer and his wife. The challenge was to create two separate accidents where they each appeared to perish in a catastrophic mishap that would leave no reasonable thought of recovering their remains. *This would be much easier if I could extricate both of them at the same time. I could easily make them both disappear. But, one at a time . . . Crap!* Cole snickered. *Buried under an avalanche? Lost at sea? Airplane crashes into the ocean? Eaten by cannibals?*

Cole stood by the window that overlooked the Admiralty and scratched his cheek. *First things first. Do they have any travel plans in the near future where I could stage an accident? Or a mysterious disappearance?* He gazed at the street below. *I need to talk to Kulakov.*

Cole left the hotel, walked to the Admiralteyskaya Station and took the metro to a shopping district. He found an electronics store where he purchased a pre-paid cell phone and one hundred minutes provided by the Russian Megafon service. He then strolled through a small park nearby and found an empty bench then sat and phoned the number provided by the CIA. When the male caller answered, Cole stated, "My name is Stanislov, and I knew your father."

The call was disconnected, but the message had been sent. A meeting with Slow Dancer was set for dusk the next day near the statue named The Bronze Horseman.

CHAPTER THIRTEEN

St. Petersburg, Russia
24th of November

It was two hours before dusk. Cole gazed at the low sun in the sky west of St. Petersburg. He left the Four Seasons and walked an extensive circuit that included subway rides from the Admiralteyskaya station to Nevsky Prospeckt station. From there, he walked to Mikhailovsky Garden where he took a tour of the colorful domed church of the Savior of the Spilled Blood. Satisfied that he had not been followed, Cole took a long walk on the Palace Embankment back to The Bronze Horseman statue.

Kulakov stood, with his hands in his coat pockets, on the large lawn behind the statue. He motioned with his head for Cole to cross the street and meet him on the embankment. Cole turned and crossed the cobblestone walkway in front of the statue, then eluded some light vehicle traffic as he made his way to the embankment and stood next to Kulakov.

"Have you been followed?"

Cole grimaced and replied, "Captain, let's dispense with this right now. I'm a professional, and I can assure you that I have not been followed and that I will ensure the same each time that we meet." He spread his arms and opened his palms then asked, "Are we good?"

"One cannot be too careful."

"Uh huh," Cole replied.

Kulakov said, "My boat is ten meters in that direction." He cocked his head toward the walkway behind Cole and said, "Shall we?"

The boat was docked on the English Embankment across the road from the massive two-hundred-meter wide yellow brick building that housed the Constitutional Court of Russia. Cole gazed upward across the embankment at the eight-columned recessed portico of the separate buildings connected by a triumphal arch.

"The sculpture on the arch is that of Justice and Piety and the Imperial Russian Empire Coat of Arms," said Kulakov. "It symbolized the unity of church and state and of social and religious rule in the days of the Tzars."

"How'd that work for the Tzars?" baited Cole.

"Pretty well for over three hundred years," replied Kulakov. "Please do not lecture me about your separation of church and state, Mr. Draper. I do not believe that the American system of government is perfect either."

"Yet you want to defect." Cole cast off the line, and Kulakov backed the boat out of the berth and onto the Neva River parallel to the court.

"The sculptures should now be replaced with the symbols of the seven deadly sins," declared Kulakov. "Russia's current leadership has no honor."

Cole moved forward in the boat and stood next to Kulakov. He turned his gaze toward Kulakov and asked, "What will happen if we fail to extricate you and your wife? If we are caught?" asked Cole.

"I will be executed with my head held high."

Cole grimaced and nodded. "Unfortunately, if we fail, I may be standing right next to you."

"Let us hope that does not happen."

"Right," replied Cole sardonically. He walked to the other side of the boat, leaned his backside against the bulkhead and gripped the rail with both hands. "Well, I have approval from my government to develop a plan to extricate you and your wife."

Kulakov turned his gaze toward Cole and nodded. "Very good."

"My bosses also agreed that I should take your wife out first. So, to do that, I would like to stage what would be a believably fatal accident. It must appear like there is no reasonable chance of finding her remains."

"This will be difficult to do in St. Petersburg."

"St. Petersburg would not be my first choice," replied Cole. "I would like to stage the accident in a more remote location." Cole paused for a moment of thought then continued, "I need to know, does she have any trips planned, like, to the country, or maybe to Moscow to visit her family? We could stage something on a highway in a remote region."

Kulakov crossed his arms over his chest, and he pursed his lips. After a few moments, he confided, "I will be on assignment in Provideniya from December through March. Oksana will join me to celebrate the birth of Jesus Christ on the seventh of January."

Cole stared at the dark wood floor of the boat and pondered what Kulakov had shared with him. *I've never heard of Providenya.* He lifted his gaze toward Kulakov. "Tell me about Provideniya."

"It is a small town far north on the Bering Sea. There is a remote navy port there where two to three ships are stationed to serve the eastern end of the northern sea route. It is a port that provides deep-water harbor close to the limits of the winter ice fields."

Cole thought quietly for a moment. "Is the water deep enough along that route for a submarine?" he asked.

"For a skilled commander, yes."

Cole straddled his chair and rubbed his chin. "When exactly will she visit and how will your wife travel there?"

"I have a navy executive jet that I will use to bring her to me on the last day of December. She will return to St. Petersburg on the fifteenth of January."

Cole gazed thoughtfully at the floor of the small boat, then asked, "Will there be other passengers on the executive jet?"

Kulakov turned toward Cole. He smirked then said, "I can arrange for there to be no others."

Cole paced back and forth in the small cabin for a few minutes and developed a rough plan. *That region is so far north, humans could not survive there without Arctic training and equipment, and it would be easy to ditch an airplane up there.* He stopped pacing and gazed ahead at the river traffic. *If I can get into this small town and get on board that plane, I might just be able to stage a terrible accident.* He faced Kulakov, stretched his arms and cracked his knuckles. "Captain, I propose that we extricate your wife on the return trip from Provideniya to St. Petersburg."

"That will be an opportune time," he agreed. "But how?"

"Are you familiar with what happens in an aircraft when the cabin slowly depressurizes?"

"Hypothermia and Hypoxia."

Cole nodded. "I'll be leaving soon and return home to make arrangements with my people. Then I'll be in touch with you through your contact at the consulate."

"I think I see what you are planning. It will be very dangerous."

CHAPTER FOURTEEN

Toronto, Canada
26th of November

T he flights, Lufthansa from St. Petersburg to Heathrow in London, then Air Canada to Toronto's International Terminal, were long. On an east to west flight, sleep was hard to come by. Cole operated the onboard entertainment system and called up three movies during the flights, but he could not recall how any of them started or ended. Instead of relaxing with the entertainment offered, he deliberated and ruminated over his plan to extricate Oksana Kulakov, and what the Captain had said to him said about marriage.

As the Airbus A360 began its descent and the flight attendants began their pre-arrival checks, Cole peered out the window at an overcast sky. The thought of holding Diana in his arms caused him to smile, which was reflected in the airplane window. *I'm really looking forward to seeing Diana. I was busy enough in Russia that I didn't have much time to think about her. But, now that I'm this close, I realize how much I missed her.*

The flight landed at the renovated and ultra-modern Terminal One. After a quick debarkation, it took another fifty minutes to clear customs and immigration then hike down the long glass-enclosed corridor to the public gateway and baggage claim.

Finally, the frosted glass sliding door opened. When he saw Diana, he took in a deep breath and exhaled. She stood in the baggage claim area with her hands joined in front of her. In spite of the cold rain outside, she wore a yellow above-the-knee dress with a plunging neckline. After a week apart from one another, she looked fabulous. Just the sight of her was like a shot of adrenaline. She hurried to him.

They embraced and held a long kiss. She patted his behind and said, "I missed you, comrade."

"Smartass," replied Cole as he hugged her tightly again. He took her hand in his and joined the crowd as they waited for the luggage carousel to start up. As a passenger in first class, his luggage was one of the first to be off-loaded. He grabbed the handle of his roller bag with one hand and took Diana's hand with the other, and they turned toward the exit.

"How did it go?" asked Diana as they snaked their way through the airport crowd.

Cole turned his gaze from side to side to ensure that others were not monitoring the conversation. He spoke softly. "Well, I satisfied myself that this guy is for real. He's not playing us. He definitely wants to defect, and in the process, he wants to hurt Russia, and in particular, the Russian President—he calls him the Tzar. But getting him and his wife out is not going to be easy."

"Why is that?"

"He wants to do it in two parts. His wife goes out first. Then we come back for him."

Diana cocked her head.

"Yeah, no shit," commented Cole. "This guy is head over heels in love with his wife and getting her out safely is a higher priority for him than anything else, including himself."

"That doesn't sound all that bad," replied Diana. She bumped him with her hip and smiled.

Cole half smiled at her response. "I think I may have a workable plan to get his wife out. That will be the first milestone," he explained. "But going back a second time . . ." He exhaled, and his lips fluttered. "I probably need to have my head examined for agreeing to do this."

"What's your plan?" she asked.

"I'll fill you in on the details when we're alone. I have a rough idea of what I need to do, and I have a good time frame." Cole paused. "But I have a few details that need to be worked out. I'll need to talk to Ramburt as soon as we get home." Cole looked around again to ensure no one was listening in on their conversation. He smirked, then asked, "You think he'll let me borrow a couple nuclear submarines and a SEAL team?"

Diana leaned into him and laughed out loud then said, "I don't know, but you'll be able to ask him soon. He has called every day asking me if I've been in touch with you."

Cole frowned. "He should know better than that. I was under cover."

They left the terminal and stayed under the corrugated metal awning to protect them from the pouring rain and joined the queue waiting for a taxi. When their turn arrived, Cole placed his luggage in the back, and they jumped into a black and yellow Chrysler minivan. The beat of the windshield wipers seemed to match the rhythm of the Arabic music that played softly in the front of the cab for the driver's benefit.

Thirty-five minutes later they were dropped off at the Ritz-Carlton Hotel. They quickly walked across the brightly lit lobby then took the elevator to their room on the eighth floor.

Cole placed his bags on a luggage stand and turned to face Diana. She stood between him and the bed. "I missed you, stud-muffin," said Diana. She bit her lower lip.

Cole looked over her shoulder at the neatly made king size bed.

"You have that look in your eye," Diana teased. She dropped the straps off of her shoulders, wiggled out of her dress, then dropped it on a chair next to the bed.

***

They checked out of the hotel at eight-thirty the next morning, took a taxi to the airport and returned to Norfolk, via Chicago's O'Hare Airport. They were met at the Norfolk terminal by Katie, Cole's irreverent niece who lived in an apartment above his garage while she attended Old Dominion University.

Katie was standing near the door that led to the parking garage as they came down the escalator. She waved her hand high above her head and said, "Mr. Draper, I'm Katie. I'll be your Uber driver today."

Cole shook his head and turned toward Diana. "Not a shred of timidity in that girl."

They reached the floor level. Cole gave Katie a long paternal hug.

"I missed you, Cole."

He felt her hug grow a little tighter.

"Oh, and so did Cooper. I think that poor dog needs a doggie shrink anytime you go out of town," she said.

Katie then hugged Diana. "That house is boring when you guys aren't around!" As they walked toward the baggage conveyor, she asked, "So how did you guys like Toronto?"

Cole and Diana locked eyes and shared a grin.

The East Beach neighborhood in Norfolk where they lived was a one-hundred-acre peninsula situated on the southernmost point of the Chesapeake Bay. It was a golf-cart community where houses with large porches were clustered around bayside greens and linear parks that extended water views to non-waterfront homes. Part of Norfolk's Ocean View area, the neighborhood sat on the Bay to the north and the Little Creek Inlet which opened to a small body of water named Pretty Lake to the east. On the east side of Little Creek Inlet sat the Little Creek-Fort Story Joint Expeditionary Military Base. To the west, approximately twenty miles away as the crow flies, sat the largest Naval base in the world, at the point where the James River opened into the Bay.

The short ride from Norfolk International Airport to Cole's house in East Beach lasted less than ten minutes, though it seemed longer in Katie's tightly packed red Mini Cooper two-door hard top.

"You could have borrowed my SUV, Katie. The ride would have been a little more comfortable," said Diana as she handed a roller bag to Cole and contorted out of the backseat.

"That car is too big. I love my Mini," replied Katie.

They entered the house through the back door. The aroma of roast turkey waft over them as they were enthusiastically greeted by Cooper, Cole's three-year-old Irish Setter. She rotated between the three of them, trumpeting and wagging her tail.

"You baked a turkey?" asked Cole incredulously.

Katie stood with her hands behind her back and wore a wide smile. "I thought I'd give it a try. Happy Thanksgiving!"

Diana hugged Katie. Cole started laughing.

"Dinner will be ready in thirty minutes," Katie decreed. "Don't be late."

"I wouldn't think of it," replied Cole. He left his bags in the kitchen, and as he entered the nook that was his home office, he said, "But first, I'm going to call Ramburt and get the ball rolling on phase one." He closed the door behind him.

CHAPTER FIFTEEN

Norfolk, Virginia
28th of November

Ramburt chose the time and location. Cole met him the following morning at the Joint Military Base Little Creek golf course which was located at the mouth of the Chesapeake Bay.

"Not a cloud in the sky, boss. I like your idea of mixing business with pleasure," said Cole as they loaded their golf clubs in the back of their cart. He wiped a small bit of perspiration from his brow. "I also like your idea to take advantage of the unusually warm temps."

"This will give us plenty of time to talk out of earshot of others," replied Ramburt. "And," he grinned before he continued, "we're having an office scramble on Friday. I need the practice."

Cole chuckled and shook his head. "You are the ultimate planner, sir."

"Never pass up an opportunity to get the edge."

Cole sat in the passenger seat. Ramburt drove the cart to the first tee.

It was a mid-morning tee-time, and the course was fairly deserted. The rush of early morning golfers was well into the back nine and the afternoon rush was not expected to start for another three hours, so they teed off as a twosome.

"I don't understand why Kulakov wants to be extricated separately from his wife. Did he say why?" asked Ramburt.

"He sure did. He's concerned that, because of his position in the hierarchy, he will always be under observation which will make it hard to get them out together. His main concern is his wife. Above all else, he wants to ensure that she is successfully extracted. He believes the chance of success is better if I take her alone. When he's sure that she's safe, he'll be ready to come out."

"Doesn't that make it more dangerous for you?"

"Yeah. No shit. But, those are his terms. They weren't open for negotiation."

"Well, I'm not real thrilled about that," replied Ramburt.

"I'm not either."

"Neither is our legal counsel. If you want out, I can justify it."

Cole turned toward Ramburt and narrowed his eyes. "Something you're not telling me?" he asked.

"No. I just wanted to give you a chance to back out if you think that this will be more dangerous than we originally anticipated."

"It's odd," replied Cole, "but I kinda like this guy. So, I'd like to give this a try. If it gets too dicey, I'll let you know."

"If it gets so dicey that you're stuck in a Russian gulag somewhere, we probably won't be able to help you."

"I plan to be very careful so that doesn't happen."

"So, what's your plan?" asked Ramburt.

"Big to small. I'll start with the logistics. I'm going to need a couple of submarines with experienced commanders and two SEAL teams."

"What?" Ramburt replied in a high-pitched voice.

"Well, I'll need one team to help me covertly sneak into a small town in the Russian Bering Sea and a second team to help me extract Kulakov's wife undetected," Cole replied.

Ramburt stopped the cart and turned to face Cole. "Is that all?" he asked credulously. "Are you kiddin' me?"

"Brother, you gave me a tough problem that requires a unique solution." Cole turned sideways to face Ramburt. "Captain Kulakov made his intention perfectly clear. We extricate his wife first then come back for him. So, to do that, we're going to have to stage two separate accidents. Each one must be staged to make it appear that there was no possibility for survival. And—this part is critical—the accident wreckage cannot be reached. The accident has to appear real enough that Russian security will accept those results without any physical evidence."

Ramburt faced forward and tapped his fingers on the steering wheel. He turned back toward Cole and said, "Yeah, that's going to be a challenge. Can you pull it off?"

"I think so, but like I said, Kulakov was very clear on this. I'm going to have to take them one at a time. So, step one is the captain's wife, and that's the phase that I will need help from the Navy on. Phase two, to get him out, his conditions need to be changed. He needs to get reassigned to a remote location. I've discussed this with him, and he is confident that he can make that happen," said Cole. "I will stay engaged with him after phase one is successfully executed, and when he gets reassigned, we can extract him. Same game plan, stage an accident."

"A two-step plan goes against every instinct I have," said Ramburt.

"A two-phase plan is less than ideal, but this is the whole ball game. His rules. We take or leave it."

Ramburt stepped out of the cart with a fairway iron in his hand and stood next to his ball. He faced Cole. "Okay, what's your plan for the wife. I'm listening."

CHAPTER SIXTEEN

Moscow, Russia.
30th of November

Tasha saw her friends' wave as she entered the Bosco Bar in the high-end GUM shopping mall adjacent to the massive Red Square and Lenin's Mausoleum. She loosened the top button of her green and blue striped, belted shirt dress then sashayed across the room, which caught the attention of several men in the room. She joined her friends at an L-shaped, four-seat, red-leather booth in a corner, away from the windows that overlooked the historic plaza. Tasha set her shopping bags from Burberry and Christian Dior on the floor next to the table. Her three friends scooted over and made room for her to sit at the end of the booth.

"Tasha, I swear that you are unable to walk past a fashion store without buying something," declared Maria over the clanging of dishes and din of the busy lunch hour crowd.

"Well," Tasha replied, "the winter designs were on display in the Dior window, so I thought I would stop and look."

"You obviously did more than just look." Nika was sitting closest to Tasha. She leaned closer to her and tried to peer in the bag.

"Stop being so curious," said Tasha as she moved the bags behind her.

The foursome giggled about that as a buxom waitress wearing a tight blue-and-red jumper approached and asked Tasha if she would like to place an order.

"I would like a vodka and tonic with a lime twist," answered Tasha. The rest of the group declined any refills.

"You look so tanned," observed Nika.

"I've managed to keep the tan I got during my holiday in Sochi with Oksana."

Nika reached, placed her hand over Tasha's, and leaned closer. "It was so sad to hear about her son," she said. "Is she well?"

"Ana wouldn't want me to talk about that," Tasha replied. "You know that she likes to keep things to herself."

"Come on, Tasha," urged Maria, who sat at the far end of the booth. "Ana is our friend, too. I think we would all like to know how she is."

"Well, alright but, don't you dare tell Ana that I told you this."

The waitress returned with Tasha's cocktail and placed it on a blue-and-red napkin on the table in front of her. She turned and walked away with an elegant swing of her shapely hips that caused the foursome to titter with their hands over their mouths.

Tasha continued, "As you can imagine, Ana is hurting about the loss of Nicolay. It was so unnecessary."

"He was a soldier," stated Maria. "It's sad, yes, but these things happen."

Tasha lowered her voice and said, "Yes, but he was killed in the Ukraine after the President said that he would not send troops there."

"But he had to say that," replied Maria. "Everyone understood that he *was* sending troops there."

"Well Ana didn't think that," replied Tasha. She narrowed her eyes and faced Maria. "She said that the President had assured Pyotr that he was not going to send troops there and Ana doesn't like that Pyotr was lied to." They maintained eye contact silently for a few moments.

"Well, at least she has that very handsome husband of hers to help her through the rough days," interjected Vera.

"Unfortunately, not always," answered Tasha. "Pytor is gone much of the time on assignments. Ana gets lonely. That's why I think it was good for her to spend a week with me in Sochi."

Tasha took a sip of her cocktail as Nika asked, "How does she stay busy then?"

"She stays busy mostly by gardening in her yards, but when she's not doing that, she is involved organizing clothing and food drives for the less fortunate."

"Aaaggh," shrilled Maria. "Ana and her causes!"

"Well, Ana has a big heart," replied Tasha. "She sees that there are many people in Russia that are less fortunate and she feels badly for them. And as she told me, there is a lot of oil money coming into

Russia, and soon there will be more as oil wells open in the Arctic. Oksana is afraid that as that happens, all that new money will only benefit a small group of politically connected insiders and she doesn't think that's right."

"What does her husband say about that?" snapped Maria. "I would be concerned if he thought the same way as Oksana!"

Tasha raised her voice a bit and angrily replied, "Ana didn't say, and I didn't ask."

"Alright ladies," said Nika as she leaned forward and alternated her gaze between Tasha and Maria, "Let's not fight over this. In fact, let's change the subject."

CHAPTER SEVENTEEN

Washington, District of Columbia
9th of December

Dmitri Pukalova, Minister Counselor of the Russian Embassy, walked south on Wisconsin Avenue and tried to blend in with other walkers. He wore a brown overcoat. A folded-up compact umbrella attached by a lanyard to his wrist danced at his side.

A powerful thunderstorm had recently left the metropolitan area and moved northeast, leaving behind a fresh, clean scent which he breathed deeply. He was followed at fifty yards by two Russian field agents dressed in jeans and black leather jackets.

Pukalova stopped at the intersection of 37th Northwest and hailed a Yellow Cab. Before he stepped inside, he looked over his shoulder toward the agents and nodded. A black Ford Expedition rolled to a stop, and the agents entered.

Twenty minutes later, the taxi dropped Pukalova off on M' street, near 19th, in Foggy Bottom. Pukalova waited until the Expedition that followed him stopped. One of the agents hopped out and walked towards him. Muscle, if needed. He nodded toward the agent to acknowledge his presence, then entered the Castle Show Bar and walked up the steps to the second-floor lounge.

The techno-music pulsated loudly, and the flashing blue-and-yellow lights reflected off of the mirrors on the back of the stage. He took a seat at a small table in the first row of the crowded exotic dance show. The pungent smell of spilled beer hung heavy and mixed with the greasy smell of the first-floor burger joint. The Russian agent bellied up to the bar near the stairs.

An athletic young woman on stage spun upside down with her leg wrapped around the center stage pole. She flipped off the pole and landed feet first. Her entire body gyrated with the rhythm of the music as she removed her G-string and dropped it on the floor.

Pukalova periodically shifted his gaze from the perfectly sculpted dancer on stage to his wrist-watch. The dancer marched to the edge of the stage in front of Pukalova, fell to her knees and spread her legs wide then flipped backward on her hands and landed back on her feet. He smiled at her then looked at his watch.

At exactly a quarter past the hour, he stood, left his drink and umbrella on the table to indicate his intent to return, and walked to the front of the hall and into the men's room. He pushed open the door of the second stall and was met by a tall, thin transvestite with rose-colored cheeks, long thin painted eyebrows, purple lipstick, and shoulder-length brown hair.

"Hi sugar," said the transvestite in Russian. "I have what you came for. What do you have for me, honey?"

Pukalova reached down, pulled up his right pant leg and removed four bundles of twenty-five one-hundred-dollar bills. He handed them to the transvestite who tossed them in a pink-and-white beaded tote.

Pukalova placed his open hand in front of him and spoke in his native language. "Give me the flash drive."

"Of course, baby. But what's your hurry?" The transvestite reached around and removed a small flash drive from the rear pocket of the skin-tight red leather shorts and handed it to Pukalova. "Would you like to have some fun before you leave?"

"No," replied Pukalova. He opened the stall door and walked out of the bathroom, the transvestite close behind. He turned the corner toward the table where he had left his drink and met the exquisite dancer face to face. She had finished her dance, put on her tiny costume and exited the stage.

Pukalova fished a twenty-dollar bill out of his pocket and slipped it in the front of her G-string and said, "You are a beautiful woman."

"Thank, you honey," she replied. She side-stepped around him and threw her arms around the transvestite and they embraced in a long kiss.

By the time Pukalova returned to his table, a pair of identical blonde twins named Farah and Sarah, were on stage. They had already stripped out of their costumes and were synchronized as they twirled around the two gold poles.

Pukalova stopped a bare-breasted waitress, gave her a hundred-dollar bill, then finished his drink and stood. He left the Palace Bar. After he confirmed that his agent was in tow, he hailed a taxi and returned to the Russian Embassy.

***

Pukalova sat at a spartan desk in the darkened basement security center. This was in stark contrast to the palatial offices assigned to the Minister Counselor. A grey cubicle and an integrated desk with a small desklight substituted for the thick designer fabric wallpaper, ornately sculpted crown molding, and crystal chandelier of his formal office. An electronically firewalled Samsung desktop computer in the security station substituted for his elegant top-of-the-line twenty-seven-inch iMac computer in his office.

Pukalova shivered as he pulled a sweater over his shoulders. There was a great deal of computer hardware running in the security center, so the technicians set the thermostat in the room at fifty-eight degrees. He placed the thumb drive he had received from the transvestite into the USB drive and lit a cigarette as he waited for the computer to acknowledge the new drive.

A pop-up menu appeared with several files that referenced Slow Dancer. Pukalova opened the first file labeled Slow Dancer First Contact. It was a copy of a heavily redacted nine-page report from the Director of the Central Intelligence Agency to the National Security Advisor and the White House Chief of Staff. The report detailed how a senior officer in a military branch of the Russian Federation had contacted a junior foreign services officer and opened a dialogue about defecting.

Pukalova read the report. He pulled a drag on his cigarette and pondered the information. The contact occurred in Moscow. The traitor explained that he is in possession of strategic information, but the exact type of information was redacted from this report that was destined to be briefed to the American President. *What is that information that was redacted?*

Pukalova opened the second file labeled Slow Dancer Terms for Extraction. This file was from the Director of the Central Intelligence Agency to the President of the United States. Again, the file was heavily redacted.

Pukalova lit another cigarette. The traitor wants to have his wife extracted separately. *That will make it harder for the Americans. Why does he want to defect separately from his wife?*

The third file was lightly redacted and labeled Rationale for Slow Dancer to Defect. He read it twice. *So even the Americans do not know why this traitor wants to defect.*

Pukalov looked at his watch. It was forty-five minutes after midnight, and there was a seven-hour time difference with Moscow. *Most of the staff will arrive for work soon. The business of the Federation will be starting, and this information must be sent to the Chief of the Investigation Directorate. We have a traitor in our midst.*

CHAPTER EIGHTEEN

In a second-floor office of the sparsely populated south wing of the yellow brick building on Lubyanka Square, Major Nicolas Ogorodnik of the FSB sat in front of two like monitors that displayed information from his desktop computer linked to a secure server located in the basement.

On the monitor to his right, he scrolled through a file that contained recent reports on citizens that were submitted by informants—citizens that were either loyal to the bureau, or simply greedy goons that would turn in their mother for a few rubles.

The monitor on his left displayed dossiers compiled over time on several citizens. In the course of the previous two hours, Ogorodnik had updated and reconciled six dossiers with the new information provided by the informers.

This work is below me, he brooded. *Each day I spend hour after endless hour reviewing informant reports. This is clerical work. I should be a field agent, undercover and at work in an adversaries' backyard.*

He picked up a lighted cigarette from an ashtray and took a pull as he worked on a synopsis of a case file titled *Kulakov, Oksana*. The file included an update provided by a community organizer in the URPP, the United Russia Political Party, within the last thirty-six hours. His curiosity was drawn to a statement provided by the reliable source.

The report read: Informant name is Maria. Informant recently participated in a conversation over lunch and cocktails with a close friend of Oksana Kulakov. The friend, Tasha Bolkonskaya, provided intimate details of Kulakov's current state of mind. Bolkonskaya, is a prominent financial analyst at the Gazprombank in Moscow and a friend of Kulakov since college.

Ogorodnik took another pull on his cigarette then leaned closer to the computer screen and continued to read. According to the informant Maria, Kulakov was recently on holiday in Sochi during which she communicated to her friend Tasha Bolkonskaya the following sentiments:

1. *She was angry that her son, a lieutenant in the army, was killed in Ukraine. Stated that the President lied to Russians about military involvement in Ukraine.*
2. *Critical of the President and United Russia Party. Believes the Party represses the working class.*
3. *Stated her belief that wealth is targeted toward the ruling party at the expense of the average family.*
4. *Resents the lifestyle of the ruling party and stated that she believes they live a life of excess.*

Ogorodnik opened a desk drawer and removed a pad of yellow legal paper and a pencil. As he continued to read the file, he wrote; *Update the color code on Oksana Kulakov to orange.* That signified a moderate threat equivalent to a minor dissident report.

He adjusted the eyeglasses on the bridge of his nose as his gaze shifted between the two computer monitors. He noted on her dossier that, Oksana Kulakov had a long history of dissent against government authority. As a student at the University of St. Petersburg, she participated in the Pushkin Square demonstrations against the Soviet Government in 1989. A few years later as a tennis professional on tour in western Europe, Oksana Kulakov, (maiden name Gursky), made statements critical of the Russian Parliament in the days leading up to the constitutional crisis and stand-off against then-President Yeltsin.

He added to the report. *Oksana Kulakov continues to communicate a distrust of the President and Ministers of the Russian Federation.*

Ogorodnik heard hard heels clapping across the old wood floor. He looked up and away from his computer. Two officers were engaged in a spirited conversation that echoed in the hallway. They slowly ambled past his open door. *The emptiness of these hallways is an embarrassment,* brooded Ogorodnik. *When my father worked here as KGB, these offices were filled with Russia's most knowledgeable and dedicated comrades. Now it is only the home of a simple prison and police force.* He gazed out his window across the courtyard at the larger wing of the yellow brick building. *The intelligence directorates are in the main building, and that is where I will work someday.*

With the distraction gone, Ogorognik returned to the dossier and added additional notes to his legal pad. He lit another cigarette and continued reading. The dossier highlighted the significance of the name Gursky.

Oksana Kulakov's older brother was First Lieutenant Victor Gursky. In November 1987, during the years of the failed Perestroika movement, he and a fellow officer chained themselves to a lamppost outside the defense ministry to protest the state of affairs for Soviet soldiers. Their many complaints included low pay, often missed pay, low morale, and crime within the ranks. Lieutenant Gursky was arrested and expired while awaiting trial in Lubyanka prison. The dossier stated that Oksana Kulakov was overheard saying, "She will never forget or forgive what happened to her brother."

The two officers returned toward his office, still engaged in an animated discussion that echoed in the hallway. Ogorodnik stood and quietly closed his office door. He pondered the case he was reviewing as he returned to his desk. *Oksana's brother died in custody of the secret service and recently, her son was killed in a secret military operation. Sad, yes. But, taken in context with statements she has made among her confidants, these are classic signs of someone who could be motivated to betray Russia.*

Ogorodnik sat, then took a pull on his cigarette. As he leaned back in his chair, he blew a few smoke rings. *This Oksana Kulakov is certainly worth investigating.* He reached for his computer mouse and continued to scroll through Oksana's file.

The source from the URPP mentioned to the interviewer that he thought Kulakov's attitude and comments were disturbing given the status of her husband in the Russian navy.

Ogorodnik flinched. *Status in the Russian Navy?* He scrolled the file backward until he found an annotation for Oksana's marriage in 1996; Married to Lieutenant Pyotr Kulakov. Son of Admiral Anatoly Kulakov. Married in Moscow. The list of guests included most of the significant military hierarchy of the time frame.

He gazed upon the smiling photo of the newly married couple. "Hhmm," he murmured. *Let's see what Lieutenant Pyotr Kulakov is doing today.* Ogorodnik opened a browser and typed a command that opened a list of all the active Russian navy officers. He typed a search for Pyotr Kulakov and found three. The first was a lieutenant first rank. *Too young.* Ogorodnik discarded that file. The second file he opened was Captain First Rank Pyotr Kulakov. He studied the photos then dragged the wedding photo from Oksana's file and placed it side by side with Kulakov's command photo. *That's a match*, he thought. *Pyotr Kulakov, you have aged well. You do not look much different than your wedding photo more than twenty years ago.* Ogorodnik then ran his cursor to Kulakov's current assignment. Commander of Baltic Fleet, Naval Forces of the Russian Federation.

He sat back in his chair and ran a hand through his wavy, sandy blonde hair as he puffed up his cheeks. *This woman with such dissident tendencies married to a senior leader.* He then whispered, "She could be a source of intelligence for unfriendly nations."

I must bring this to the attention of the deputy director. He will surely be pleased that I have uncovered this potential national security risk.

CHAPTER NINETEEN

Moscow, Russia
12th of December

T he cafeteria in the Lubyanka building was Ogorodnik's favorite place to eat. The price of a meal that included succulent sturgeon fish pie, a beet soup called Borsht and a Salat Olivier on the side would be well above the means of an FSB major at a restaurant in Moscow. In the headquarters building, the meal was free to junior officers and served on cheap china with faux silverware. He sat at a corner table with a yellow plastic tablecloth.

Ogorodnik waited for his meal to be served, and sipped mineral water imported from France, out of the bottle. His table had a clear view of the senior officer's dining facility where the same quality meals were served, except the senior officers ate off of fine china, real silverware, and sat at a table draped in a fine white cloth.

He placed his elbows on the table and gazed through the door to the separate dining room and smirked. *I will have my place at the table someday. I will make sure of that.*

His view was interrupted by the arrival of his customary lunch partner. He stood to greet her. Lieutenant Veronika Kuragin was twenty-six years old, and with heels, stood an inch taller than him. She wore her long strawberry blonde hair pulled up in a neatly packed bun.

Ogorodnik touched her elbow. She kissed him on the cheek. *She is such a beautiful young woman, and I am fifteen years her elder. If only I were a few years younger, I could make her love me.* He smiled and shook his head. *I do love our lunch dates, though. Yes, this is my favorite part of the day.*

"I apologize that I am late," said Kuragin as she seated herself across the two-person table from Ogorodnik. "I was distracted by a conversation with some of my peers." She raised her hand to get the attention of the server assigned to their table. "There are rumors that a high-ranking officer from one of the services will try to defect. I overheard the deputy director say that this rumor should be taken seriously."

Ogorodnik sat as the server arrived and Kuragin ordered her lunch from the 'al a carte menu.

The deputy director has taken note of this. It must be important, surmised Ogorodnik. He leaned his right shoulder over the table. "Tell me what you have heard," he urged his friend.

Kuragin leaned over the table closer to Ogorodnik and lowered her voice. "What I heard was, an undercover agent at the American Central Intelligence Agency alerted our chief of residency in Washington of an operation in planning that the Americans call the Slow Dancer Case."

"The Americans always attach a clever title to their operations," replied Ogorodnik sarcastically. "What does Slow Dancer refer to?" he questioned.

"I don't know for sure, but the agent in Washington provided marked-up copies of secret documents about the case. I overheard the deputy director say that Slow Dancer is a traitor that has offered to provide the Americans with highly classified strategic information in exchange for extracting him and his wife."

"At least we know the traitor is married," said Ogorodnik. He placed his elbow on the table and rested his chin on his thumb and forefinger. "I should imagine that will eliminate a large number of possible suspects."

"What would you do?" asked Kuragin. "Arrest every married officer in the military and question them?" She snickered, then said, "You would be placed in an asylum for a long period of observation."

Ogorodnik smiled. "Perhaps it is not a matter of what I would do. It is more like, what I will do."

"What are you talking about?" Kuragin grinned, wide-eyed.

"I will look into this matter. On my own time if I must." Ogorodnik glanced toward the senior officer's dining facility. "Imagine the acclaim that will be awarded to the agent that identifies this Slow Dancer."

"Phew," spat Kuragin. "And how would you propose to do that?"

"First I would make a list of married senior officers with strategic positions."

"There could be hundreds."

"There will be hundreds. Yes, that is true. But the search must start somewhere."

"Then what would you do?"

"I would review their records and look for any indication of dissent."

"That would be tedious and painstaking."

"Yes, yes it would. It would be the kind of tedious and painstaking work that would get the attention of my superiors and make them look favorably on me for promotion."

They paused the conversation as the server arrived with Kuragin's lunch and placed the plates on the table. Ogorodnik placed his elbow on the table again and rested his chin in his hand, then narrowed his gaze at his lunch partner. *Can I trust my friend to help me quietly or would she want to alert others whom I would have to share credit with?*

Kuragin chewed a forkful of meat pie. After she swallowed it, she asked, "Do you really intend to pursue this?"

"I don't know," lied Ogorodnik. "Maybe this is just talk." He shifted his gaze away from Kuragin toward the senior officers.

Kuragin chuckled. "Good. I'm glad it's just talk." She placed her fork on the table and continued, "Because your approach is all wrong, anyway. If I were going to do this, I would start by questioning my American boyfriend." She smirked and blinked her eyes like an owl. "Remember, he is the bee in *my* honey trap. And, now I think that he is in love with me. I think that, if he knows anything about this, I might be able to find a way to get him to slip up and tell me something about this Slow Dancer during one of our meetings, as he calls them."

Ogorodnik grimaced as he dipped his fork in his Sturgeon pie. "So, you will help me then."

"Sure. Why not. If we are successful, it would benefit my career as well."

Ogorodnik clenched his teeth. *I can't stand the thought of you with him, in that way. I have a better idea. And, it would also be a reason for you to stop seeing this man.* "Excellent!" he exclaimed. "But rather than trying to coax him to say something to you in your bed, I think we could cause him to become very cooperative if we threatened to expose his liaisons with you to his people."

Kuragin smiled. "I think you are a devious man Nicolas Ogordonik." She paused. "Let's do this today!"

***

Ogorodnik sat across the small wooden table from Michael Hewlett. The basement interrogation room inside the Lubyanka building was kept cold to contribute to the intimidation of the invited "guests." The room was small, and with the exception of the bright light that faced Hewlett, not very well lit. Located in a wing that housed the small holding cells where, at the height of the KGB's power under Soviet rule, thousands of political opponents disappeared.

Hewlett's gaze moved around the room. He appeared to take note of his surroundings; a concrete floor, cinder block walls painted grey, a single toilet, with no seat cover, and a stainless-steel sink. Ogorodnik understood that these rooms still held a sense of intimidation.

Hewlett leaned back in his seat on the opposite side of the small wood desk from Ogorodnik. He placed his hands on the armrest and tapped his fingers. "I would like to contact my embassy."

Ogorodnik ignored Hewlett's annoying tap...tap. He placed a cigarette in his mouth then flipped open a metal lighter and lit it. He shook the cigarette pack in his hand to expose one and offered it to Hewlett.

"No, thanks," replied Hewlett. "In fact, in these small confines, I'd appreciate it if you didn't light up. There's real danger in second-hand smoke, ya know."

"Yes. Yes, I'm sure there is." Ogorodnik took a long pull on his cigarette then placed it in an ashtray situated between them. He leaned forward and folded his hands on the table.

"How are you enjoying your assignment in Moscow?" asked Ogordnik. "It is a modern metropolis, is it not? More cosmopolitan than most Americans believe. No? And the women of Moscow. Do you think they are attractive?"

Hewlett's gaze rolled upward. "Major, you don't give a damn if I like Moscow or not. Can we cut the crap and you tell me why you had your goons *request* my visit here? I've committed no crime. Not even a traffic violation. You have no legal grounds for detaining me."

"Ahh, but Mr. Hewlett, I was told that your visit here is purely voluntary."

"Look, four men in suits stepped out of an unmarked van, each of them clearly armed, and asked me to step inside the van. That's not voluntary."

Ogordnik pushed his chair away from the table and crossed his legs. He took a pull on his cigarette then exhaled. "Then you may leave whenever you wish."

Hewlett pushed his chair away from the table and stood. As he did this, Ogorodnik said, "But first, would you mind answering a few questions?" He pressed a button under the table, and two of the four men in black suits entered the room and stood by the door.

"Yes, as a matter of fact, I do mind answering a few questions," Hewlett replied. "I demand to be allowed to contact my embassy."

"Of course, yes, of course you do. But first, my colleague and I have some questions."

A hidden door behind Ogorodnik opened. Lieutenant Veronika Kuragin entered the room. She wore a tightly fit double-breasted gray jacket and matching above-the-knee skirt. Her shoulder-length strawberry blond hair was pulled back in a ponytail. She stood behind Ogorodnik, her shoulders back and her hazel eyes fixed on Hewlett. "Hello, Michael. I think we have much to talk about." She smiled smugly.

Hewlett's posture stiffened and his eyes widened. "Veronika?" His gaze alternated between the two Russian officers. "What the fuck is going on here?"

"Michael, may I call you Michael?" asked Ogorodnik. "Perhaps you would like to sit down. I would like for you to be comfortable."

***

The Russians used a good cop, bad cop, with a charm twist routine on Hewlett. Ogorodnik placed a stack of compromising photos on the table in front of Hewlett. They were high definition photos that showed Hewlett and Veronika engaged in numerous sexual positions. Veronika's face was obscured, but the rest of the photos were crystal clear.

Hewlett perused several of the photos off of the top of the stack then tossed them back on the table.

"Please, Mr. Hewlett, don't stop," said Ogorodnik. "There are over a hundred photos. I'm sure you will be impressed with our photographer's artistic ability."

"Fuck off," replied Hewlett. His heart pounded, and in spite of the chill in the room, he perspired.

Veronika walked behind Hewlett, placed her hands on his shoulders and whispered in his ear, "Michael, my love, please cooperate with Major Ogorodnik. He only wants to ask you a few questions."

He welcomed the familiar touch of her fingers and lavender scent of her hair.

"There is nothing to worry about, Michael. All you have to do is cooperate with the Major. Then we can go back to the apartment and act like nothing has happened."

Hewlett sat rigidly, and with a frown, he gazed over his shoulder at Veronika. She leaned into him and her soft breasts pressed against his back as she gently massaged his neck and shoulders.

"Baby, you are so tense. Let me help you relax."

Hewlett closed his eyes, placed his hands on his forehead and leaned his head back. *What the hell of have got myself into?* He visualized the two of them on the large bed at the apartment. He kissed her breast, then the other, then down to her navel, then lower. *Her taste, her touch, she pleasures me so much. I want to be with her.* He sensed movement in front of him and opened his eyes.

Ogorodnik stood then walked around the table. He leaned his backside on the table and leaned toward Hewlett. "Tell me what you know about a case called Slow Dancer," he demanded.

"What are you talking about? What is Slow Dancer?" replied Hewlett.

"He is a traitor, and I want his name."

"I don't know what the hell you're talking about."

Ogorodnik slammed the palm of his hand on the table and raised his voice toward Veronika. "Talk some sense into this idiot! I'll be back in ten minutes." Ogorodnik and the two other agents left the room, slamming the door closed. Hewlett was left alone with Veronika.

Veronika's hand moved down his arm, and she interlocked his hand with hers, then guided Hewlett to stand. She put her arms around him and leaned her head on his shoulder. "Baby, I don't want you to get hurt, and I don't want to lose you," she whimpered. "Major Ogorodnik will send those pictures to your embassy. If he does that, you will be sent back to America. I will never see you again."

Hewlett held her shoulders and pushed her an arm's length away. "Did you set me up?" he hollered.

"No." She turned away and clenched her fists. "I did not. Oh, Michael, this has gone so wrong. It is not what you think. I did not set you up." She turned and faced Hewlett again. "Yes, I did arrange to meet you at one of your embassy parties. I did that, with no oversight from my superiors. I thought if I could get an American diplomat to trust me, then I could impress them. I wanted them to see that I was a self-motivated and valuable officer. But that all fell apart when I realized that I am in love with you." She moved closer and hugged Hewlett tightly. "Just tell Major Ogorodnik what he asked you for and I will convince him to leave you alone after that. Then things can be like they were with us."

Hewlett put his arms around Veronika and closed his eyes. *She is so beautiful.* His thoughts returned to a scene in the bedroom. *Veronika held his head in her hands. Her back arched as her body convulsed and she moaned.*

The door crashed open. Ogorodnik returned to his seat behind the desk. "It would appear that you have only two choices, Mr. Hewlett. You can cooperate with me. Give me the information that I have asked for. In this case, you may continue living, and working, here in Moscow, as if nothing has happened." He smiled a toothy grin. With his palms extended, he continued, "And nothing changes. I'll even allow Lieutenant Kuragin to continue using the apartment for your meetings together." He sat and lit a cigarette. "As I say, nothing changes."

Hewlett gently pushed Veronika away. She moved to stand beside him. "And if I don't play ball?" he asked.

"Well, if you don't play ball, as you say, that is your second choice. In that case, copies of these photographs will be delivered to your Ambassador in a diplomatic pouch with an anonymous note included that explains that you have been engaged in an amorous relationship with an officer in the Russian Federal Security Service for many months." He took a pull on his cigarette then, continued, "That would be very embarrassing for you, I think. Very embarrassing indeed."

His pulse pounded like a bass drum in his ears as Hewlett weighed the options. *Crap, I'm smack in the middle of a rock and a hard place.* He turned his gaze toward Veronika. Her eyes were widened and glassy. Her lips were slightly parted. He had seen that look before when they were together, and she didn't want him to leave.

Hewlett turned toward Ogorodnik. "I don't know anything about Slow Dancer. That's a term I have never heard. But, a few months ago an officer contacted me and indicated that he wanted to defect."

Ogorodnik stood. "What was his name?"

"I don't recall his name."

"What did he look like?"

"I never saw him."

"What service was he in?"

Hewlett shrugged his shoulders and blew out a puff of air.

"Was it navy, army, air force, security service?"

"Shit, I don't know!"

"Then how did he contact you?"

"He left a note on my car. The note explained that he wanted to defect and included a telephone number to call and instructions if we were interested in helping him defect."

"What was the number?"

"I don't know, damn it. That was a long time ago. I read the note, placed it in my pocket, and later gave it to the defense attaché and never heard a word after that."

Ogorodnik sat, elbow on the desk and chin in hand. "Then you must find out who this man is." He picked up the stack of photographs and thumbed through them.

Hewlett's heart thumped. He loosened the collar of his shirt, and turned his gaze toward Veronika. She smiled and blinked her moist eyes. "Well, I'd say that you haven't left me with much of a choice."

"It won't be as bad as you think, baby" she replied.

***

"You do not have to continue whoring yourself to this American," said Ogorodnik after Hewlett was escorted out of the room. "We have him where we want him now. He will do what we need."

"I don't mind," replied Veronika. "It might expedite the gathering of information if I, shall we say, motivate him along the way."

"But you have accomplished your objective. It is no longer necessary," Ogorodnik insisted. *And the thought of that cowardly American doing to you what I have seen on those photos sickens me.* He visualized Veronika's milky white skin. Her flawless complexion. Her ample breasts with excited nipples. *You and I should be together.*

"I don't mind." She had a wide smile, her teeth perfectly white and straight. "In fact, he is a good lover. He makes me feel good. I will continue to see him. Then when we're through with him, eh." She waved the back of her hand.

"I forbid it," said Ogorodnik.

Veronika stood next to the door and faced him. "Remember Major, Michael wants to see me. That is why he will cooperate." She closed the door quietly as she left.

CHAPTER TWENTY

Moscow, Russia
3rd of January

"How have your meetings with Hewlett been going?" asked Ogorodnik. "Has he told you anything?"

"I have been with him twice since we confronted him and he has told me nothing about Slow Dancer. The only name he has given me is someone named," she pulled a pocket-size notebook from her hip pocket and opened it, "Cole Draper. He may be the American agent that is handling Slow Dancer."

"Hhmm. That is a good start."

"Michael told me that he loves me and that he is confused about this situation he finds himself in. He is distressed." She smiled. "But, he will find out who Slow Dancer is. I am sure of it."

Ogorodnik's desk on the second floor overlooked the courtyard between the two wings of Lubyanka. Veronika pulled a chair from a nearby desk and sat to his left.

"I have spent most of the last two days reviewing the records of high-ranking officers that have protested orders or resisted conformance to federal constitutional laws. Most of the senior officers are quite reticent to criticize publicly, but a few *have* been overheard to do just that. Subsequent reports were filed by patriots concerned about that officer's true allegiance." Ogorodnik turned the computer monitor so they could both read what was displayed on the screen.

"What have you found?" Asked Veronika.

"I have located records of two dozen officers that could fit the profile of someone willing to defect. Some that were passed over for a promotion they thought they deserved at one time; or given a reprimand they thought they didn't deserve. But, I still ask myself, in the end, these are all very successful officers so why would they even consider defecting?"

Veronika bit her lower lip and shook her head.

"So, what else could it be? What other factor could influence someone to betray their country?" Ogorodnik turned toward Veronika and grinned.

She smiled, nodded, then replied, "Love. Love and sex."

"Exactly. So, I wondered about the wives, or perhaps the girlfriends of these officers. We know that the traitor is a man. So, could a woman be the reason that this man is willing to turn against his country? And then I recalled a dossier that I updated a few weeks ago." He pointed his computer cursor to a name that was two from the bottom of his list and opened the file. "Captain Pyotr Kulakov. You may remember his wife. She is a former tennis professional." He placed his hand on the second computer monitor on his desk and moved that to a position where Veronika could see the screen that displayed the dossier titled: Kulakov, Oksana.

Veronika leaned closer to the monitor. "You recently changed the color code on Oksana Kulakov to orange based on comments made by a friend named Tasha," she observed. In a low tone, as if speaking to herself, she continued, "She blames the President for her son's loss in Ukraine. Resents lifestyle of the party." She turned toward Ogorodnik and her eyes grew wider. "A history of demonstrations against the government in her youth." Her forehead scrunched up. "She has made comments that indicate that she does not trust the government."

"Keep reading," said Ogorodnik.

Her gaze returned to the computer monitor and she continued to read. Veronika gasped and placed her hand just below her throat. "Her brother died while in custody in Lubyanka and she vowed never to forgive the government!" She turned her chair toward Ogorodnik. "She is married to a navy captain first rank. Major Ogorodnik, this is why I like working with you. This is magnificent research."

She touched his forearm. He closed his eyes for a moment, and the picture of her making love to Hewlett raced through his mind. There was a tingle in his groin. He pulled back, stood and turned his back to her.

Veronika stood and stepped in front of him. "We must learn more about Pyotr Kulakov. We should talk to this friend named Tasha."

Ogorodnik nodded.

***

The brown and white trolley clunked down the center lane of Kaphobkorp Boulevard in the academic district. Tasha Bolkonskaya sat in her usual seat on the right side in the back row of the first car. The light from the late afternoon sun was brightest there, which allowed her to read her sexy romance novels that provided an escape after long days as a financial analyst at one of Russia's largest banks.

"Next stop, Pectopah Street," announced the trolley driver.

Tasha looked out the window and lifted her gaze at the twenty-six story KYKCY apartment complex, a grim reminder of Stalin's architectural re-planning of Moscow. *Ugh. How can people stand to live there? It is such an eyesore*, Thought Tasha. *Someday I will move closer to the business district. Then I will not have to look at that building, and I will not have to make this miserable commute every day.*

She tossed her backpack over her shoulder and disembarked at the stop adjacent to the KYKCY complex and walked on the cobblestone path past a black Mercedes SUV with darkened windows. The SUV was parked parallel to the other curbside angle parked cars. She headed south on Kaphobkorp Boulevard next to a long row of white concrete columns that had once fenced in the large estate of a Romanov Prince.

The SUV's engine started, and it slowly passed Tasha as it moved in the same direction she was walking. It stopped a few yards ahead of her. *What is this?* Tasha stopped. *I don't like this.* She decided to cross the street and as she stepped off of the curb, the Mercedes quickly backed-up and stopped next to her. The front and rear doors sprung open, and two men wearing jeans and black leather jackets grabbed each arm. She screamed and resisted, but they overpowered her. In a matter of a few seconds, Tasha was forced into the back seat of the Mercedes, between two men with broad shoulders.

***

She was locked in a small room and stood with her back to the door. Her gaze darted from side to side; green concrete cinder block walls and a grey poured concrete floor with a drain in the middle of the room. No desk. No chairs and one lone light bulb hung from a cord hanging from the concrete ceiling.

Her pulse thundered in her ears as she began to pace the small room. *I've done nothing wrong. This must be a mistake.* She wiped a small tear off of her cheek. *I will just explain to them. I have done nothing wrong. Then it will be alright. But I must not cry.*

The door opened. A small man wearing the dark green uniform of a major in the FSB stepped inside. He carried a brown metal folding chair, walked to the back wall, opened the chair and sat.

Tasha stood in the corner of the room with her back to the wall. She felt her shoulders slumping, so she bravely stood tall and asked, "Why did you bring me here?"

Ogorodnik crossed his legs. "My name is Major Ogorodnik."

She brushed a lock of hair off of her forehead. Her lips trembled. "Do you know where you are?"

"This is Lubyanka. I want to know why you brought me here."

"You will stand in the middle of the room now," commanded Ogorodnik. "I have a few questions that I want to ask you."

Tasha looked at the drain in the middle of the floor. A tear dribbled down her cheek as she shook her head. "No."

"Stand in the middle!" shouted Ogorodnik as he stood.

Tasha flinched then shuffled to the center of the room and stood over the drain. "I have done nothing wrong," she whimpered.

Ogorodnik paced in front of her. He scratched his chin. Then he sat in the chair again, crossed his legs and lit a cigarette.

Tasha wiped tears from both eyes.

"You are friends with Oksana Kulakov."

"Yes, but I still don't understand why you brought me here."

"How long have you been her friend."

Tasha scrunched up her forehead and cocked her head. "Since we went to the university together," she replied.

Ogorodnik stood and closed the distance between them. The pungent odor of his cigarette wafted over her like a wave. "Is she a dissident?"

Tasha turned away and tried to put more space between them.

"You will stand where I tell you and not move unless I allow it!" shouted Ogorodnik.

Tasha returned to the center of the room and wiped another tear from her cheek.

"Tell me why your dear friend Oksana Kulakov objects to the ruling party," said Ogorodnik as he returned to the chair and stood next to it.

"I don't know what you are talking about," replied Tasha.

Ogorodnik placed one foot on the chair and glared at her. After a few moments of quiet, he asked, "Do you know what this room was once used for?"

Tasha shook her head to imply that she did not.

"Interrogations."

He stood quietly for a moment and Tasha shuddered at the thought.

"Not like this of course. I'm just going to ask you a few simple questions that I would like you to answer. This is not an interrogation. Those were, shall we say, disagreeable." Ogorodnik's gaze turned toward the drain in the floor. "Do you know why there is a drain in the middle of the floor, in the lowest spot?"

Tasha shook her head. "No, but — —"

Ogorodnik cut her off. "Blood and other body fluids were easily washed down the drain after those interrogations."

Tasha covered her mouth with her hand.

Ogorodnik closed the distance between them. "I'm sorry. I didn't mean to upset you. But please tell me what your friend talked about while you took holiday together in Sochi."

"It was nothing. It was just girl talk."

Like a shot, Ogorodnik slapped Tasha's cheek with a vigorous open hand. The heat of the blow intensified on her cheek, and a warm feeling trickled down her thighs. She dropped to her knees and whimpered, "Please stop."

"Will you tell me about Oksana Kulakov?"

Tasha raised her gaze and with tears in her eyes answered, "Yes."

***

After Tasha broke, Kuragin entered and escorted her to a small water closet where she was provided with a washcloth, and under the lieutenant's watchful eye, she was allowed to clean up and dispose of her soiled panties.

As they walked the hall toward Ogorodnik's office, Tasha wiped a tear from her cheek and sniffled. "I don't want to get Oksana in trouble. She is my friend. She is a good person."

Kuragin retrieved a facial napkin from her handbag and handed it to Tasha. "Mrs. Kulakov may already be in trouble, Ms. Bolkonskaya. By telling us what you know about her, you may be able to help her."

Kuragin opened the door to the office and told Tasha to sit on a worn, red leather couch with little cushion. She sat next to Tasha as Ogorodnik opened and sat on a padded folding chair facing them.

"Where am I," asked Tasha.

"You are in my office," replied Ogorodnik. "I think it will be more comfortable for you here while we talk." He smiled a reassuring smile with narrow, closed lips and raised eyebrows. "Would you like something to drink? Coffee perhaps?"

"I'd like some water," replied Tasha.

Kuragin stood and retrieved a plastic bottle of water and handed that to Tasha. Her hands trembled as she took it. She twisted the cap off and swallowed some as Ogordnik leaned back in his chair. He crossed his legs and clasped his hands over his knee. Tasha responded to his scrutinizing glare by dropping her gaze toward the floor.

"Tell me about your holiday in Sochi," demanded Ogorodnik.

"Oksana meant no harm by what she said. She is a caring person."

"Is she an angry person?"

"No. No. She is not angry. She only talked about being lonely since her son, Nicolay, was killed."

"And she is not angry about that?" probed Ogorodnik.

"Well, yes, I suppose a little bit. She didn't think that he should have been in Ukraine."

"He was a soldier following orders."

"Yes, but, the President told Pyotr that he would not send soldiers there."

Ogorodnik unclasped his hands and leaned forward. "Is Captain Kulakov also angry that his son was killed?" He raised his voice, "What is his state of mind. Will he betray the Federation?"

"No, of course not. He is —— —"

"Tell me the truth," shouted Ogorodnik as he stood over her.

Through a gush of tears, Tasha placed her head in her hands and said, "I don't know. Maybe. Please. I just want to go home."

CHAPTER TWENTY-ONE

Onboard the USS Jimmy Carter
Under the Bering Sea
NW tip of St Lawrence Island
15th of January

The coffee was hot and strong. Cole had been warned that navy coffee had a reputation for being that way and it was no different on a nuclear-powered attack submarine. Cole wore navy-issue blue coveralls and sat across the small wardroom table from Navy Lieutenant "Bobby" Choesler, an experienced SEAL assigned to Team Two out of Little Creek in Norfolk, Virginia. Cole poured a small amount of cold water in his coffee mug to bring the temperature down and to dilute the strength.

Cole and Choesler had trained hard for this mission. Time and time again, they'd practiced the docking and un-docking procedures with the submersible SEAL delivery vehicle. Over and again, they'd rehearsed the timing of the submerged run into Provedniya. Choesler had simulated the path that they would run so many times he claimed that he could do it blindfolded.

Cole sat with the cup in both hands. His gaze fixed on it like he was studying the cup.

"Nervous?" asked Choesler.

Cole snickered. "What do you think?"

"I think you'd be crazy if you weren't."

"I'm concerned about the intel coming out of the station chief in Moscow."

"It's pretty sketchy stuff," replied Choesler.

"Sketchy? Yes, but it's pretty clear the FSB knows about Slow Dancer. They have agents actively working the case." Cole raised his mug to his lips with both hands and sipped his coffee.

"You have a lot of courage, man. I respect that."

Cole nodded. "There's a fine line between courage and insanity, my friend. Not sure what side of that line I'm on right now."

Choesler drummed his fingers on the table. "It would be insane if you weren't prepared, shipmate, but you are the most prepared warrior I have ever worked with. You could do this in your sleep."

"Yeah, but in addition to not knowing what the FSB knows, the other unknown is Slow Dancer. Will he hold up his part of the plan?"

"At this point, you just have to trust him. You've checked him out thoroughly."

"Uh huh. But it concerns me that we placed a lot of information and instructions in one dead drop, and we never received a response. Shit, I could be walking into a trap for all I know." Cole placed his mug on the table, slid his chair back and exhaled. He looked up, toward a clock on the wall. "Well, what's gonna happen is gonna happen." He paused. "Skipper said we're about an hour away from our launch point. I suppose we ought to gear up." Cole stood.

Choesler stood and placed his hand on Cole's shoulder. "Hey. You're ready for this, but be careful."

Cole's gaze locked on the SEAL.

"And," continued Choesler, "good luck."

Cole nodded.

Ramburt had arranged for the Carter to be fitted with a four-man SEAL delivery vehicle and dry-dock shelter that mated with the deck hatch aft of the conning tower.

They left the wardroom and walked aft to the sub's transfer compartment and suited up in their scuba gear. They each attached diving knives on their calf. Cole draped a small pickaxe over his shoulder and a sound suppressed Glock nine-millimeter handgun in a holster on his other calf. When they were ready, they each signaled with two thumbs up. A chief petty officer opened the shipboard hatch.

Cole followed the SEAL up the ladder into the torpedo-shaped vessel. He attached the seat harness, inserted his breathing mouthpiece, and signaled that he was ready. The hatch closed with a metallic thud. The locking mechanism was rotated closed.

Choesler flipped several toggle switches. The compartment of the mini-sub flooded and the battery-powered motor and propeller started with a whir. The SEAL then pulled the latch that released the mini-sub from the docking station. It deployed from the host submarine with a lurch.

The vehicle was powered by a single rear propeller and was not much bigger than a Volkswagon bug. After hours of slow, calculated movement through water too shallow for the Carter, the onboard LED radar screen indicated they had reached the deployment point in Emma Cove, a half-mile from the tip of the Provedniya Peninsula. Still underwater, the SEAL slid back the top canopy of their vessel. Cole shook hands with Choesler, then released his harness. He pushed himself upward and away from the sub, gave a hand salute to the SEAL. Still submerged, he swam the last stretch to the shore under cover of night.

The only illumination Cole had was a small battery powered light attached to his headgear. He used his multifunctional wristwatch to guide him and swam on a compass bearing of three five zero until he reached a depth of five feet. He stopped there and chiseled through the eight-inch ice cover with the pickax. Within a few minutes, he broke through the surface of the ice. He was then able to stand and place his hands on the surface of the ice and lift himself out of the water.

He took one last look at his wristwatch before he turned off the headgear light. It was four ten in the morning. Twenty minutes before his arranged rendezvous time with Kulakov. "Shit!" he cursed. *Too early and it's friggin cold.*

Cole took off his flippers, and with only the rubber soles of his dive suit to protect his feet, he trotted across the ice to the snow-covered shore. There he crouched behind a large rock that provided some protection from the wind and removed his small oxygen tank. He surveyed the area around him. As far as he could see in the darkness were snow-covered rock outcroppings. He smelled the smoke from the coal-fired plants in the industrial city of Provideniya and saw the lights from the city that he knew from his readings during the planning stage was five to six miles northeast from his location. There was one small road that looked like it led out of the village and curved around the tip of the peninsula and headed northwest. It looked like it had been recently cleared of snow.

Kulakov should come on that road.

Cole crouched down behind a rock near the small road and held his knees next to his chest for warmth. After ten minutes, the sun began to peak over the horizon. Cole shivered. his fingers and toes started to feel numb.

At exactly four-thirty, he heard the sound of a vehicle's wheels crunching over the salted road. The vehicle stopped. A door creaked open.

"Mr. Draper," a man asked in a whispering voice. "It is Captain Kulakov. Are you here?"

"Hell yes, Captain. I'm here, and I'm freezing my ass off!"

Cole stepped out from behind the rock he had been cradled under and approached the silver Range Rover.

"I thought that you might be cold." Kulakov handed Cole a heavy down jacket, which he eagerly placed on his back and zipped it up.

"Now we must hurry," said Kulakov. "Place your gear in the back and get in." He pressed the dashboard switch to open the rear hatch.

Cole tossed his diving tanks, flippers and mask in the cargo area then got into the passenger seat and closed the door. Warm air blew out of the dashboard vents. Cole took off his gloves and warmed his hands in front of the vents. He turned toward Kulakov. The two of them appraised one another quietly.

Kulakov spoke in English. "Your submarine was not detected. Our admiralty would be wise not to underestimate your navy's capabilities."

A few moments passed in awkward silence, then Cole said, "Look, Captain, I'm here, and my ass is kind of dependent on you to have made the arrangements we agreed to. The other's that will help me extricate your wife will be at their designated place and time." Cole subtlety placed his hand on the handle of his ankle-holstered handgun. "I hope you haven't changed your mind."

Kulakov's gaze followed Cole's hand. "Intimidation is not necessary, Mr. Draper. I have not changed my mind. I am, as I said earlier, all in." He placed the vehicle in gear, did a Y-turn and headed on the road in the direction he had come from. "There is a small shack that is sometimes used by fishermen. It is about four kilometers from here. You will be safe there. It is warm, and you can rest."

Light snow started as they drove toward the shack. "The aircraft will arrive in approximately six hours. The crew will be changed, and the jet will be refueled at that time. It is scheduled to depart at eleven. There is a uniform at the shack that will fit you. You must wear that when I return."

"And the crew arrangements?"

"The co-pilot will become ill and unable to make the trip. You will replace him."

"And your wife. What does she know?"

Kulakov stopped the vehicle in front of the shack and faced Cole. "Oksana, of course, is ready to defect. We have talked of it often, and she knows the moment will be soon. But she is not aware that you will take her out today."

"Will that be a problem?" Cole asked.

Kulakov smiled. "I will leave that to you." He opened the car door. "Come, let's go inside."

Shit, I'm placing a lot of trust on this dude. Who knows what's behind that door. Cole adroitly pulled his pistol from his leg holster and slipped it into the pocket of the down jacket as Kulakov walked around the front of the car toward the shack. He placed his hands in the pockets and his finger on the trigger as he disembarked the Range Rover and followed Kulakov inside.

The shack was about-four hundred square feet of space. It had a wood-burning stove, a sleeper sofa, a small refrigerator, and a water closet with a toilet and sink with running hot water. Kulakov had stopped at the shack and started a fire before he rendezvoused with Cole.

"There are a few cans of beans, some black bread and a pound of sliced beef in the refrigerator. You are probably hungry after your journey."

Cole gazed around the small room. *Small. Nowhere to hide. Not a trap.* He took his finger off of the trigger, removed his hands from the pockets, then removed the parka.

Kulakov stood by the door. "I will pick you up in six hours." His brow furrowed. "I suppose if I were in your place, I might act this way as well, but you must learn to trust me. The gun was not necessary." He opened the door and before he stepped outside said, "Keep this door locked until I return."

Cole smirked. *I will trust you, Captain, but I will still keep my Glock close by, thank you.*

The stove provided more than enough heat for the small shack. Cole took off his dive suit and stripped down to his shorts and t-shirt. He ate a small meal with what was provided. His eyes felt heavy, so he crawled under a wool blanket and fell asleep.

***

Cole awakened when he heard the clicking of the doorknob being turned. He rolled off of the sleeper-sofa onto the floor and grabbed his Glock off the adjacent cocktail table. Crouched behind the thick side cushions, he slid the handle back and chambered a round. Cole's mind snapped to attention. His heart pounded like a jackhammer. He looked at his watch. *Seven o'clock. Too damn early for Kulakov.*

Two shadows hovered behind the iced over window. They appeared to be trying to see inside. Cole low crawled to the doorway and stood behind it. He held his Glock with both hands, finger on the trigger.

He heard voices outside. *Sounds like no more than two people. But there may be more if they arrived in a vehicle.* The doorknob turned again, and Cole stepped away from the door. He raised his Glock and prepared to shoot at whoever opened the door.

"Who is in there?" shouted one of the intruders. "Is that you Nicolai? Come on, it is Leo, and it's fucking cold out here. Let us in!" The doorknob turned again. "Damn you! We've been out fishing all night. We just want to warm up."

"C'mon, Leo, let's go." said the other voice outside. "Other than the captain, Vasili is the only one with a key. There is no car here. He probably skied here with one of his ladies. He's probably not in a state that he can accept visitors."

"Is that true, Vasili?" shouted Leo. "Are you in there with a town girl?" Cole heard a thud on the door. "You're an ass, Vasili!" Another thud on the door then it was quiet for a few moments. "Fuck you, Vasili. I hope your dick falls off."

The extended start of a cold ignition was followed by the rumble of an un-muffled engine then the crunching sound of tires rolling over icy gravel.

Cole sat on the edge of the sofa bed. "Sorry, Vasili. If you're dick falls off, I guess that's my fault." He smirked. *Well, that rules out any more sleep tonight.* He sauntered into the small kitchen and started a pot of coffee.

He washed and shaved with some products that had been left there for him, then dressed in the Russian officer's uniform that was provided.

***

Cole was lacing up and tying the bootstraps on the above-the-ankle, black boots when he heard the door being unlocked from the outside. With his hand on the Glock, he stood and faced Kulakov as he entered the hut.

Kulakov's gaze wandered to the handgun.

"I had some visitors this morning."

"Yes, I know. Lieutenant Vasili has been explaining to his comrades that he was in barracks all night."

"Well, I hope his dick doesn't fall off."

Kulakov looked quizzically at Cole. "Why would you say that?"

Cole snickered and said, "Never mind."

"Fine," replied Kulakov. "Here is your identification." He handed two plastic cards on a lanyard to Cole.

"Vladimir Rostov." Cole smiled. "No doubt a descendant of Count Nicolay Rostov."

Kulakov's eyebrow raised. "I'm not surprised that you know the characters of *War and Peace*. You are a learned man."

"Required reading in The History of Europe. Junior year at the University of Virginia."

Kulakov laughed heartily then said, "Come, we should go."

An inch of snow had accumulated while Cole was holed up in the shack. The road was slippery in places. Kulakov had no problem navigating his all-wheel-drive vehicle in those conditions. Still, he drove slowly.

"Let's talk about what happens after your wife is extricated," said Cole.

Kulakov turned his gaze toward Cole.

"That will start phase two of my plan."

Kulakov returned his attention to the road ahead of the car. "I will do what is necessary," he replied.

"Have you been reassigned to a job that is not as visible as fleet commander? Perhaps, something that will require you to travel?"

Kulakov grinned. "Will you make my aircraft disappear as well?"

"That would be a little obvious, don't you think?"

"After Oksana disappears, I will become depressed. I will also drink too much. My command leadership will be forced to make a decision."

Cole smirked at the thought.

"I will be reassigned when my depression and alcoholism affect my performance. But I do not yet know where. On this, we must be patient."

Cole nodded his agreement. "Good plan. That will work."

It took twenty minutes to reach the gate of the small naval facility. Kulakov slowed as he approached the guard and was prepared to stop. The guard saluted and waved him past. "The guard is a petty officer that has found himself in some trouble with alcohol and women. I have had to talk with him often lately. He does not want to inconvenience me by asking me to stop."

"And did you have anything to do with him being posted at the gate this morning?"

Kulakov turned toward Cole. "It's good tactics to place the chess pieces where you want them."

They drove another ten minutes and stopped at a small hangar in an area that looked relatively new. The hangar sat at the end of a runway that was unusually wide and long for an installation as remote as this was.

"I assume the runway is new, and part of your strategy to dominate in the Arctic?" Cole asked. "Long enough to accommodate your largest cargo jets?"

"You assume correctly."

Inside the hangar, a white with red trimmed tri-engine Yakovlev-40 passenger jet sat on a wet tarmac, fuel hoses attached to both wings. The center line rear cargo door was open and boxes of used electronics parts were being stowed onboard, along with Oksana Kulakov's luggage. The pilot was a short, stocky, senior lieutenant. He was walking around the aircraft and checking the condition of the tires and brakes, as well as ensuring fuselage integrity. Kulakov and Cole approached him.

The pilot stood at attention. "Captain, I wasn't expecting you so soon. Is your wife here already?"

"No. My wife will arrive soon. I came here to tell you there has been a crew change. Your co-pilot has suffered from food poisoning and is unable to fly. This is Lieutenant Rostov. He will be your co-pilot."

CHAPTER TWENTY-TWO

In flight above Siberia
15th of January

T he flight plan from the port of Provideniya on the Bering Sea to St. Petersburg was expected to take seven hours and thirteen minutes. It was just over three-and-a-quarter hours into the flight as the aircraft passed over the town of Nord'sk in the Siberian Plain. The clear, bright, blue horizon ahead was a stark contrast to the vast unbroken, snow-white plain below.

Cole poked the arm of the captain to confirm the strong dose of eszopiclone he had laced in the captain's coffee had taken effect. With the pilot in a deep sleep, Cole set the cabin pressure controller on a slow reversal, which began the process to slowly open the outflow valve and begin depressurization of the aircraft. He placed the aircraft on autopilot to cruise at an altitude of thirty-five thousand feet at four-hundred-twenty miles per hour, then unbuckled his seat harness and stepped out of the cockpit. At over six-feet tall, he found it necessary to turn slightly and duck his head as he walked through the cabin door toward the passenger area.

The VIP passenger area of this Yakovlev-40 was configured for eight guests. Four sets of two heavily cushioned, coffee colored leather seats that faced one another. A cocktail table made of aluminum and glass sat between them. There were two sets on either side of the beige, plush carpeted aisle. The only passenger was Oksana Kulakov.

Oksana was seated in the second seat on the right side, facing forward. She wore a light-blue one-piece above the knees dress, that accentuated her thin waist. Oksana was in her mid-forties and wore her light-brown shoulder-length hair parted down the middle. Her dark brown eyes and long, curvy eyebrows were set above high cheeks and luscious full lips. She closed the book she had been reading and placed it on her lap as she looked out the window at the frozen tundra below.

Dressed in the dark blue dress uniform of a Russian navy lieutenant, Cole slid into the seat across from Oksana. As he did so, she shifted uncomfortably and turned to face him. Her cocked head and raised eyebrows showed her surprise at this breach of protocol. *Yeah, I know. You are, after all, the wife of a captain, first rank.* He leaned forward, his elbows on his knees and hands clasped together, and spoke in Russian. "Mrs. Kulakov, my name is Cole Draper. I am an American, and I am here to help you defect."

Oksana inhaled deeply through her nose, sat upright and turned her gaze through the window, towards the clouds far off in the distance. After a brief pause, she turned to face Cole. "I was not expecting — —"

"I know." Cole cut her off and looked directly into her eyes. "You weren't expecting to defect today, not during this flight. I'm sorry, but that was intentional. Your husband is aware and agreed to do it this way. Not knowing the specifics of when and how I would take you out eliminated the chance that you could have said something that might have alerted a friend or an acquaintance. Your security service has spies everywhere."

Oksana looked out the window again. "I had hoped to visit my son's grave in Moscow."

"I'm sorry," replied Cole as he stood and walked toward the back of the airplane to a floor-to-ceiling closet. "That won't be possible." Cole opened the closet and pulled out two cardboard boxes and returned to where Oksana was still seated. He stood in the aisle next to her. As she looked up at him, Cole opened one box and pulled out a blue suit and handed it to her.

"Mrs. Kulakov, this is a thermal, high altitude jumpsuit." He pulled out a small cylinder and mask. "And this is a parachutist oxygen system." He handed that to her.

Oksana placed the suit, cylinder, and mask on the table in front of her, then sat back in her seat and folded her arms across her chest. "You're crazy, sir. I am not going to jump out of this airplane. You are going to have to — —"

"I need you to trust me Mrs. Kulakov." Cole cut her off again and sat on the edge of the seat across from her. "We don't have a lot of time. I need you to listen to me and focus." He waited a few moments to ensure he had her undivided attention. "In a few minutes, this aircraft will lose cabin pressure. This suit and oxygen will protect us from hypoxia and from freezing to death."

Oksana leaned over and looked forward toward the cockpit cabin door.

"Your pilot is sleeping. He will not be protected," said Cole sternly. "I will guide the plane to a predetermined location, and we will do a tandem jump." Cole took hold of her hands and looked her straight in the eyes. "Mrs. Kulakov, I have done this many times. I promise you will be safe."

Oksana shook her head as she said, "No. No. I cannot do this."

"Mrs. Kulakov," said Cole. He dipped his head slightly to maintain eye contact. "There is no turning back. The plane is depressurizing. You have to trust me."

She continued to shake her head, "The plane — —"

Cole cut her off again, "The plane will fly until it runs out of gas and then it will fall through the ice somewhere in the Laptev Sea, far away from any civilization. The ice will refreeze. It will be many years before the crash site will be discovered."

"The pilot has a family." She frowned.

Cole fixed his gaze on her and showed no emotion.

"What about us? How will we survive in Siberia?"

"Where we jump, we will be met there by an American special operations team. They will quickly take us out of Russia."

Cole stood and began to remove his uniform to change into his jumpsuit. "Mrs. Kulakov, this has been well planned. You can't turn back now."

Oksana sat wide-eyed as Cole stripped down to his shorts. Her hands shook as she slowly unfolded her jumpsuit.

With his jumpsuit on, Cole stood in the aisle next to Oksana. She looked up at Cole.

"I'm frightened," she said softly while she wiped a tear from her eye. Her lips quivered.

"Don't be," replied Cole. "Mrs. Kulakov, this is what I do."

Cole held out his hand, which Oksana accepted. "Let me help you put on your suit." He helped her to her feet, and they stood facing each other.

Standing just above Cole's shoulder height, Oksana smiled nervously, looked up and said, "I will trust you." She removed her dress by lifting it over her head and tossed it in the seat on the other side of the aisle.

Cole furtively admired her very fit physique as she stood in front of him wearing only her very skimpy black lingerie. He held the jumpsuit as Oksana stepped in, one leg at a time. Cole zipped up the front of her suit, helped her put on her gloves, then taught her how to breathe through the oxygen system.

As the cabin became noticeably colder and the air thinner, he attached the tandem jump harness across her chest and snapped the harness closed on the center of her back. He tested the tandem strap snap hooks to ensure they worked as he described the jump procedure to Oksana.

"I'm going to disconnect our harness now, and go back in the cockpit." Cole grabbed Oksana by her shoulders and looked through her mask and into her eyes. "But when I return, this is how we will connect our harness, and then I will open the rear door. Do you understand?"

Oksana nodded. "Yes."

After he ensured she was breathing properly through her cylinder, he unlatched the snap hooks, helped her into her seat and headed back into the cockpit where he piloted the aircraft to the designated jump altitude and coordinates.

***

Two of the most experienced cold weather warriors from the U.S. Navy's SEAL Team Two wore white cold weather suits and rode their white painted snowmobiles to a designated location eight miles inland from the small, ice-covered, cove at the north end of the Yamalsky district in Okrug, Russia. The two chief petty officers reached the assigned GPS coordinates and stopped less than one hour after they'd driven away from the site where the USS Scranton, a Los Angeles class nuclear submarine, had broken through the ice surface long enough to disembark the pair.

"Wind is coming out of the west. I'll set up the tent," said the senior ranking of the two chiefs. "You can start packing the snow cover from the leeward side. No telling how long we'll be here."

"Senior Chief, I've been on some wild assignments, but this one ranks right up toward the top."

"Not our job to question why, we just do or die," he replied as he pulled his backpack off.

"Yeah, I know, but I can't help but wonder who these dudes are." The chief petty officer pulled a shovel out of his backpack and started pilling a wall of snow that would eventually cover their tent and provide an additional layer of insulation from the cold. "The dudes are jumping from an airplane just so we can take them back to the Scranton and then take them to Norfolk. Doesn't make much sense. Why not just fly the plane?"

"Don't worry about that, just shovel."

***

Cole attached a harness to the handle for the hydraulically operated door then pulled the lever. The door opened slowly. "This is it." Cole spoke into the microphone embedded in his jump mask. The loud noise of the air rushing past the open door made it difficult for Cole to hear her response. He tapped her on her shoulder to ensure that she was paying attention. Cole raised his voice as he spoke into the microphone. "When we jump, the harness attached to the handle will reverse the door position lever, and the door will slowly close. We'll only have a few seconds to jump before the opening gets too small." He pull-tested their latches on the tandem rig then asked. "Are you ready?"

Oksana's gaze was focused on the sky outside of the open tail door of the aircraft. She nodded then her eyes closed and, as Cole had told her to, she knelt down at the edge of the door.

Freefall time is ten seconds for the first one thousand feet then approximately five and a half seconds for every thousand feet at terminal velocity. Cole did the math in his head. *Two minutes and forty-nine seconds to reach five thousand feet.*

He started the stopwatch on his wrist and pushed forward out the cabin door. They tumbled downward. Slow at first, but they rapidly accelerated. Soon, they were in a one hundred and forty mile per hour freefall. The force of the air against their bodies felt like they were being pushed upward. The wind howled, and the sky was an intense blue until they passed through a fluffy white cloud at twelve thousand feet. Then the snow-covered surface below approached rapidly.

Cole maintained focus on his digital watch, and when two minutes and forty-nine seconds passed, he opened the parachute. With a jolt, they dramatically slowed, and Cole maneuvered the risers to gently spiral the chute toward the ground. As they approached the landing, Cole tapped Oksana on her shoulder, and she lifted her knees to her chest the way Cole had instructed her to, and he slid into the landing on his backside.

Cole unlatched the rig to separate them and stood.

Oksana sat on her knees and quickly removed her mask. "I'm feeling light-headed."

"Give it a few seconds. It will pass."

She raised her head and looked at Cole, then blew a puff of air. She smiled. "That was amazing! It was breathtaking!"

"You were amazing. You did everything exactly the way I told you to do it. That made the jump easy."

Oksana stood and squinted. She completed a three-hundred-sixty-degree scan of the horizon. "The sun's reflection off of the snow is so bright. It hurts my eyes."

Cole pulled in the parachute, folded it up, and placed it in a backpack.

"What do we do now, Mr. Draper?"

"Well, we'll just take a ride with our friends over there." He pointed toward two white objects on the horizon.

"I don't see anybody." Oksana squinted and raised her hand above her eyes.

The SEAL's approached rapidly and became easily distinguishable.

"Now, we'll take a short snowmobile ride. Then a long trip in a nuclear submarine. Destination, America," Cole said as he placed his and Oksana's oxygen mask in his backpack and buckled it up.

The pair of SEALs rolled to a stop a few yards away from Cole. The senior chief took off his cold weather goggles. "Holy crap sir, I ain't never seen a tandem jump from altitude. That took guts."

The second chief took off his goggles. When he saw Oksana, he visibly flinched and said, "You're a woman."

Oksana looked at Cole and asked, "What did he say?"

Cole replied in Russian, "He noticed that you're a woman."

She turned toward the chief and laughed.

"Sorry, sir," replied the chief. "I didn't mean anything by it, I just wasn't expecting a woman."

"Gentlemen," Cole said. "My name is Cole Draper, and at this moment I am working with the Central Intelligence Agency." He turned and faced Oksana and said, "And this wonderful lady is named Oksana Kulakov. Now, I believe you have a submarine somewhere nearby."

The senior chief chuckled and handed artic goggles to Cole and Oksana. "You'll need these. Jump on."

Cole and Oksana each placed the goggles over their eyes and climbed onboard the back seat of one of the snowmobiles and the SEAL's accelerated toward the ice-covered cove to rendezvous with the Scranton.

***

"Red Dog Two, this is Red Dog One, this YAK appears to be in distress," radioed the lead pilot of the two-ship formation of SU-30 fighter jets dispatched to check on the Yakovlev-40 that had veered far from the course that was registered with the Federal Aviation Administration of Russia. "Bogie appears to be flying on auto," the pilot continued in a clipped tone.

"Affirmative," replied Red Dog Two.

"Have you established comms?" asked Red Dog One.

"Negative."

"Have you observed any structural damage on your side?" asked the lead pilot.

"Negative dog one."

"Dog two, I'm going alongside to peek into the cockpit," radioed Red Dog One. With a sinking feeling in the pit of his stomach, the lead pilot continued, "I may be able to make contact with someone inside, then we may be able to help them land safely."

"Affirmative."

"Dog two, maintain position on his tail."

"Affirmative. Be careful, sir. He's been porpoising between thirty-two and thirty-nine thousand."

Red Dog One keyed his mike to acknowledge, then eased the throttle for a gradual acceleration and eased the stick to carefully move close alongside the YAK-40. The SU-30 drew within a meter of the YAK-40's port side wingtip. The lead pilot gazed to his right but was unable to see into the cockpit. He closed his eyes and shook his head, then reported, "Windows frosted over. Unable to see into the cockpit."

A few moments passed in silence. "God rest their souls," replied Red Dog Two.

These experienced pilots knew that if the windows were frosted over, then the temperature inside was well below freezing and that the cause of that was a loss of cabin pressure. At an altitude of thirty-five thousand feet, the pilot probably succumbed to hypoxia and lost consciousness in less than twelve seconds. The passengers and crew had no chance of survival.

Red Dog One veered away and took position behind the Yak-40 on the port side. The two pilots maintained position for more than two minutes without conversation until Red Dog Two said, "Red Dog leader, I have three minutes of fuel before I need to return to base."

"Acknowledged," replied Red Dog One. *Proper procedure would be to request permission to shoot this YAK down.* He shook his head. *But, the aircraft is on a course that will take it over frozen water. There is no chance that it will crash in a populated area. I won't shoot it down. I can't do that.* He shook his head. "Red Dog Two, let's go home."

***

The foursome on the two snowmobiles slowed down as they approached the icy cove and the senior chief signaled for the others to stop. He removed his goggles and looked at his watch, then turned toward Cole and said, "We're a little early. We need to wait here."

After thirty minutes, a loud crunching sound like crystal breaking, followed by the screeching of steel against the heavy ice surface, caused Cole to step off the snowmobile and observe. The black conning tower of the Scranton, with the wings positioned vertically, poked through the ice layer then rose up like a time-lapsed spring flower.

Cole smiled, then said to Oksana, "Our ride has arrived."

She wore a wry smile. "Mr. Draper, when will I see my husband?"

"Soon, Mrs. Kulakov. Soon," replied Cole. *I'm sorry that I had to lie to you, honey, but right now, your guess is as good as mine.*

Cole sat back on the snowmobile. The SEAL drivers accelerated in the direction of the submarine. When they arrived, the submarines' commanding and executive officers were climbing down the ladder from the conning tower. Steam vented from several vents on the surfaced hull.

The commanding officer walked over to Cole and said, "I assume you are Cole Draper." He extended his hand. "Welcome to the Scranton."

CHAPTER TWENTY-THREE

Moscow, Russia
17th of January

Hewlett had insisted on a change of location for his continued rendezvous with Veronika. The new apartment was located in the industrial Dobrovsky District near the Sheremetyevo International Airport.

"I'll feel more comfortable away from the city," he said when they had made the arrangements. "I'm afraid someone from the embassy will see us together, and I would then be asked to explain who you are. It's better this way."

Veronika sat on the end of the bed, naked, her legs crossed in a lotus position. Her strawberry blonde hair brushed her breasts. She twirled a few strands between her fingers. Hewlett sat on the black leather sofa. He wore only his white boxer shorts. His shirt and slacks were draped over the side of the sofa.

"What is the matter, Michael. Why won't you come to bed?" asked Veronika.

Hewlett gazed at a faded painting on the opposite wall. A painting he had seen many times in his past visits to this room, but had never paid it any attention. He studied the garden scene until he recognized it. "That's funny," he said, "as many times as we have been here, this is the first time I noticed the painting is a scene from Swan Lake in Gorky Park."

Veronika scrunched up her face and slowly turned her gaze toward the painting. "Yes, yes, it is." She stood and joined him on the couch.

Her warm skin pressed against him and her hand slipped under his boxers. She began to fondle him.

"You're very distracted, love," said Veronika. "Let me see if I can get your attention."

Hewlett leaned back and closed his eyes as he slowly became aroused. Veronika removed his shorts. A warm moistness enveloped him as she took him in her mouth. There was a pleasure, yet at the same time, he seethed with a rising sense of anger at her, and at himself. *I've betrayed everything that was important to me. Veronika used me, and I let her.* "Stop," said Hewlett. He pushed her away.

Veronika sat upright. Her face wore a frown. "Michael, what is the matter?"

The rumble of a large jet on final approach caused the room to shudder. Hewlett stood and began to pace the room. "Damnit, Veronika," he snarled. "I don't know who I am anymore. I haven't felt well lately." He stopped pacing and faced Veronika. "What I've been doing is wrong. Yes. I have strong feelings for you. But I'm an American. I come from a patriotic family. My father, my grandfather, my uncles, they have all served America. All proudly, and with distinction." He turned his back to her and paced again. "They all said, 'We're so proud of you,' when I was appointed to the foreign service." He shook his head then turned, and with a thud, he fell back onto the couch next to Veronika. He placed his head in his hands. "What I have done is unforgivable. Sometimes I think I should just kill myself."

Her hand touched his leg. "It will be alright, darling."

He turned to face her. "You don't understand. A few days ago, I received an email from my younger sister."

Veronika's eyes glistened. She took his hands in hers. "Tell me, darling. I *will* understand."

They leaned toward one another and kissed. Her lips were soft and tasted like berries. Hewlett closed his eyes. *No woman has ever made me feel the way I do when I'm with her.*

He reclined against the back of the sofa and Veronika leaned against him. He put his arm around her. "My sister just graduated from Yale University."

"A very prestigious school," interjected Veronika.

"Yes." Hewlett stroked her hair, and continued. "In her email, she gushed on about how proud she was of me and that, because of me, she sought an appointment to the foreign service, and was accepted. She worships me. I've always been a hero to her, no matter what I did. Now, because of what I've done with you—when it's discovered that I have provided top secret information to the Russians—her career will be over before it ever gets started, and it will be my fault. Then, there will be the embarrassment my entire family will endure. It will be unbearable for them." He leaned his head back and closed his eyes. "I can never go home," said Hewlett.

Veronika shifted her position. Her warm breast pressed against his chest. He lowered his head and gazed into her eyes.

"You don't need to go home," said Veronika. "Once you find out who Slow Dancer is, you can defect." She sat upright, smiled, and with an enlivened voice said, "You can stay with me. I will make you happy."

The room began to shudder again.

Hewlett grimaced. "I already know the identity of Slow Dancer. I've known it for several days."

Veronika's eyes widened. She placed her hands on his shoulders. "Tell me!"

As the large jet flew overhead, Hewlett said, "It's as Ogorodnik suspected. Slow Dancer is Captain Kulakov."

Veronika's mouth was agape with incredulity. "Oh my gosh!" she blurted. "Major Ogorodnik will be so happy to hear this." She stood and went to her neatly folded pile of clothes at the edge of the bed and started to dress.

"Where are you going?" asked Hewlett.

"I am going to tell the major that he was right."

"Right now?"

"This is important, Michael. This will be very good for me. When my record is reviewed, and it states that I discovered who Slow Dancer was . . ." She paused with a smirk as she reached around her back to clasp her bra. "It will be very good for my career."

Hewletts' pulse surged like a dam had been opened. *That's it, then. She's completed her assignment, and she'll be through with me.* He raised his voice. "Don't go yet. Stay with me."

"You should come with me. I'll make sure that you're rewarded for this information." She sat and picked up her jeans from the pile.

Son-of-a-bitch. So, it was all just an act, thought Hewlett. *She never cared about me. Sex was just part of the job for her.* He gritted his teeth, narrowed his eyes and balled his fists. *My life is ruined, my family name is ruined, my sister will be devastated, and Veronika doesn't give a damn because she will get what she wants.* "You bitch!" hollered Hewlett. He stood, and as Veronika turned toward him, he swung hard and landed his fist on the upper edge of her right eye.

Blood splattered from the force of the blow. She fell backward onto the bed, unconscious. A dark red puddle grew on the white sheet of the bed where her face lay.

Hewlett's mouth was dry. He swiped his hand across his mouth then mounted the bed on top of her. He rolled her onto her back and straddled her.

The paper-thin floor of Veronika's right eye socket was ruptured. The eye was colored purple and had begun to swell closed. The pupil in her left eye raced rapidly from side to side. Her nose bled profusely. Then, as his eyes watered and his pulse thundered in his carotid arteries, Hewlett placed his hands around her neck with a vice-like grip, and squeezed until Veronika turned purple and she stopped breathing.

CHAPTER TWENTY-FOUR

Moscow, Russia
23rd of January

The audio and acoustics technician sat across the table from Ogorodnik in the soundproof audiometric room in the center of the ground floor of the Lubyanka building. Designed and constructed as a room within a room, the facility was structurally isolated from the host room. Double walls isolated the facility from ambient noise in the surrounding rooms to achieve a 75dB reduction.

In spite of assurances to both Hewlett and Veronika that he would discontinue monitoring their rendezvous, Ogorodnik had continued to do so. On his orders, technicians placed a laser listening device in a hotel room across the street from the small apartment they met at in the Dobrovsky District near the airport. The device worked on the Doppler principle of frequency shift. The technique used an infrared laser beam focused on the window of the apartment. The beam was then reflected off the glass back to the receiver, which captured all of the tiny vibrations of the glass. Those vibrations resulted in a pattern of higher and lower frequencies that the receiver then reconstructed and recorded as voices.

The technician handed Ogorodnik a set of Bose acoustic headphones that matched his and said, "I have listened to this conversation at least fifty times, and I have tried to isolate the American's voice, but the interference from the airliner was just too much. The jet's engines caused the windows to vibrate more than the voices in the room."

"Then we will listen another fifty times until you can eliminate all other sounds and capture the distinct voice which will answer my question." Ogorodnik lit a cigarette and placed the headphones over his ears. "Start the recording before the interference."

The technician started the recording. The voice was clear. It was Veronika Kuragin

"You don't need to go home. Once you find out who Slow Dancer is, you can defect. You can stay with me. I will make you happy."

The interference started, and it sounded like a soft drum roll.

Hewlett's words became distorted by the interference, *"I already ... the ... of ... Dancer."*

The drum roll grew louder.

"Tell ..." Was all that could be established from Veronika's answer.

"... Ogorodnik ... Slow Dancer ..."

The interference lessened, and Ogorodnik clearly identified Veronika's voice again. *"... gosh!" Major Ogorodnik will be so happy to hear this."*

"Where are you going?" Hewlett asked Veronika.

"I am going to tell the Major that he was right."

"Right now?"

"This is important, Michael."

Ogorodnik closed his eyes and blocked out the remaining conversation as he visualized Veronika in the room with Hewlett.

"You bitch!"

Ogorodnik flinched. He opened his eyes and removed his headphones as he heard the loud crack of Hewlett's fist impacting Veronika's face.

The technician removed his headphones and placed them on the table. He leaned forward. "I'm sorry that you heard that, Major. I know that Lieutenant Kuragin was more than just a colleague. I know that you had feelings for her. This must be hard to listen to."

Ogorodnik took a pull on his cigarette then exhaled the smoke through his nose. He nodded. "Yes. I wanted her to stop seeing the American once we had him compromised. But as you can surmise from the recording, she must have had feelings for him."

"I'm very sorry, Major."

"He beat her. Then he strangled her." Ogorodnik blinked as his eyes began to tear up. "Then he laid in bed with her, placed a gun in his mouth and pulled the trigger." He took another pull on his cigarette and wiped a tear off of his cheek. "Run the recording again." He placed the headphones over his ears. "I must hear what they said about Slow Dancer. It must be Captain Kulakov. That is why I must have clear audio on the recording. When I confront him, I want to be able to prove to him that I know he is the traitor called Slow Dancer."

CHAPTER TWENTY-FIVE

St. Petersburg, Russia
2nd of February

The Black Mercedes-Benz GLS stopped on Liteyniy Avenue in front of the massive red marble establishment known only as the Government Building. After thanking the FSB driver that met him at the airport, Ogorodnik stepped out of the backseat and onto the curbed sidewalk. A young couple walked hand in hand toward him then stopped when they saw him. They crossed the street, which made him smile. *Does this uniform make you uncomfortable?*

He lifted the collar of his black wool peacoat to ward off the cold wind and walked a hundred meters to the solid mahogany doors that served as the entrance to the Government Building. Inside, the large atrium had polished white marble floors and yellow painted walls almost entirely covered by paintings and sculptures.

Ogorodnik stepped up to the substantial, built-in, polished redwood reception desk and announced, "I am Major Ogorodnik of the Second Division of Internal State Security. I am scheduled to meet with the Director of Fourth Division."

The clerk lifted her gaze away from the computer monitor. She narrowed her eyes and seemed to scrutinize Ogorodnik. Her braided, light brown hair protruded from the back of her red beret, and her light-green uniform indicated she was in the navy. Her youthful complexion suggested an entry-level rank. She raised her hand and flicked her index finger, and an equally young petty officer marched across the room and stood in front of Ogorodnik.

"The director is expecting you. Follow me." He turned and marched toward the wide marble stairway that led to the second floor.

Ogorodnik followed and was seated in a comfortable brown leather chair in the anteroom where he waited briefly before being escorted into the director's office.

"Major Ogordnik, please have a seat," said Colonel Vasily Yustitsiya. "May I offer you a drink? Vodka? Or a glass of this fine French brandy that was a gift to me from my wife."

"Thank you, Director. Brandy sounds fine. It will deflect the chill from outside."

As the director poured two brandies in crystal snifters, he said, "I understand from your emails that you would like to discuss the plane crash that killed Oksana Kulakov." Ogorodnik accepted the brandy offered. They took their seats across the desk from one another. "It's such a shame. Do you remember her from her days as a tennis player?"

"Yes, indeed I do. But that is not my interest in her now."

The director's eyebrows raised and he took a sip of brandy.

"Oksana Kulakov is one of several individuals that I have been investigating in the context of a possible high-level defection."

"But she is dead, Major. What is your possible interest now?"

"Is she dead, sir? Have her remains been discovered?"

"Major, I've read the reports from the pilots who intercepted her aircraft. It was in distress and crashed north of the Laptev Sea."

"I have read the report as well, sir."

"Then I do not understand what you are asking, Major. This seems very unnecessary."

"I have reason to believe that Mrs. Kulakov did not perish in that incident. In fact, I have reason to believe that she was not on that aircraft when it fell to the earth and that, furthermore, I have reason to believe she is involved in a plan to betray The Federation."

"What proof do you have to make such an accusation?"

"A colleague of mine was able to compromise an American foreign service officer. She uncovered evidence of a senior officer of the Federation that intends to defect to the Americans. This man is code-named Slow Dancer by the Americans, and I have reason to believe that this man may be Captain Kulakov, and I believe that the Americans have already helped Oksana Kulakov defect to America."

"Come now," replied Yustitsaya. "That's absurd. To make this accusation against the captain now? I think that he has suffered enough. Don't you? We shouldn't bother him and make it harder for him to cope at a time like this." He refilled his brandy sniffer and did not offer a refill to Ogorodnik.

None offered to me. Your subtle message is understood, Director. I cannot expect any cooperation from you in this investigation. "Yes.

Well, Director, I have fulfilled my obligation to inform you that my investigation will require me to interview someone in your jurisdictional area and that I will do so today." Ogorodnik stood and placed the empty brandy sniffer on the director's desk. "Thank you for the brandy, sir."

"And who do you plan to interview?" asked Yustitsaya.

"Captain Kulakov. I have arranged a meeting with him for this afternoon."

The director craned his neck forward and squinted. "You're going to interview the husband of the recently deceased Oksana? One of the most decorated and respected naval officers in the fleet?" He shook his head. "You're going to go into Captain Kulakov's office and accuse him and his wife of being traitors? Major, I would be surprised if he does not cause you great physical harm, and I would not blame him if he does."

"When I confront him, you will see that I am right."

"That is absurd. I must ask again, what proof do you have to make this accusation?"

"I have a recording of a conversation that technicians are working on to clean up background noise. I believe that this recording will electronically isolate the voices of my colleague and her informant. When this is done, I will formally charge Captain Kulakov with treason."

With his brandy sniffer in his hand, the director pointed toward the door. "Good day, Major. I do not wish to be any part of this."

Ogorodnik stood and met Director Yustitsaya's icy glare with one of his own. "You will see that I am right." He turned and eased the door closed as he left.

***

The click of a door handle opening caused Yustitsaya to turn around and face a hidden door on the wall behind him. The Deputy Director of Fourth Division stood in the doorway.

"Did you hear everything that little man said?" asked Yustitsaya.

"Yes, sir, Director. The accusation that he made against Captain First Rank Kulakov is preposterous. It is based solely on circumstances. No real evidence."

"Yes, it is." Yustitsaya drummed his fingers on the table for a full minute. "Still, what if there is *some* substance to his suspicion? What if the recording that he mentioned holds credible conversation, as he suggested?"

"Then the evidence would be better than circumstantial."

"And," Yustitsaya paused, "it would be very embarrassing if an arrest is made within our area of responsibility without my full participation."

"Indeed."

Yustitsaya continued to drum his fingers as he contemplated the situation. After two minutes, he stood and walked to the door to his private office. With his hand on the doorknob, he faced the deputy director. "Place Major Ogorodnik under surveillance when he is in Fourth Division District. I want to know what hotels he stays in, and I want to know who he meets with. If there is any substance to his accusation, I will know when to exert my authority over this operation, as it occurs in my district."

The deputy director nodded. "I will take care of it."

***

The windy minus-six-degree centigrade temperature was average for January. Ogorodnik was not offered a ride, so he walked one block north on Liteyniy Avenue and then followed the Kutuzov Embankment. The cold, moist air blowing off of the Neva River caused a thin layer of ice to form on Ogorodnik's coat and fur-lined winter hat. He wore sunglasses, which left nothing exposed to the raw elements.

After thirty-five minutes, he arrived at the Admiralty Building. After depositing his coat and hat in a cloakroom near the entrance, he was escorted to a small conference room and was seated at a faux wood round table.

***

Kulakov entered the room. Ogorodnik stood. "I am Major Nicolay Ogorodnik of the Federal Security Service. It is my pleasure to meet you, sir, and thank you for agreeing to meet me here instead of your headquarters in Kaliningrad." Ogorodnik extended his hand.

Kulakov appraised the agent from the FSB. *Late thirties, Skinny. Probably smokes a lot. Large dark bags under the eyes. Perhaps a heavy drinker. Shifty eyes.* He sat without completing the handshake. "I understand you want to ask me some questions about my late wife."

Ogorodnik shifted his gaze away from Kulakov and answered, "Yes, I — —"

"What are you looking at. Look at me. I am the one you are talking with."

They made eye contact, and Kulakov fixed his stare at the agent. "What do you want?"

Ogorodnik ran his hand across his mouth. "Sir, please allow me to express my sympathy for your loss."

"Thank you." Kulakov placed both elbows on the table and leaned toward Ogorodnik. "But I should tell you, Major, that I was informed only moments ago that you are leading an active investigation into the disappearance of my wife. Had I known that earlier, I would not have agreed to meet with you."

"Captain, I am sure you understand that if you had refused to meet with me voluntarily, that the service has methods to compel you to cooperate."

Kulakov stood. "Is that a threat, Major?"

Ogorodnik remained seated, his hands trembled slightly.

"Are you nervous, Major?"

Ogorodnik steepled his hands and placed them on the table, the slight tremble continued. "Captain, please sit down. I don't want this to be any harder than necessary. I am sorry for your loss, but I must ask you some questions."

Kulakov sat. His pulse surged. He leaned forward again with both elbows on the table and his fists balled. "What do you want?"

"Captain, are you aware of your wife's activities while she studied at St. Petersburg College?"

Through gritted teeth, Kulakov answered, "Yes, I am. That was over twenty years ago, and that was all reported and investigated long ago."

"Yes. But are you aware that she was recently overheard making subversive comments about our government."

"When and where was she allegedly heard making subversive comments, and by who?"

"I'm sure you understand that — —"

"I'll tell you what I understand, Major." Kulakov raised his voice. "I understand that you are implicating my late wife, and by association, me, in some kind of plot that you have not yet defined to me. Now if you can't show me some piece of evidence and tell me what the alleged crime that Oksana and I are being linked with, then it is time for you to leave." Kulakov pressed a call button under the table. Two armed petty officers entered the room. He stood and said, "Do I make myself clear, Major?"

Ogorodnik stood. They glared at one another angrily.

"I thank you for your cooperation, Captain. I'm sure we will talk of this again."

Ogorodnik was escorted out of the room. Kulakov sat. His lips trembled and his heart pounded like a jackhammer. *I must get this information to Cole Draper.*

***

Outside, Ogorodnik glared angrily at the door to the room where Kulakov sat. *Captain, you are a foolish man to treat the FSB with such disrespect. We have many resources. If your wife is in America, I will find out. I will send a message to our undercover operative in the United States and ask him to investigate. We have people deeply embedded in the clandestine services of the United States. If your wife is there, I will find out.* Ogorodnik turned up the collar of his jacket, and stepped into cold streets of St. Petersburg. He hailed a taxi to the airport.

CHAPTER TWENTY-SIX

Davi Keenan had two children who attended the International School of St. Petersburg, located across the north bank of the Neva River, and well beyond walking distance from the American compound. The consulate provided transportation for the children but recently, on most mornings, Keenan drove his children to school, and they returned on the bus with the other children in the afternoon.

Keenan had a specific reason for doing this. Before Cole returned to the United States, he had instructed Kulakov to leave a small red mark on a "Children Crossing" traffic sign in front of the International School anytime he needed a dead drop recovered.

It was a cold, drizzly morning, so the children were appreciative about getting a ride in a warm car instead of one of the nine-passenger vans provided by the consulate. With the children chattering in the back seat, he approached the entrance to the school property. Keenan slowed as he passed the Children Crossing traffic sign. A six-inch red line spanned half the width along the bottom of the rectangular yellow sign. He recalled Cole telling him, *"Half line drop is at the coffee house in Mikhailovsky Garden. Full line drop is Pushkin House on the Fontanka River."*

He stopped the car in front of the school entrance. As the rear door popped open, the children called out, "Bye dad. See you this afternoon." The door closed with a thud, and Keenen was alone in his quiet sedan.

He drove back to the consulate and parked in his designated spot. *Can't just drive a diplomatic vehicle to a dead drop, so I guess I'll have to hoof it.*

Bundled in a brown hooded winter parka, he exited the gate on foot onto Furshtatskaya Road. Five minutes later, he boarded a city bus which he rode to Letniy Garden across the Fontanka River. An old woman with a two-wheeled shopping cart and a young man wearing a denim jacket also got off the bus at that stop.

Keenan boarded a second city bus headed south toward the shopping mall on Nevsky Avenue, where most of the passengers disembarked. Keenan entered the west side door of the mall and walked at a fast pace through it. He exited on the east side where he and two others boarded a city bus going north. Five minutes later, the bus stopped at Mikhailovsky Garden. He was the sole passenger to disembark. On foot, he followed the bus for two hundred meters to the next stop and observed only a young woman get off. She trotted in her high heels to catch a transfer on an adjacent road.

So far, so good. No watchers.

Wet snow started to fall as he walked under the evergreen arch and along the gravel walkway toward the coffee house. The air temperature was just below freezing. The smell of coffee mixed with that of the wood fireplace from the coffee shop filled the crisp air. Keenan was warm inside his parka. Warmer than he should be considering the outside temperature. His mouth was parched, and his heartbeat thumped as he walked to the back of the coffee house and approached the pile of neatly stacked firewood.

Cole's instructions had been very clear. *"Kulakov has made the arrangement. You must find the log of a different color. It will be a hollow log, and the package will be inside."*

Keenan scanned the pile of firewood logs. They were all sections of white birch wood except for one log that stood vertical and leaned against the back of the pile. It was thicker and a darker color. *Oak, probably. Like that matters.* He picked up the log and reached his trembling hand inside.

"Hey, you! Get away from that firewood. It is for the use of the coffee shop," scolded a middle-age woman with a streak of grey that mingled with her long brown hair.

Keenan clutched the small leather package in his hand and dropped the log. His heart pounded. "Yes. I am sorry," he said in Russian. "I was walking by the pile, and this log fell off. I was just placing it back on the pile."

"You should not be back here. This area is for employees only."
She stood just outside the rear door with her hands on her hips.

"Yes. I am very sorry." Keenan placed his hands, and the leather
sack, in the pockets of his parka and walked towards the garden
entrance. When he reached the gravel walkway, he looked over his
shoulder. The middle-aged woman was engaged in an animated
discussion with another woman. She pointed at Keenan. He stepped
up the pace and left the garden. Cold sweat beaded on his upper lip.

At the first bus stop outside of Mikhailovsky Garden, Keenan
boarded a bus headed south on Sadovaya Street along with three
workmen. They wore dirty denim jeans and layered tops under hooded
sweatshirts. Keenan sat facing forward near the rear door. The three
men sat side by side on a bench seat that faced the inside of the bus.

On three occasions, Keenan made eye contact with the largest man
in the group. His head was shaved, and he wore a goatee. His hooded
sweatshirt was colored burnt orange. Each time the man
acknowledged Keenan with a nod. *Who the hell are you*, thought
Keenan. He wiped the sweat off of his forehead with the back of his
hand. In his other hand, he held the leather sack in a tight grip.

One man got off at the second stop. Keenen looked at the transit
map that hung on the wall of the bus across from his seat. *Six more
stops and I'll be near the consulate. I need to do something to see if
these men are watchers.*

At the third stop, one lady got off. Keenan waited until the driver
was almost ready to close the door, then he abruptly stood. As he
disembarked, the large man smiled and nodded again. The bus pulled
away from the curb, and Keenan noted that one of the workmen had
disembarked as well.

Keenan crossed Sadovaya Street and headed north along the busy
pedestrian walk for one block, then turned a corner and waited behind
a building wall for the workman to approach. After three minutes, he
stepped out from behind the wall. There was no sign of the workman,
so he walked briskly in a north direction toward the consulate. As he
made the final turn onto the road that ran parallel to the consulate gate,
Keenan saw the backside of a workman with a shaved head and a burnt
orange hooded sweatshirt walking away.

CHAPTER TWENTY-SEVEN

T he Defense of the Fatherland Holiday fell on the first Friday of February. Patriotic flags flapped in the brisk breeze along the main road on the naval base. Three feet of snow lined both sides of the recently plowed road. Kulakov pulled his Range Rover into his assigned parking space behind the office building at the naval base headquarters in Kaliningrad. He quickly scanned the area around him and saw that he was not alone. He reached under the seat and found the bottle of Stolichnaya vodka he had placed there. He lifted the bottle to his mouth as two junior lieutenants walked past the car. He quickly slipped the bottle under the seat again then looked up. The two lieutenants had passed the vehicle and were both looking over their shoulders towards him.

Yes, I just took a drink, and yes, I know that you saw me.

He got out of the car, entered the office building, and walked through the foyer into the office area for the senior staff. As he entered the room, Kulakov stepped unsteadily and bumped into a water cooler, nearly knocking it over.

Captain Pantelyov, Kulakov's second in command, caught the large bottle and steadied it. "Good morning, Captain." Kulakov noted his stern gaze. "Sir, the staff was concerned. You are over an hour later than your normal arrival time."

"Yes. I overslept." He glanced around the room. The others in the room were staring at him, and they averted their gaze when he met theirs.

"I understand, sir. That can happen to any of us," replied Pantelyov. "You have a meeting scheduled at ten to discuss the fleet maintenance schedule. Will you be attending that?"

"Of course. Why wouldn't I attend?" Kulakov answered tersely.

"Yes, sir. I was just reminding you."

Kulakov walked to his office. Along the way, he took occasion to rest his hand on desktops to steady his balance. He shut the door behind him and closed the blinds to the outer office.

***

Pantelyov shook his head and walked away. Three junior officers approached him in the hall before he reached his office. "Sir," the shortest of the trio said. "Begging your pardon, sir, but we've talked about this among ourselves, and . . ." He looked around at the other two.

"Go on," said Pantelyov.

"Well, sir, we think that it is our duty to state our concern about Captain First Rank Kulakov."

Pantelyov fixed a hard gaze on the trio.

"Sir. Kulakov is —— —"

"Captain Kulakov," Pantelyov corrected the speaker.

"Yes, sir." The lieutenant stood at attention. "Captain Kulakov is not fit to lead the fleet. He is an alcoholic. He is drunk when he comes to work, and he is drunk when he goes home. He has become an embarrassment to the uniform that he wears. We believe it is our duty to raise this concern."

"Captain Kulakov is a hero of the navy." Pantelyov raised his voice above the conversational level and continued, "How dare you speak of him in this way? He has suffered a great deal. He lost his son to a sniper and his wife to a tragic accident in a matter of months. How dare you denounce him in this manner!"

"Sir, what happened to Captain Kulakov is regrettable, but in the best interest of the fleet we urge you to ask the Admiralty to replace him." The three officers continued to stand at attention, their back straight and eyes focused on a spot directly in front of them.

Pantelyov took a step closer to the trio and replied, "I will take your concern under advisement." He balled his fists. "But I warn you, if I ever hear any of you speak of this again, to me or anyone else, your career path will take a decisive turn for the worse."

"Yes, sir," the trio responded in unison.

Pantelyov entered his office and sat behind his desk. He turned his chair toward the window and stared absently at the snow-covered banks of the Pregolya River. *Damnit. Those officers are right. I've known that for several months, but Pyotr is my friend.* He turned toward the desk, placed his elbows on the desktop and his head in his hands. He lifted his gaze to a framed picture of Kulakov and himself on graduation day from the Academy. *I'm sorry my friend, but those young officers are correct, you are no longer fit to lead this fleet.* He raised his head and saw several other pictures on his wall of he and his friend Pyotr as they progressed together in their careers. *But maybe there is a way to get you reassigned without making this a medical issue that would ruin you.*

He picked the handset off of his desk phone and dialed the number for Admiral Kletsov, a mutual friend and the highest-ranking officer of the Russian navy.

CHAPTER TWENTY-EIGHT

Light snow showers over the Elizabeth River did little to dampen the enthusiasm of the homecoming crowd that waited at the pier as the Scranton returned to its homeport. Cole thanked the captain for the professionalism and hospitality the crew had shown them during the four-week journey under the ocean. They shook hands. Cole then faced the United States Flag that flapped in the breeze on the boat's tail and briefly stood at attention before he escorted Oksana, wearing navy coveralls, and a heavy wool pea coat, across the gangway and onto the pier.

It was a bone-chilling cold as they walked toward the end of the parking area where Diana and Katie waited. Oksana was shivering, so Cole put his arm around her shoulder and pulled her closer to him for warmth.

"You are a very kind man," said Oksana. She flashed her broad smile at Cole. "It is very cold, but I am also shaking because I am very nervous."

Cole reassured her. "There is nothing to be nervous about. The hard part is behind us. Everything will be fine."

Before they exited through the security gate at the end of the pier, and into the throng of friends and loved ones, Oksana turned and observed the scene surrounding three attack submarines moored pierside. Hammers clanged, and powered ratchets screeched as sailors in their blue work coveralls performed maintenance. Others moved about on yellow forklifts, and loaded parts and supplies. "There is so much activity," she said.

"There always is," Cole replied. He took her hand and led her through the gate.

They passed through the crowd. Diana stood about twenty yards beyond and wore a red overcoat and a fluffy wool cap. Her blonde hair extended to her shoulders. She smiled and waved her hand above her head when she saw him then walked quickly toward him. They embraced and kissed.

"Happy Valentine's Day, lover," she whispered.

"Are you kidding? I didn't realize what day it was."

Diana's whole face radiated a smile. "You will tonight."

Katie, wearing big wool mittens and ear muffs, bounced up next to them. Cole gave her a bear hug and kissed her forehead. "I missed you guys."

"Missed you, too," replied Katie.

Cole disengaged from Katie then stood side-by-side with Diana, his arm draped over her shoulder. He spoke Russian, and introduced Diana and Katie to Oksana. He then switched to English and completed the introductions.

As Cole's business partner, Diana's assignment in the Slow Dancer operation was to help Oksana assimilate to life outside of Russia. She extended her hand to Oksana. Also speaking in fluent Russian, she introduced herself.

"Ramburt wants us all to meet at the safe house at Eaton's Landing," Diana said as the group walked toward the black Cadillac Escalade with government plates parked in the lot next to Katie's red Mini Cooper. "If we leave now, we might be able to avoid the beltway traffic nightmare."

"I'm all for that," replied Cole.

They reached the Escalade. Katie turned toward her Mini Cooper and placed her hand on the door handle, then stopped and asked, "How long will you be gone, this time, Uncle Cole?"

"I'm not sure."

"Well, okay. You guys have been spending a lot of time away from home lately. What's going on?"

"It's business, Katie. You know I can't tell you everything."

"Yeah, yeah, I know. Secret agent stuff, huh?"

Cole pointed his forefinger toward Katie. "You just worry about school, young lady."

Katie broke into a wide smile. "Cooper misses you too, ya know."

"Have you been letting her sleep in your bed?"

"That's against your rules."

Cole shook his head and turned toward Diana. "She's been letting Cooper sleep in her bed, hasn't she?"

Diana smiled and stepped into the Escalade.

"See ya soon, number one niece," he said to Katie.

Katie smiled and raised her fist, thumb up, then entered her Mini Cooper.

Diana sat in the driver seat and Cole in the passenger seat. Oksana sat in the back. As they buckled up their seatbelts, Diana said, "I talked with Ramburt while the boat was pulling in and he told me he already sent a request to the foreign service officer in St. Pete to dead drop the confirmation that Oksana had arrived."

Cole smirked. *Great! Commence phase two.*

Diana continued, "Ramburt will be at the safe house when we arrive. He needs to talk to you. He said there have been some developments. It's important."

"Not sure that I like the sound of that."

***

The sun had set by the time the entourage arrived at the safe house in Eaton's Landing. After brief introductions, room assignments and two shared take-out pizzas, Cole followed Ramburt to the backyard deck overlooking Crab Creek. He closed the patio door behind him and they sat at a black, wrought-iron circular table with two matching chairs next to a circular fire pit and a crackling three log fire. Lights from the nearby docks and estates across the river flickered as the wind shook the tree branches of the mature landscape that surrounded them. Ramburt poured two glasses of eighteen-year-old single malt scotch, neat, and handed one to Cole.

"Glad you made it back safely, Cole. What you did was pretty daring." Ramburt raised his glass in a toast.

Cole clinked glasses. "Thanks. Now I have a second sense that tells me that phase two will be a little more challenging and that you have something you need to tell me."

"The news out of Russia has not been good, Cole," said Ramburt.

Cole sipped his scotch then placed the glass on the table. "Would you care to elaborate?"

Ramburt drummed his fingers for a few seconds, then said, "There have been two incidents. They're most likely related," he paused. "Shit! Cole, I think that that Slow Dancer has been compromised."

Cole leaned back in his chair and crossed his arms over his chest. "Son-of-a-bitch," he muttered.

"The first event happened a few days before you pulled Mrs. Kulakov out. It took a while to unravel this, but we know that a foreign service officer stationed at the Moscow embassy was involved in what State has designated a murder-suicide."

Cole narrowed his eyes and cocked his head.

"What's clear from the evidence the Moscow police have shared with the investigating team at State is that our FSO murdered a young Russian woman. He beat her and strangled her. Then he laid in bed next to her and blew his brains out with nine-millimeter. The Russian version is that he had an affair with this young lady. They had a lover's quarrel. He did what he did, and as far as they're concerned, the case is closed. The FSO was sent home in a flag-draped box, and condolences were offered to all concerned."

"And when the other shoe dropped?"

"The other shoe, we've discovered, is that the dead woman was a lieutenant in the FSB."

"Holy shit," replied Cole. "A sparrow, no doubt."

"Yeah." Ramburt took a sip from his scotch then continued, "Trading sex for secrets. The oldest game in spycraft. On top of that, we think the kid knew about Slow Dancer and probably shared some information with the sparrow."

Cole finished his drink, picked up the bottle and poured another. He held the bottle over Ramburt's glass.

"Yeah."

Cole gave Ramburt a two-shot pour.

"It turns out that this was the young man that was Kulakov's initial contact. Espionage was not in his dossier, so he did the right thing at the time, and turned the information he had to the station chief who took it from there. But after he offed himself, his colleagues have come forward and reported that he was subtlety asking questions about Slow Dancer, a code name that he would have no professional reason to show interest in."

Cole placed his hands behind his head and leaned back. "Shit!"

Ramburt stood and walked to the back of the deck. "Then there's this note we received from Kulakov. It's on the table in the envelope."

Cole reached over the table, retrieved the note and read;

Mr. Draper,

I trust when you read this note that Oksana will already be under American jurisdiction. I look forward to that confirmation. However, it is with grave concern that I inform you, I have discovered that Oksana has been the subject of an investigation by an agent from the Federal Security Service. I have reason to believe that investigation has now expanded to include me. I am concerned the plan has been compromised. I wish to meet with you to plan an expedited departure.

Cole placed the note on the table. "This is not good."

"Yeah," replied Ramburt. "There are some at headquarters who think we should pull the plug on the operation." He turned and faced Cole.

"What do you think?" Cole asked.

"You first."

Cole sipped his scotch and tapped his fingers on the table. He took a moment to contemplate then replied, "I can't do that. The deal we made was to extricate both of them. What would we tell Oksana?"

"Yes. The deal was for both of them, but if he's been compromised, the degree of difficulty is much greater now. It may be too risky."

Cole stood and joined Ramburt near the back of the deck. "We made a deal. I intend to honor that deal."

"You told me that Kulakov's priority was to get his wife out safely," Ramburt replied. "We've done that. I think our priority now needs to be getting our hands on the information he said that he would provide."

"And if we go thumbs down on bringing him out, just what do you think would motivate him to give us that information now?"

"We could tell him it's too hot right now. Maybe in a year or so, if he keeps a low profile, we can look at mounting an operation to get him."

"Ahh, bullshit. Brother, you know as well as anyone, the FSB are like vultures. If they're already circling overhead, in a year Kulakov will either be dead or lost in their penal system. The Gulags are still there and functioning efficiently." Cole narrowed his eyes. "Is there something else you're not telling me? Because it sounds like you're getting cold feet. And that's not like you."

"POTUS is worried. She asked if I thought we should pull the plug. She's concerned about the optics. If you get caught, well, she's afraid we could have another Gary Powers spectacle. An American spy on public trial. Highlights on every television, every day."

"She's concerned about appearances! You can tell POTUS to go to hell."

"Cole. she may have a point. If nothing else, think about Diana."

Cole slammed his glass on the table. "Diana has nothing to do with my decision."

"What the hell is the matter with you, Cole?"

"No. What the hell is wrong with you?" replied Cole angrily. "I told you before to stay out of my affairs. My relationship with Diana is not in your wheelhouse!"

Ramburt placed his glass on the table and glared at Cole. He then calmly said, "You're right. But the Slow Dancer operation is directly in my wheelhouse. Maybe I should pull the plug on it right now."

"Screw you, Todd. We made a commitment. You can't do that."

The swoosh of the patio door opening caused them to break eye contact. Both men turned and looked towards the sound. Diana stepped halfway out of the door. "What's going on out here? We can hear your voices raising inside. Is everything alright?"

Oksana stepped on the patio behind Diana.

"Everything is fine," replied Cole. "I was just telling my old friend that I am going back to Russia to meet with Oksana's husband and begin the next phase of this operation."

"So, you're still committed," replied Ramburt, matter-of-factly.

Cole nodded.

"You're on a short leash, Cole."

"Fine." Cole turned toward Diana. "Professor Madison needs to do some more research in St. Petersburg. "I'll be leaving soon."

Ramburt poured himself another glass of scotch. "I'll tell POTUS that we're going to stay active."

Cole nodded.

"Cole, if Kulakov is being monitored . . ."

"I know. It's dangerous. Thank you for pointing that out, Captain Obvious."

CHAPTER TWENTY-NINE

T he spacious room was cold and drafty. An eight-log fire burned in the large fireplace under a black marble mantel on the dark, wood-paneled north wall. The south and east walls were almost entirely covered with artwork depicting Russian navy ships and naval battles.

The rectangular, six-seat conference table that Ogorodnik was seated at was small, considering the size of the room. He faced four floor-to-ceiling windows accented with heavy drapes the color of merlot wine. They were closed at the top and fixed open by sashes along the sides. Behind him was the main entrance on the east wall, where an armed petty officer stood at attention by the door. Three crystal chandeliers hung from the high ceiling and lit the room with a dull, incandescent glow.

Vladimir Kletsov, Admiral of the Russian Navy, entered the room from a hidden door on the paneled north wall. Kletsov was a large man, shorter than Ogorodnik expected, with a large nose and thick eyebrows. He wore a grey double-breasted blue uniform with one thick gold and four narrower stripes on the sleeves, and gold epaulets on the shoulders. A single row of five narrow rainbow-colored ribbons adorned his barrel-like chest.

The admiral was followed by his chief of staff, who was a head taller than Kletsov. His uniform was similar with one fewer narrow stripes and was adorned with gold aiguillettes that hung on the right shoulder of his double-breasted coat.

Ogorodnik stood as Kletsov and the chief of staff took seats on the opposite side of the table.

"Please sit down, Major Ogorodnik," said the chief of staff in a gruff voice.

Kletsov pushed his chair away from the table. He crossed his legs at the ankles and folded his hands in his lap.

Ogorodnik sat. His heart hammered under Kletsov's scrutinizing gaze. The admiral remained silent.

"Thank you for seeing me, Admiral," said Ogorodnik. "I know that you are a busy man, so I will get right to the point. It is a concern of grave national security." He shifted his gaze between the admiral and chief of staff, then continued, "Sir, I am afraid that a senior naval officer under your command is planning to defect to the United States."

Kletsov pursed his lips and narrowed his eyes.

Ogorodnik fiddled with the top button on his shirt and glanced at the fire as a few moments of uncomfortably warm silence passed.

The admiral leaned forward and placed his elbows on the table. "That is a very serious accusation," replied Kletsov, his voice a deep baritone and his five-second glare penetrating. "My staff has informed me that the officer that you have accused of this is Captain First Rank Kulakov."

"Regrettably sir, that is correct."

"I have known Pyotr Kulakov many years. I attended his wedding and drank cognac with him to celebrate the birth of his son." Kletsov folded his arms across his chest. "Major, you are utterly wrong to make such an accusation against this outstanding officer." His scowl intensified. "I also understand that you met with Pyotr and raised your concerns with him. Did his answers not satisfy you?"

"No, sir. I do not believe that Captain Kulakov was truthful with me when I interviewed him." Under the table and out of Kletsov's view, Ogorodnik wiped the sweat from his palms on his pant legs. "Admiral, may I request the courtesy of allowing me to describe the evidence and the reasons that I believe Captain Kulakov is the man the Americans call Slow Dancer?"

Kletsov leaned back in his chair and nodded.

Ogorodnik licked his lips and ran his hand over his mouth. "My case started with confirmed reports about Captain Kulakov's wife and her seditious comments made in public to her group of close friends."

"Oksana?" replied the admiral incredulously.

"Yes, sir. In the federal security service archives, I have discovered several reports about her past and that of her family that caused me great concern."

"I am aware of the history of her brother," replied Kletsov.

"And her dissident activities after her brother passed."

Kletsov placed his elbow on the table and rested his chin in his hand. "She was a young woman then, and she was angry that her brother died while waiting for a trial. I do not find that hard to understand."

"While touring as a tennis professional, she developed a reputation for, shall we say, an abundant appreciation of the lifestyle of Western Europe."

"That was a different time, Major. That lifestyle is no different than what she had available to her in Russia today."

Ogorodnik wiped his hands on his pant legs again. "Yes sir. May I continue?"

Kletsov nodded.

"Her frequent seditious comments were confirmed by her long-time friend during a simple interrogation. She — —"

Kletsov interrupted, "Enough! You are wasting my time, Major. You must be aware that Oksana perished in an aircraft accident just over a month ago."

"Admiral, I am not convinced of that."

Kletsov tapped his index finger on the table. "Get to your point, Major."

"Sir, the wreckage has not been located. There is no proof that she perished in that plane crash."

"Air Force fighters were scrambled. The pilots confirmed that the crew and Oksana were dead before the plane crashed."

"What if she wasn't on the plane when it crashed?"

"You're mad."

"Admiral, I believe that Oksana Kulakov has already defected and that she is somewhere in the United States waiting for her husband to join her."

"Are you saying that you believe Oksana Kulakov parachuted out of that airplane? That's ridiculous!"

"Perhaps she was never on the plane, sir. Perhaps — —"

Kletsov's face reddened. "Major Ogorodnik, Captain Kulakov is one of the most respected officers in my command. I don't like what you are accusing him, and his wife, of. He is a patriot. Don't ever accuse him of being anything less. Have some respect. He recently lost his son. Within a few months, he lost his wife to a tragic accident."

Kletsov slammed the palm of his hand on the table and then pointed his index finger at Ogorodnik. "Let me be clear about this, Major. My concern as it relates to Pyotr is to get him through this period of grief and mourning and get him back to work in the capacity that I know he is capable of. I trust that you will do nothing to impede his progress in that respect."

"Yes, sir, I understand, but given the strategic information that Captain Kulakov can access — —"

"I have complete confidence in Captain Kulakov, and you have given me no reason to think otherwise." He raised his gaze toward the guard at the door.

Ogorodnik felt the grip of the petty officer on his shoulder. He looked up at him, stood, and replied tersely, "Thank you for your time, Admiral."

***

"That impertinent bastard," said Kletsov after Ogorodnik had been escorted out of the room. "To come into my headquarters and accuse one of my best officers of treason. With no proof. I would have liked to punch him in the face."

"Yes, sir, Admiral," replied the chief of staff. "But with all due respect to Captain Kulakov, you must take this report in context with the reports that have surfaced regarding his excessive drinking, and the loss of confidence from his subordinate officers at fleet headquarters."

Kletsov turned his angry glare toward his chief of staff. "Just what are you implying? And remember, Pyotr is my friend."

"I consider him a friend as well. He has dealt with much personal tragedy within the last year. But the fact remains that Pyotr is in a critical and strategic job. In his current state of mind, he may be susceptible to manipulation, or at the very least, susceptible to error."

"And what do you suggest?"

"My recommendation is to consider reassigning him. At least until he accepts what has happened and moves on."

CHAPTER THIRTY

St. Petersburg, Russia
17th of March

Cole arrived at midday and checked into the Four Seasons Hotel. He was greeted by a brunette with wide eyes and a flawless, milk-white complexion that needed no makeup. She spoke English with a sing-song French accent. "I see you have been here before. Welcome back, Professor Madison. I can place you in a second-floor room with a view of the gardens in front of the Admiralty building, if that is acceptable."

"That will be fine," replied Cole. "I'm curious, your English is lovely. Were you schooled in France?"

"Oh, no sir." She gave him an embarrassed smile. "I learned to speak English in my secondary school."

Makes sense. French culture is still an influence in Russia, particularly St. Petersburg.

The receptionist raised her hand to get the attention of a bellhop. Cole was escorted to his room. After he shelled over six hundred rubles and bid goodbye to the bellhop, Cole showered and changed into fresh clothes. A short time later, Cole again located the large painting of a nude woman wrapped in a red shawl on the third floor near the spa. He stood in front of the painting and the same short, elderly man and with a pronounced limp and blue beret, approached Cole. Without stopping, he handed over a sealed envelope.

Back in his room, Cole read the note. *There is a boat club at Fermy Park, near the Military Institute of Railway Troops in Peterhof at a distance of forty kilometers. Meet me on the dock at the boat club at precisely nine o'clock.*

Cole picked up the house phone and dialed the concierge. "I will need a rental vehicle tonight at half-past seven o'clock. Yes, a Mercedes Benz will be fine."

***

There was a dusting of snow on the ground when Cole retrieved the rental from the concierge in front of the hotel. The engine was running and the interior was warm when Cole closed the door and adjusted the seat. The Benz was a black E-class sedan with a beige colored soft napa leather interior. He adjusted the two side view mirrors with the electronic control and then reached up and adjusted the overhead rear view mirror.

He gazed into the mirror. A dirty white Volvo SUV was parked in a Parking Prohibited area behind him. Exhaust billowed from the dual tailpipes. *That is too obvious. Shit, I hope I haven't picked up a tail already.* Cole rubbed the sweat from his palms on his pant legs. *Please don't let that be a watcher on me.*

He waited for an opening in traffic then quickly merged with the vehicles on the road outside the hotel and monitored the scene behind him for signs of a tail, specifically, the white Volvo.

The city streets were congested and a little slippery, so Cole placed the dynamic select transmission in manual and used the paddle shifters on the steering wheel to manage the gear selection and obtain the best traction under the conditions.

Traffic was heavy and moved slowly. An accident on the Obvodnly Bridge that spanned the Ekateringofka Canal blocked one lane of traffic ahead. A tall, burly man in a dirty grey-hooded sweatshirt emerged from a seafood delivery van and began directing traffic ten cars at a time. The first group to cross came toward Cole, then he moved ahead with the traffic as the second group of ten crossed. As he waited, Cole shifted his gaze between the rear view and the two side view mirrors. After two cycles, Cole was across the bridge and was relieved to accelerate ahead. Two white-and-blue Muscovite police sedans with flashing blue lights passed on the other side of the road. *If the Volvo was behind me, I'll definitely lose it now.*

It was eight o'clock. *Shit. That accident cost me a good fifteen minutes, and I suspect when Kulakov says precisely, he means it.* Cole shifted the transmission back to automatic as he accelerated on the

Western Diameter High-Speed Toll Road. The nine-speed transmission shifted gears imperceptibly as Cole easily merged into traffic and accelerated to 140 kph. After ten minutes, Cole moved to the right lane and slowed to 100 kph. He shifted his gaze between his mirrors and the road ahead as other vehicles with headlights flashing changed lanes and quickly passed him on the left, often accompanied by the universal one finger salute.

Cole repeated the acceleration and deceleration two more times on the toll road, and when he was comfortable that there were no watchers on him, he followed the signs and exited at Peterhof. He glanced at his watch. *Twenty minutes to park and find the pier.*

To Cole's surprise, the marina appeared abandoned. He had no problem finding a place to park in the large gravel lot. The lot contained dozens of rows of small boats set in wood dry docks and covered with tarps under several inches of melting snow and ice. He glanced around at the midway and mused, *I suspect this must be a playground for the wealthy in the summer months.*

Cole zipped his brown leather aviator jacket tight as he walked toward the largest of three piers that extended several hundred feet into the Gulf of Finland. The cold wind bit at his exposed face, and a mist hovered several feet above the frigid water as he ambled down the longest pier.

Lightning flashed behind dark clouds over the Gulf of Finland.

Cole blew warm air into his cupped hands and stomped his feet to stay warm. At the low rumble of inboard engines, Cole turned his gaze to the left. Dim lights gradually brightened through the mist. He looked at his watch. *Precisely nine o'clock.*

The boat was different. A hard cover enclosed the pilothouse, but Cole recognized Kulakov under the glass in the illuminated interior as the boat slid sideways next to the pier. The sound of a window sliding open was followed by Kulakov's voice, "Get on Draper. We will talk when we are underway."

The height of the pier was level with the boat's deck. Cole stepped onboard. Kulakov eased the throttle as Cole made his way to the pilot house and entered. "Welcome, Draper," said Kulakov. "The seas are more active where we are going. I hope you are not prone to sickness." He looked over his shoulder with a stern look as he fastened his seat harness.

Cole narrowed his gaze and cocked his head. "I'll be fine." He removed his jacket and warmed himself near a heating vent.

"Good. That is good." Kulakov opened the throttle, and Cole lost his balance briefly as the bow of the boat lifted out of the water. "We have much that we must discuss but first, tell me about Oksana. Is she well?"

"Oksana is fine." Cole sat on a wood bench, with little cushion, along the rear bulkhead a few feet behind the conning station and faced Kulakov. "She's in a safe house near Washington with some of my partners who will teach her to speak English and help her adjust to life in the free world."

"Life in the free world," rejoined Kulakov. "You make it sound like Arthur's Camelot." His eyebrow lifted and he shook his head. "Don't be so smug, Draper. We both know there are many problems in your so-called free world. Let's not pretend it is that much better than life in Russia."

Cole leaned forward and placed his elbows on his knees. "Yeah, well allow me to point out that I am helping you escape Russia and not the other way around."

"It is a complicated world, Draper." Kulakov stoically gazed at the seas ahead. "But we do what we must do."

Kulakov maintained the speed and trim of the boat as he headed northwest into the wind and seas. The sea state gradually became more active, with water coming over the bow as the small boat pounded over the surf. After forty-five minutes, he turned with the seas and placed the boat controls on auto-pilot, with just enough throttle to maintain steerageway in the rough seas. He turned his captain's chair toward Cole and said, "I'm very sorry."

CHAPTER THIRTY-ONE

St. Petersburg, Russia
17th of March

The Petr Hotel stood fifty meters northwest of the Four Seasons Hotel on Admirateyskiy Prospeckt. Located between a restaurant that served Mediterranean cuisine and a pharmacy, the Petr lacked the elegance of the Four Seasons. Colonel Yustitsiya, from the St. Petersburg office of the FSB, was parked in the white Volvo SUV next to the wide, red brick sidewalk in a Prohibited Parking area midway between the two hotels.

It's a pity that the Major's per diem rate only allowed him to stay at the Petr when there are much nicer rooms to be had. He gazed toward the Four Seasons. *Or, maybe this Major Ogorodnik is just a cheap bastard, and he pockets the difference between the rate and what he pays at the Petr.*

Yustitsiya placed an FSB placard on the dashboard of the vehicle allowing him to leave the Volvo unattended. He stepped out, crossed the wide sidewalk and entered the hotel. A slight garlic aroma from the restaurant next door diffused through the small, well lit, lobby. Yustitsiya approached the brightly colored yellow-and-brown marble reception counter and was greeted by a blonde woman seated behind the desk that appeared to be no more than in her mid-twenties.

"Good evening, sir. Can I help you?" She stood, and her hair fell loosely over her black blazer and low-cut blouse.

"Yes. I'm sure that you can," replied Yustitsiya. He leaned over the counter and studied the backdrop. An aged, red brick wall that Yustitsiya assumed was a remnant of the building before it was renovated stood under a lighted arch. Several framed photographs of, what was likely her family, adorned the desk where she was seated and countertop behind her.

Yustitsiya glanced around the room for situational awareness. A well-dressed elderly couple was seated in a dimly lit lounge area. A man with brown hair and wearing jeans and a blue button-down shirt descended the red brick stairs at the far wall and reached the lobby floor. Yustitsaya removed his FSB badge from his pocket and placed it on the counter.

The blonde receptionist's eyes opened wider, and her wide smile turned to pursed lips.

"You have a man registered here under the name Ogorodnik. Is he in?"

"I . . . I can check." She sat and typed Ogorodnik's name on her computer keyboard. After a few seconds, she looked up. "It appears that Mr. Ogorodnik left the hotel several hours ago."

"Good," replied Yustitsiya. "Then I will need you to let me into his room."

The receptionist stood and leaned toward Yustitsiya and spoke under her breath. "Sir, this is very unusual. I don't know if I can do this. I will have to ask my supervisor."

"I am a Colonel in the FSB. I will take the responsibility. You have nothing to worry about."

Her eyes narrowed and she nodded. Then she turned and pulled a key attached to a large brass ring from a row of wooden boxes on the back wall and placed it on the counter. "Room 305. You'll have to take the stairs." She pointed to her right toward another aged red brick wall and an old stone staircase with black wrought iron railings. A six-foot tall, stuffed grizzly bear stood sentinel. "We do not have an elevator."

Yustitsiya nodded as he scooped up the key.

***

This is an extraordinary room, thought Yustitsiya. His gaze proceeded from side to side as he closed the door to Ogorodnik's hotel room. There was a king-sized bed with a black leather headboard and pink satin bedspread. A rectangular mirror on the wall above the headboard reflected an image of the unmade bed. Patterned pink wallpaper covered all four walls, dark hardwood floors, a white ceiling with a 12-bulb chandelier, and a pink velvet sofa, led him to one conclusion. *This is a honeymoon suite! Very curious.*

His gaze moved to the wall opposite the bed and to a large dark wood roll-top desk. The wall behind it was filled with grainy photographs thumbtacked to the wall. Pictures of a man and woman engaged in numerous sexual encounters. *There must be at least a hundred of these. The same man and woman.* She was beautiful with long strawberry blonde hair and a curvaceous body. The man had brown hair and an athletic physique. An X had been marked across the man's face with an ink pen in each photograph. "There is a story in these pictures," he said softly.

Yustitsiya studied the photographs. A dozen on the top row were different. *Ogorodnik and a young woman wearing the uniform of the security service.* He removed one from the wall and held it next to a picture of the naked couple entwined in each other's arms. He then compared it to another of the sex photographs. *This is the same woman.*

Row after row, Yustitsiya examined the photographs. *Who are these young lovers and why would Ogorodnik have these photos?* He moved his gaze to the bottom row and found forensic photographs that showed Veronika Kuragin and Michael Hewlett in their last, grisly embrace. He gasped, and made the sign of the cross over his forehead to his shoulders. "We pray for those who have died and for the forgiveness of their sins," he recited softly.

She was his partner. Yustitsiya remembered an internal security service memoir he had recently read that paid tribute to an anonymous female agent who was murdered by her American collaborator. *Of course*, he thought. *That would make sense, but why does Ogorodnik have these photographs pinned to the wall? And why in a honeymoon suite?*

Yustitsiya placed a hand on his cheek and walked to the roll-top desk. He attempted to roll up the desktop, but it was locked, so he removed a Swiss army knife from his pocket and used it to force the drawer open. There were two folders on the desktop. The top folder contained a stack of handwritten letters from Ogordonik to Veronika Kuragin. Yustitsiya sat in the desk chair and read them.

The letters spanned a period over two years. In them, Ogorodnik professed his love for her. Over time, the letters became longer and more passionate. In the last six months, the tone of the letters changed. Without consulting with Ogorodnik, Veronika had chosen to befriend and entrap a foreign service officer from the United States Embassy.

When the relationship turned sexual, Ogorodnik's letters turned angry. In his last letter, Ogorodnik wrote: *How could you act like you love this man and offer to protect him? This makes me very angry. You have broken my heart.*

Yustitsiya turned his gaze toward the wall of pictures and the X marked across the face of the man. He steepled his fingers and placed them under his chin. *This Ogorodnik must have been in love with his partner.* He placed the folder on the desk then stood and paced the room. *He did not deliver these letters, yet he kept all of them. Did she know that he loved her? Why is this man's face is blocked out? Did he fantasize that he was his partner's lover? Did Ogorodnik kill his partner and her lover?* He picked up the picture he had removed from the wall and focused on the beautiful young woman. *One thing is certain, this Major Ogorodnik is a disturbed man.*

Yustitsiya sat at the desk and opened the second folder. It contained all of Ogorodnik's evidence against Captain Kulakov. Yustitsaya took his time as he perused the pages. There were twelve pages of notes that described Oksana's history, including a transcript of her friend Tasha's interrogation. There were another twelve pages that transcribed Hewlett's interrogations. There were one hundred and twenty pages of notes that rendered graphic exemplification of six months of taped encounters between Lieutenant Kuragin and the American. Finally, he read the transcript of the acoustic tape that captured the night Hewlett killed Kuragin and took his own life.

He placed the folder on the desk. *Major Ogorodnik is a desperate man who may believe that Captain Kulakov, or his wife, is responsible for what happened to Lieutenant Kuragin. He must be found and stopped.*

CHAPTER THIRTY-TWO

Gulf of Finland
17th of March

Major Ogorodnik emerged from the inside cabin area of Kulakov's boat. He wore a black leather coat and carried a Makarov nine-millimeter pistol. "Good evening, Mr. Draper. I am Major Ogorodnik of the Russian Federal Security Service."

Cole stiffened and made eye contact with Kulakov. "You son-of-a-bitch." He leaned forward as he attempted to stand.

"Stay seated," ordered Ogorodnik.

With the engine at slow speed, the boat heaved in the rough seas.

"I'm very sorry, Draper," Kulakov unfastened his seat harness. "I am afraid that our plan has been compromised. Major Ogordnik confronted me before I came to meet you. I had no choice."

The boat rocked heavily to the starboard side. Ogorodnik steadied himself by grabbing an overhead beam with one hand, his gun in the other. "Tell me, Mr. Draper, what was your plan to extricate Captain Kulakov? Were you going to cause another plane to disappear? I'm very interested. It could be educational," said Ogorodnik.

Cole narrowed his eyes and glared at Kulakov then he turned his gaze back toward Ogorodnik. "Go to hell."

"I'm curious. Who do you work for? Are you CIA?"

"Justice League of America."

"You're a very funny man."

Cole looked past Ogorodnik and addressed Kulakov. "You know that you'll never see Oksana again."

"We both knew the risk."

Cole tilted his head to one side. *That was not the response I would have expected.*

"Mr. Draper, is there someone in America who loves you?" asked Ogorodnik.

"That's none of your business. Besides, that hardly matters now, does it?"

"You're wrong, Mr. Draper. It matters a great deal." Ogorodnik lifted his pistol and aimed it at Cole's forehead. "You see, I lost someone that I loved, and it hurts." Ogorodnik raised his voice, "It is your participation in this ridiculous attempt to help Captain Kulakov defect, that is to blame for my loss. So, it will give me pleasure to know that your last thought before you die will be about the hurt that your loved one will feel when she learns of your death."

"You kill me and then what? You'll kill the captain?"

"We have made an agreement. He will retire. Eventually, my government will make an arrangement for the return of his wife, and they will be allowed to live together at one of their many properties. Under FSB guardianship, of course." Ogorodnik half smiled then continued, "Mr. Draper, I will be credited with exposing your agencies' reckless attempt to interfere with Russia's sovereign right to harness the resources in the areas of the Arctic that are now becoming reachable. This will be very good for my career, don't you think?"

As the boat heaved forward on a large wave, Kulakov gunned the throttle which caused Ogorodnik to lose his balance. Cole dropped to his knees on the floor and reached for a boathook on the rear bulkhead.

Kulakov tackled and wrestled with the agent for control of the pistol. Kulakov and Ogorodnik fell to their knees facing each other. Each had their hands on the pistol. The boat listed hard to starboard and Ogorodnik fell backward against the bulkhead with a loud *thump*. Kulakov grunted as he landed a blow with his elbow across the agent's nose.

Ogorodnik struck back, and Kulakov fell against the bench seat at the back of the cabin. The pistol fell to the floor. Ogordnik stood and lunged toward him. Kulakov kicked his leg up and caught him in the chin which caused him to gasp for air. Kulakov then took hold of Ogorodniks shoulders and threw him against the bulkhead. His forehead hit hard, and he fell to the floor, his arms flailing.

Cole used the boathook to snag the pistol and pull it toward him.

The small boat accelerated to a high speed in the rough seas. Green water crashed over the bow and the boat violently pitched and heaved.

Cole attempted to stand but was thrown sideways and to the floor. His shoulder crashed into the bench seat. A sharp pain radiated down his arm. He dropped the boathook and the pistol spun away on the floor. Kulakov and Ogorodnik dove for the pistol and wrestled for control.

Cole grasped the slats in the flooring. Ignoring the pain in his shoulder, he crawled to the cockpit area. At the control station, he gripped the arms of the captain's chair and pulled himself to a standing position then throttled down and turned the boat so the stern rose with the prevalent seas. As the pitching subsided, Cole turned to face the others. Kulakov held the pistol. Ogorodnik had a gash on his forehead that bled heavily. His head tilted and bobbed.

Kulakov tossed the Macarov on the floor and placed Ogorodik in a bear hug with his arms pinned behind him. "Help me, damn it. Open the door," shouted Kulakov.

Cole turned his gaze toward the pistol on the floor.

"Forget the gun. Open the door!"

Cole nodded. The boat heaved heavily to starboard. He fell against the bulkhead next to the weatherdeck door. He grimaced as he reached for the door handle and opened the rear door to the weather deck. Cold and damp air surged into the enclosed cabin. Ogorodnik weakly resisted as Kulakov pushed him through the door and into the weather.

With no one steering, the boat was turned by the seas. Large waves now came from the port side front quarter. A large wave crashed into the quarter, and the boat shuddered. Cole fell forward into the weather deck door frame. He steadied himself and poked his head through the frame. Rain and sea water splashed against his face. He squinted and raised his hands to protect his eyes, and scanned the back deck and saw no one.

"Take my hand, Draper."

Cole turned towards Kulakov's voice. He was seated on the deck with his back against the outer bulkhead of the cabin. He was sliding on the slick deck toward the back of the boat. With his good arm, Cole reached and gripped Kulakov's forearm, and pulled him into the inside cabin then closed the door as another wave crashed over the bow. Cole was tossed onto the back bench.

Cole squeezed his eyes in an angry glare. "You want to tell me what the hell is going on?"

"We should return to port." Kulakov got to his feet and gripped a handrail around the inside of the cabin to help him return to the wheel and throttle.

Cole located the Makarov on the floor and reached for it.

"You will have no need for the weapon," said Kulakov as he gained control of the boat and headed southeast toward Peterhof.

Cole picked up the pistol and aimed it at Kulakov. "Where is the FSB major?"

"Do not worry about the major. He will not survive more than a few minutes in these waters."

"He fell overboard?"

Kulakov turned toward Cole. "I pushed him overboard."

Cole grasped the railing and pulled himself to stand. He glared at Kulakov. "I deserve an explanation."

"Yes, you do. But please, not at gunpoint."

"Why don't you tell me what the hell is going on. I'll decide if we should talk at gunpoint."

"Major Ogorodnik boarded my boat as I was preparing to cast off to meet with you. We argued for some time. He knew your name, but not much else. Regardless, I became concerned that he knew about our plan and that he knew where Oksana is." He turned his gaze toward Cole. "I think he knew too much."

Cole cocked his head. "I was afraid of that."

"One of your embassy officers in Moscow was reckless. He fell for a Russian woman who was an FSB officer. She used him, and information was leaked."

"Yes. I was aware of that. Do you know how much information was compromised?"

"That I do not know. I think that Major Ogorodnik was speculating much of what he said to me. I don't believe he had any evidence. He used the information he did have to develop a theory. He used his theory to accuse me. To see how I responded."

"And?"

Kulakov faced Cole again. "He said he knew that I was Slow Dancer."

Cole puffed his cheeks and exhaled. "Shit." Cole set the gun down and took a seat next to Kulakov at the front of the pilot house.

"You should also know that I believe that Ogorodnik was under surveillance when he boarded my boat."

"What?" Cole replied. "Who was watching him?"

"I do not know for sure but, it seems only logical that it would be either local police or federal security."

"Why would they watch one of their own?"

"There is a phrase that we use in Russia that applies to government agencies like the Federal Security Services. When you're sitting at the table with card sharks, you can't trust anyone. There is competition for promotions among the officers in the services. They are the card sharks. They do not trust one another."

"You believe he was being watched to see what he was investigating."

"That is a possibility," replied Kulakov.

Cole puffed his cheeks, exhaled, then muttered, "Shit."

"What should we do?" asked Kulakov.

Cole placed his fingers on the bridge of his nose and shook his head. "Stay the course. It's all that we can do. Stick to the plan."

Kulakov raised his eyebrows.

"If you get back to your dock tonight, if I get back to my hotel tonight, and we're taken into custody, then we'll know. Otherwise, stay the course. You said that you don't think he had any proof. If that's true, and he's dead, someone else will have to pick up the case. If Ogorodnik couldn't prove anything, then a new case officer won't be able to either." Cole rubbed his hand over his mouth then continued, "Captain, we know for certain the FSB is working this case. Ogorodnik's disappearance will buy us some time, but get that reassignment as soon as you can."

Kulakov turned toward Cole, and their gazes met. "As you wish."

The seas calmed as they neared the coastline. The lights of Peterhof grew more distinct as the fog cover lifted.

"You fell on your shoulder. Are you alright?" asked Kulakov.

Cole rubbed his shoulder. "I think so, but I expect that I will have a very large bruise here."

"I am sorry."

They each remained thoughtfully still and gazed at the calming seas ahead.

Kulakov broke the silence. "Oksana." He turned to face Cole. His eyes twinkled mischievously as the light reflected off of the instrument panel in the darkened pilothouse. "Did she perform well the day you took her out?" he asked.

"What?"

"Oksana, was she frightened when you parachuted?"

Cole scrunched up his face. "Oksana was a trooper." He turned toward Kulakov and smiled. "She showed no fear when we jumped, and was just as tough as our SEAL team in the harsh weather."

"Good. I'm glad," replied Kulakov with a satisfied grin as he stared at the lights of Peterhof ahead of him.

CHAPTER THIRTY-THREE

St. Petersburg, Russia
21st of March

The naval base on Kotlin Island at the entrance to the St. Petersburg harbor was accessible only on highway A-118. The road runs over a complex system of flood dams that protect St. Petersburg from storm surges by separating the Neva Bay from the rest of the Gulf of Finland. The downside of this highway was the routine traffic backups caused by the maritime traffic that required frequent bridge openings. The twenty-five-kilometer drive from the FSB government building to the hospital of St. John took sixty-five minutes during the height of traffic.

Yustitsiya parked his white Volvo on a tree-lined boulevard in front of the hospital behind three compact Muscovite sedans. He entered the building through a set of nondescript white metal doors typical of remote military facilities constructed after World War II. Inside were narrow hallways, salmon-colored walls, and a dull yellow linoleum floor that looked like too many coats of wax had been applied. Except for several empty gurneys pushed tight against the walls, the hallways were vacant.

He had walked several meters toward the center of the building in search of a reception area when a middle-aged, slender, woman stepped out of a room and into the hallway in front of him. She wore tortoiseshell glasses, her brown hair in a ponytail, and light blue hospital scrubs. In her hand that hung at her side, she held a clipboard.

Yustitsiya stopped and asked for directions to the morgue.

The nurse held a pencil under her chin and seemed to study his light blue uniform with blue-and-red shoulder boards. "Federal security?" she asked.

"Yes. That is correct," he replied. "Colonel Yustitsiya." He nodded. "Now, if you would please direct me to the morgue."

"I will show you. Please follow me." She turned around and marched down the quiet hall with purpose. Yustitsiya followed, his hard heels tapping on the floor was in contrast to her quiet athletic shoes.

Two left turns, and two hallways later, she stopped in front wide metal swinging doors, painted white and worn to bare metal at shoulder height. "The morgue is through these doors. Have a good day, Colonel."

Yustitsiya pushed through the doors and was greeted with a blast of chilly air. A navy petty officer with a medical insignia was seated behind a dais. He stood at attention when Yustitsiya approached.

"As you were," said Yustitsiya.

The petty officer relaxed. "Yes, sir. I assume that you are here to confirm the identity of the major."

"Yes, but first, may I see the death report."

A brown folder was passed across the counter. Yustitsiya opened it. He paced around the small room while he perused the report. The cause of death was hypothermia and drowning. The body had been recovered in a tuna net by a fisherman in the Gulf of Finland thirty kilometers from the port of St. Petersburg. It appeared to have been in the water for three or four days. The condition was partially decomposed. The body trunk was bloated and liquefication of the skin covering the arms and legs had begun. Identification and personal effects were still on the body and bruises and contusions on the head were consistent with a scuffle. The report also noted these could also have been caused by a fall from a boat.

Yustitsiya stopped pacing and faced the dais. "I am ready to view the remains. May I have a copy of this report?"

"That copy is yours, sir." The petty officer stood to escort Yustitsiya into a refrigerated room to view the corpse.

***

Ninety minutes later, Yustitsiya found a coffee shop next to the green lawn of Petroskiy Park just outside the gate of the naval base. The shop had a green tent roof with a painted picture of windmills. It was juxtaposed between the green park on one side and a coal-fired power plant and industrial cranes of the shipyard behind it.

He entered and was seated alone at a small two-person table in a surprisingly upscale tea room. Blonde hardwood floors, marble counters, well cushioned beige armchairs and the strong aroma of freshly ground coffee blended with soothing jazz music at a comfortable volume.

A cigarette and a pretty young waitress were a welcome diversion before he would have to take the long drive back to the office. The viewing of Ogorodnik's remains had been grisly. The petty officer had explained that much of the decomposition evident was probably the result of an attack by prawns or other sea creatures that feasted on the carcass.

The report stated that the bruises on the face may have been caused by a scuffle. "How could that have been determined?" Yustitsiya had asked.

The petty officer explained, "When a human corpse is on land, the head is typically the first part to degrade, due to the presence of maggots and similar predators. That is not the case in the sea. In water, the head is the last part to be consumed. So, in maritime forensics, any wounds to the face that are found are very likely due to an event of some kind that occurred before the deceased entered the water."

The surveillance report stated the last sighting of Ogorodnik was at the St. Petersburg marina where Captain Kulakov docks his boat on the same night that he went missing. Did he get on that boat? Did Captain Kulakov murder Ogorodnik at sea that night?

His coffee was delivered in a large mug accompanied by a radiant smile from the waitress. Yustitsiya raised his gaze and returned the smile.

"My manager told me there will be no charge for the first cup."

"That's very kind of him," replied Yustitsiya. "Tell him, thank you."

She turned and walked away with a bounce in her step. He admired her youthful figure then looked down at his middle age paunch. *Ah, to be young.*

He gazed out the window toward the gold-domed cathedral and monument to the sailors of the Russian-Japanese War that stood in Petroskiy Park. Beyond that, a line of gunmetal colored clouds and occasional bolts of lightning moving from the Gulf toward St. Petersburg warned him of an impending storm and nightmarish traffic.

With both hands placed on the mug, he sipped his coffee and pondered what he had learned about Ogordnik and his case against Captain Kulakov. There was a documented and active case of a suspected defection operation in progress that involved a high-ranking military officer, and the Americans have code-named this action Slow Dancer. And, while Ogorodnik was probably not thinking with a clear head because of his feelings for his partner, Yustitsaya had to admit the historic evidence he had compiled against Oksana Kulakov was compelling.

He placed the mug on the table and gazed out the window toward the approaching storm. *Ogorodnik's disappearance in my area of responsibility requires that I investigate those circumstances. It is my duty to determine what happened to Major Ogorodnik, and while it is true that Captain Kulakov is a powerful officer in the navy, with the power to influence many federal ministers . . .* Yustitsaya took a long pull on a cigarette then snuffed it out in an ashtray on the table. *Regardless, at no small risk to my own career, I must investigate Captain Kulakov myself.*

CHAPTER THIRTY-FOUR

"Hell," said Cole. "It's almost as cold here as it was in St. Petersburg two weeks ago." He placed two more logs in the backyard fire pit at the safe house on Crab Creek to keep the fire going and ward off the chill of the evening air.

"This house, so near the water, it is so . . ." Oksana stopped her heavily accented sentence and appeared to be struggling to find the right word.

"I think the word you want to use is, nice," said Diana.

Oksana shook her head. "No. More than nice."

"Beautiful?"

"Yes." Oksana nodded enthusiastically. "Beautiful."

Cole took a sip of beer from a chilled Stella Artois chalice then placed it on the table next to his chair. "You're English has improved a lot these last few weeks."

Oksana smiled and nodded.

"We went grocery shopping today, and Oksana handled the transaction by herself," said Diana. "In fact, I think Oksana is almost ready to live on her own."

"Let's not rush things," interjected Ramburt as he stepped onto the backyard deck and joined the three of them near the fire pit. He sat on the edge of a chair nearest to Oksana and opened a bottle of Stella beer. The cap fell to the deck with a clink. As he poured the liquid into a glass, he said, "I heard what you said about Oksana's progress, but I think it's best to wait until the captain joins us before moving on. Wouldn't you agree, Oksana?"

"Yes. Pyotr speaks English best than me."

"Pyotr speaks better than you," Diana corrected.

"Better?"

"Yes. Better than you, not best than you."

Oksana smiled. "Yes. Better, not best."

Ramburt picked up the beer cap then stared at his beer as he swirled the liquid by rotating the glass in his hand.

Cole exchanged a glance with Diana. "Something on your mind, boss?"

Ramburt stopped spinning his glass but kept his gaze on the beer. "We received a message from Keenan this morning." He looked up. "An FSB agent reportedly met with Admiral Kletsov. He's the Admiral of the Russian navy. We have reason to believe the topic was Slow Dancer and that Kulakov might have been implicated."

"Damn it." Cole ran his hand through his hair.

"You think the agent in question is the guy that Kulakov tossed into the sea?" Asked Ramburt.

Oksana's face contorted and her gaze alternated between Cole and Ramburt.

"Well, I think that we still need to stay the course. Any report yet about Kulakov getting reassigned?" asked Cole.

"Stop," interjected Oksana. "Who did my husband toss? What is that word?" She turned her head from side to side to engage the gaze of the others around the fire. "Is this man dead? Did my husband kill this man?" She tapped the palm of her hand on her knee. Her leg shook nervously.

Cole answered, "Yes, Oksana. Pyotr and I were in trouble. He did what he needed to do. He killed an FSB agent."

"This is not beautiful," replied Oksana. "Too many people killed. They will never stop finding us."

"You mean they will never stop looking for you," interjected Diana.

Oksana turned her gaze toward Diana. "What mean, stay the course."

Cole replied, "Oksana, there is no need to worry. Stay the course means that we will stick to the plan that Pyotr and I agreed to. The next step is for him to get reassigned to a job that is not in St. Petersburg or Moscow."

"How?"

"I don't know Oksana. Pyotr will have to figure that out."

Shaking her head, Oksana answered, "No. This is not beautiful. Pyotr will talk to Admiral Kletsov. He will know that Pyotr not truth."

Cole scrunched his forehead and cocked his head. "Huh?"

"Friends a long time. Kletsov will know." She wiped a tear from her cheek.

Cole turned to Diana. "Why don't you take Oksana inside? Try and calm her. Let her know it will be alright."

Diana nodded, stood and placed her hands on Oksana's shoulders and led her into the kitchen.

"Shit," said Ramburt. "I assumed she knew about the boat incident."

Cole placed his head in his hands. "I hadn't found a good time to tell her. She's been getting a little nervous. I think this is taking longer than she expected."

"Well the news doesn't get any better," said Ramburt. "Keenan's message said that a senior FSB officer from the St. Petersburg office has taken an interest in the case. Word is that he's better connected and has more experience than the other guy."

"Shit." Cole closed his eyes and fell back into his chair, his arms draped over the side.

"I'm getting nervous Cole," said Ramburt.

Cole sat up. "Pretty easy for you to say from where you are in the cheap seats," replied Cole.

Ramburt turned his gaze toward Cole. "What did you say?"

"I said it's pretty easy for you to say that you're getting nervous when you're not the one whose ass is on the line."

"Ah shit, Cole. Here we go again. That's not fair. If you're worried, you've had several opportunities to let this go. You haven't wanted to."

"Let this go. What kind of bullshit spin is that? We can't let this go. What happens to Oksana if we don't finish this?"

"I don't know." Ramburt placed his hands behind his head. "But, every day this continues, any more time that you spend in Russia, this just keeps getting more dangerous."

"I'll decide when it's too dangerous."

"Damnit! You're not in charge. Don't press our friendship on this, Cole," warned Ramburt.

Cole's angry glare met Ramburt's.

"I put my ass on the line to get you back on the team." Ramburt set his unfinished beer on the table. "I'm getting a lot of heat on this from POTUS, and I have backed you all the way. Don't let me down." He left through the patio door and closed it with a bang.

Sorry, brother. I guess that I'm getting a little nervous too, thought Cole.

CHAPTER THIRTY-FIVE

St. Petersburg, Russia
11th of April

The black Mercedes-Benz Maybach S600 turned right off of Admiraltseskiy Prospeckt and braked to a stop at the khaki-colored brick arched road gate of the Admiralty complex. The driver pressed a button on the center console and opened the dark tinted back seat window on the driver's side. A Russian navy guard in an enlisted winter dress blue uniform approached the vehicle.

Kulakov shivered as the window opened and a blast of cold air entered the car. Without speaking, he passed his identification to the guard through the open window. He sat patiently, looking straight ahead as the guard examined his credentials. When the guard dipped his head to see through the window, Kulakov turned in his direction and half smiled. The guard then handed his identification back to him, ordered the gate open and stepped back with a smart, white-gloved hand salute. The driver closed the window and proceeded through the gate.

Kulakov had been summoned, and had arrived at the Admiralty as directed. He assumed that his intentionally uncharacteristic personal and performance issues had been reported up his leadership chain and that was why he had been called upon to report to the Admiralty. *What does Kletsov know? What will he want to do to me? Where will he want to send me?* The Maybach rolled to a stop in front of Admiralty Building. *Will this plan of Drapers' work, or blow up in my face? Will my faked drunkenness and incompetence earn me a remote transfer, or will I be placed under closer scrutiny of the Admiralty?*

A petty officer opened the door. Kulakov stepped out and gazed up at the gold-painted pediment depicting the goddess's Isis and Urania over the archway. *The protectress of shipbuilders,* he thought.

I should be the one that hopes for your protection today. He smiled wryly, folded his uniform coat over his arm and walked up the short stairway. At the building entrance, he was met by another senior petty officer who relieved Kulakov of his coat and escorted him to the office of Vladimir Kletsov.

As Kulakov entered, the petty officer softly closed the door behind him. Admiral Kletsov was seated behind a large oak desk. Behind him, a large window overlooked a snow-covered lawn, and beyond that, the Neva River. Kulakov gazed to his right where a fire burned inside a large marble fireplace. A portrait of the Russian President hung above the mantel. The remaining walls were covered with portraits of previous navy commanders that dated back hundreds of years. An ornate crystal chandelier hung from the ceiling in the center of the room.

"Pyotr. It is good to see you. Please come in," bellowed Kletsov. He stood from behind his desk and walked over to greet Kulakov. He extended his hand. Kulakov accepted it, and Kletsov guided him to a purple, heavily cushioned chair in front of the admiral's desk. Kletsov sat in a similar chair next to him. Following protocol, Kulakov waited for the admiral to be seated and then he sat rigidly in his chair.

"Pyotr, how have you been, my old friend?" asked Kletsov.

Kulakov turned and remained silent.

"Hmph," grunted the admiral. "Yes. I understand. These are difficult times." Kletsov leveled a scrutinizing, narrowed-eye glare at Kulakov. "You know that I am very sorry for your loss. It must be difficult for you to maintain under the strain."

"Admiral," replied Kulakov still seated at attention with his hands on his knees. "I suspect that you already know how I have been dealing with my loss and that is why you have summoned me here."

Kletsov slapped his hands on his knees then stood and walked behind his desk. He opened a wood box on his desk, pulled out a cigarette, lit it, took a long pull and then blew a large cloud of smoke out of the side of his mouth. "Pyotr, I would prefer to say that I invited you here. I do not consider this a summons." Kletsov placed a hand on his desk and leaned toward Kulakov. "Yes, I have heard that your performance has not been up to your usual standard and that you have been drinking too much." He sat down took another pull on his cigarette. "What you have suffered," smoke came out of his mouth as he spoke, "this is to be expected."

Kulakov said nothing. His mouth was dry.

"Pyotr, you are one of the navy's brightest officers. You have commanded a guided missile cruiser and have led a fleet of warships. I thought that after you completed this command of the Baltic Fleet, you would be competitive for a greater promotion. Then these unfortunate events happened."

"Sir, unfortunate events?" Kulakov grimaced.

Kletsov leaned back in his chair and took another pull on the cigarette. "Pyotr, a recommendation has been sent to me by several of my most senior staff. They are concerned that you are no longer fit for command. And there have been rumors."

Kulakov stiffened in his chair. "Rumors, Admiral?"

"Yes. An impertinent little security officer visited me and said he was concerned that you . . . well, it was ridiculous, what he suggested."

Kulakov shook his head and in a slightly raised voice said, "This major visited me in my office. What he said was preposterous. I threw him out. Admiral, you can't be serious. I hope that you did not believe him!"

"Tell me, Pyotr. Why does he accuse you?"

Kulakov leaned forward, his palms open. "Admiral! I do not know." He squinted. "On top of all that has happened to me, please tell me that you did not believe this little bastard."

Kletsov tapped his fingers on the desk. He focused a scrutinizing glare on Kulakov. Several tense moments passed in silence. "Pyotr, you are a valuable asset to the navy. High expectations have been placed on you." He leaned forward, an elbow on the desk, and rested his chin in his hand. "Pyotr, I tell you this as your friend, not your superior officer. Your future in the navy is in jeopardy." Kletsov's eyebrows slanted upward. "I have much invested in you, and I don't want to see that happen." He slid his hand to an ashtray on the desk and tapped ashes from his cigarette. "So, what should I do with you?"

Kulakov placed his head in his hands. "Admiral, I just need some time to work things out. If I could have some time."

Kletsov leaned back in his chair. His thick eyebrows squeezed together in a crease. "Hhmmph." He tapped his fingers on the desk. "Remember when we were at the naval academy? I was a company officer, a junior lieutenant when you were in your first year of schooling. I watched you then. I saw then that you were a natural leader, and I also know that you are an excellent teacher." He folded his hands together and placed them on his desktop. "Pyotr, I think it would be good for you to be around midshipmen again."

"Sir?"

"Summer will arrive soon. A wonderful time of year. I want you to get some rest. Rediscover your purpose, and in the process, you can help develop the skills of the navy's future leaders. Then you will come back to work for me in another capacity."

"Admiral, I don't understand," replied Kulakov.

"I want you to take command of the Kruzenshtern."

"Sir, a training ship?" He faked a protest. *Good. This is precisely the assignment I need to execute the Americans' plan.*

"Yes, I know you are overqualified for this command." More smoke escaped his mouth as he spoke. Kletsov leaned back in his large black leather chair. "What you need now is time. It is my hope that with less stress and time working with cadets, this will give you the best environment to decompress and deal with your circumstances."

Kulakov nodded. "Yes, sir." He lowered his gaze toward the floor.

"You will do this for one year, then we will meet again."

Without another word, Kletsov stood and walked toward a side door that led to a private water closet. Kulakov also stood and turned toward the door to exit the office. The senior petty officer stood next to the door with Kulakov's coat in hand.

CHAPTER THIRTY-SIX

C ole was at the kitchen sink peeling potatoes for what he proudly called his "world-famous Guinness beef stew." Diana sliced them into bite-size pieces. In the next room, Oksana exercised on a treadmill.

Cole heard the chirp of the security alarm and turned his gaze to the four monitors that received a live feed from locations around the grounds and inside the house. Ramburt had just accessed the front door and was in the foyer.

"Looks like one more for dinner," Cole said.

"I'll set another place," replied Diana.

Oksana approached and stood in the doorway. A white workout towel was draped over her shoulders. She used it to dab perspiration off of her cheeks and forehead. "I heard someone arrive," she said. "Is there news from Pyotr?"

Ramburt entered the kitchen. "Hey guys." He opened the refrigerator door and stood behind it.

The *Phaashup* of a bottle being opened, and the clang of a bottle cap tossed on the counter caused Cole to ask, "Stressful day, boss?"

Ramburt sat at the kitchen table, placed the open beer bottle in front of him. "We received a message today from the consular officer that's handling Slow Dancer." He turned toward Oksana. "Your husband has been placed in command of the Russian Federation ship Kruzenshtern."

Oksana stepped into the room, her brow furrowed. "That is not good. Kruzenshtern is an old training ship. Sails. No guns. This is a big…" She looked at Diana.

"Demotion, Oksana. I think the word you're searching for is demotion." She placed her knife on the table and dried her hands with a towel.

Oksana shook her head. "I don't understand. Pyotr is fleet commander. Why was he — —?"

"Oksana, on this training ship, who gets trained?" asked Cole.

"Sea cadets. The Kruzenshtern trains sea cadets."

Cole paced back and forth. "So, if I read this right, your husband will be in charge of a ship that will, essentially, have only a skeleton crew of active navy sailors onboard. Because when the cadets are onboard, they will perform the jobs that sailors normally do in order to learn the basics of seamanship. And, to train the cadets, the ship has to go to sea."

Oksana stepped in front of Cole. He stopped pacing.

"This is good news, Oksana."

She shook her head. "How this good news?"

He picked up his iPhone from the marble island countertop and "Googled" the Kruzenshtern. He read the search results then turned toward the others. He smiled and chuckled briefly then said, "This is brilliant."

"I don't understand," said Diana. "What are you talking about?"

Cole addressed the group as he started to pace again. "I figured that the captain would get demoted. But, I thought he would be sent to a desolate outpost and that I would have to take him out similar to the way I extricated Oksana." Cole held his iPhone with the screen toward the group. "But this is great! According to this article, every summer, the Kruzenshtern takes a three-month cadet training deployment that also serves as a goodwill cruise, stopping at foreign ports along the way. According to this article in the *Times*, it appears that this summer the Kruzenshtern will stop at two ports in America. The article goes on to say that the State Department has carefully crafted these visits with the Russian foreign ministry because the two countries are trying to ease tensions." Cole smiled, then said, "This plays right into our hands. Captain Kulakov is coming to us."

Oksana turned her gaze from Cole to Diana and then back to Cole.

Cole stood next to Oksana and told her, "Your husband purposely, and brilliantly, got himself placed in that job so he can come to America in a capacity that will not permit any FSB oversight. So, while he is in America, we will help him defect, and together you will disappear. We will then set you up in your new life."

"Jeez, Cole, do you have a plan?" asked Ramburt.

"Yes, I do," Cole replied. "And the first thing we need to do is get the Kruzenshtern's schedule. Everything will depend on that."

***

"What time is it in St. Petersburg?" asked Ramburt as Cole led the way down the stairs to the sensitive communication facility in the basement.

"St. Petersburg is plus eight." Cole looked at his watch. "So, it's four twenty in the morning. It's probably too early to talk to Slow Dancer's handler, but we can leave a message with the watch officer."

Cole sat at the desk and woke the Dell computer and large curved monitor out of sleep mode. He typed in his password, and entered the secret internet network, then scrolled through his contact list until he found the watch room at the consulate in St. Petersburg and established a secure connection.

He typed; Reference Slow Dancer case. Must have itinerary. Contact S.D. He will know.

"Very cryptic, Cole. Even if the Russians did intercept and decode it, they wouldn't know what to do with that bit of information."

Cole turned toward Ramburt and replied, "Let's just hope he doesn't get picked up by the FSB before he takes his ship to sea."

The message reply came back on the monitor; Message will be delivered.

CHAPTER THIRTY-SEVEN

St. Petersburg, Russia
15th of May

Two weeks after setting to sea for the first time on the Kruzenshtern, Kulakov returned to his solitary, and cheerless, family home in St. Petersburg. Evenings in the large villa with no companion to share the day's events with were unbearable. Dinner out, followed by a long walk, became the routine. During his usual evening dinner at the popular Evraziya restaurant near the English Embankment, Kulakov picked up a cloth napkin that was placed at his seating by a server that he did not see again. He put the napkin in his pocket, and after dinner walked the few short blocks past the brightly lit and immense nineteenth century Nikolayevsky Imperial Palace to his nearby villa.

Alone in the villa that had been in his family during the days of imperial Russia, he opened a bottle of cabernet-sauvignon, poured a small amount in a glass, and took a swallow. He then spread the napkin on the table in front of him, dipped two fingers in the glass and swiped some wine across the napkin. Partial Cyrillic scrip letters began to appear. He swiped some more red wine. After four strokes, a message began to appear. He continued to apply the red wine to the napkin. A wax substance embedded in the cloth remained white against the crimson background of the soiled napkin, and the complete message was readable.

Need the visit schedule of your ship.

***

Admiral Kletsov and the chief of staff were seated at the small rectangular, six-seat conference table in the suite of offices at the admiral's headquarters. It was not unusual for the two senior officers to work late into the evening and have their dinner served to them in the office before retiring to their respective homes and families for the evening.

As a staff of four petty officers dressed in crisp white uniforms cleared the place settings, Kletsov asked the chief of staff, "What have you heard about our friend Pyotr? Has he taken command of the Kruzenshtern?"

"Yes, he has, Admiral. Just this morning I read the first report that he filed after he took command. With a full complement of cadets, Pyotr took the Kruzensthern to sea for a two-week indoctrination cruise that he evaluated as very successful."

Kletsov leaned back in his chair and clasped his hands behind his head. "Good. Good. I'm glad to hear that. A few months at sea instructing cadets in the art of seamanship might be just what he needs to move past his unfortunate circumstances."

"Yes, Admiral. But what he has suffered, it will be difficult."

"Pyotr is a good man. He will get through this."

The chief of staff pursed his lips, exhaled, then said. "Admiral, I'm afraid I have more news. It may concern Pyotr."

Kletsov placed his elbows on the table and replied, "What is your news?"

The chief of staff formed his fingers in a steeple and placed them under his chin. "Major Ogorodnik, he was the security officer that met with us and suggested that perhaps Pyotr was considering defecting to the Americans."

"Hmph. He did more than suggest. He accused Pyotr."

"Yes, sir. Well, Major Ogorodnik is dead."

"How did that happen?"

"He drowned, under suspicious circumstances, in the gulf near St. Petersburg."

"What are you suggesting?" asked Kletsov.

"Sir, with all due respect, I think we need to step back from our personal relationship with Pyotr and review the facts."

"You have said nothing that will cause me concern."

"There is more, Admiral."

Kletsov opened a cherry wood, brass ingrained, box on the table and removed a cigarette. He lit it with his old brass lighter. "What else have you heard?"

"This afternoon, I met with Colonel Yustitsiya. He is a senior security agent in the St. Petersburg office."

"I am aware of Colonel Yustitsiya. He is a good man," interrupted Kletsov.

"Yustitsiya explained the case that Ogorodnik had prepared. He presented the evidence that had been compiled. His case was almost exclusively built with evidence against Pyotr's wife, Oksana."

Kletsov sat quietly, his arms folded over his chest.

"Admiral, the case against Oksana was compelling."

"She is dead."

"Yes, sir. That is what we all believe. But, Colonel Yustitsaya also showed me a dispatch from our embassy in Washington." He slid a folder across the table. "If you look at the chain of inquiry, you will see this dispatch is a response to a query that was initiated by Major Ogorodnik."

Kletsov picked up the folder, donned a pair of reading glasses, and studied the dispatch. The operative words read, *agents have been assigned to investigate reports that a Russian woman is being held in protective custody by the Central Intelligence Agency. This development may be in connection with the investigation of a possible defector the Americans have codenamed Slow Dancer.* When he finished reading, Kletsov gazed over the top rim of his glasses at his chief of staff and said, "I do not believe that this woman the Americans *may* have is Oksana."

"Admiral, I do not want to believe that either but, I think that we must accept that it is a possibility."

Kletsov removed his glasses and placed them on the table. He sat quietly for several minutes as he pondered the case. "Pyotr is an excellent officer, and I have complete confidence in him. However, if what you are suggesting is true, I will deal with him most harshly. But I will not take any action against him based on this suspicion alone. Contact Colonel Yustitsiya and tell him that I want to be immediately apprised of any further information in this case." He abruptly stood then lowered his gaze toward the top of the table, and snarled, "And, place a trusted officer on the Kruzenshtern crew to keep an eye on Pyotr. He will watch Pyotr closely and report directly to you if the captain acts suspiciously."

***

At his desk in the government building, Yustitsiya worked into the evening that day as well. He read a dispatch that had been received from the embassy in Washington regarding the possibility that a Russian citizen was in protective custody of the CIA. *Major Ogorodnik's unfortunate demise is in itself very suspicious. Now this report of a Russian woman held in protective custody by the Central Intelligence Agency. This is precisely what one would expect if Ogorodnik's allegations against Captain Kulakov are to be believed.*

Yustitsiya stood and walked to his window that overlooked the Liteyniy Bridge spanning the Neva River. A heavy storm with strong winds pelted rain against the windows. Yustitsiya gazed through the rain-soaked window at a coastal tanker headed northeast that had just passed the bridge. Traffic backed up on Liteyniy Road as the lighted drawbridge slowly descended. He crossed his arms over his chest and placed a hand on his cheek and contemplated his puzzle. *There are many data points that substantiate Ogorodnik's suspicions. And there is a Russian woman in America that is of sufficient value for the Americans to place her in protective custody. I do not believe this is a coincidence. It must be Oksana Kulakov.* He turned away from the window and paced. *But, Kulakov is an influential man. I would be a fool to formally accuse him without irrefutable evidence.* He stopped pacing and stood in front of his desk, his hands clasped behind his back. *I will go to America and investigate this observation. If this woman is Oksana Kulakov, I will bring her back to Russia, and I will charge the captain with treason. If it is not his wife that the Americans are holding, then at least I will know and we can be done with this case.*

CHAPTER THIRTY-EIGHT

St. Petersburg, Russia
18th of May

C atherine Park was popular with spring visitors in May. Cherry trees with white blossoms lined the walking path that led to the statue of Catherine the Great. Couples with baby strollers and young, as well as elderly, lovers strolled by, hand in hand, on a late afternoon walk. Keenan sat on a park bench near the statue each day after he'd left the message-imbued napkin with Kulakov. For three days he had waited between four and six in the afternoon without seeing the agreed-upon signal. On the fourth day, a man with blonde hair stepped up to the front of the monument and removed his coat then draped it over his left arm. Keenan counted to one hundred and thirty, and as expected, the man put on his light coat and walked away.

The dead drop is active. The left arm means Mikhailovsky Palace.

Keenan waited five minutes then left the park and headed north on Sadovaya Street. He walked for thirty-five minutes and entered the grounds of the massive Summer Garden and Peter the Great's Summer Palace. There, he walked the immaculately groomed grounds and pretended to admire many of the seventy-nine sculptures that depicted the images of the gods and heroes of antiquity. *Any other day I would enjoy this outing. Not today, though.* His heart pounded. Keenan focused on remaining calm. *Today,* he told himself, *I just need to maintain situational awareness.* As he walked, he carefully monitored his surroundings for any sign of a potential FSB watcher.

He stopped at the coffee house, sat in a wrought-iron chair and kept track of the people around him. After thirty minutes, no one appeared to have any particular interest in him, so Keenan walked to the metro station, boarded the service to the Admirateiskaya station then walked along the Palace Embankment.

The crowds thinned out considerably as the evening progressed. Keenan found it easier to maintain vigilance on his surroundings. He didn't recognize anyone from the several places he had visited over the last two hours, so he stayed on the embankment.

He reached the dead drop destination at the prominent three-story Nova-Mikhailovsky Palace. A large façade of marble columns and terracotta sculptures faced the Neva River. After he did a three-hundred-and-sixty-degree visual scan to ensure that he was alone, Keenan climbed down the stairs to the semi-circular boat landing that had once been the scene of Tzar Alexander's frequent riverine disembarkations in St. Petersburg.

On the wall that faced the river, he found a grey brick on the otherwise red brick wall. After one quick glance toward the top of the stairs to ensure he was still alone, he removed a pocket knife from his slacks and quickly removed the brick. He retrieved the computer flash drive that was hidden there and placed it in his pocket. Keenan then carefully replaced the brick and returned to the embankment walkway.

Keenan took the most direct route and expeditiously returned to the Admirateiskaya station and then to the United States Consulate. He sat at his desk and removed the flash drive from his pocket. *The schedule will be in Draper's hands by tomorrow morning.*

***

Ramburt arrived at the safe house mid-morning. Cole sat on a bar stool at the kitchen island reading national news on his MacBook computer. He held a cup of coffee in one hand while he used his other hand to move his wireless mouse, scrolling through the pages on the screen. Ramburt entered the kitchen and tossed a leather satchel on the counter in front of Cole. "This arrived last night at Foggy Bottom." He poured a cup of joe from the coffee maker on the counter.

"The schedule?"

"See for yourself," replied Ramburt. "Brother, this couldn't have worked out better if we had planned the ship visits ourselves."

Cole opened the satchel, removed the dispatch and read the first half of the message aloud. He deemed it was unimportant information. "Blah, blah, yadda, yadda." When he had read to the second half of the message, Cole raised his gaze toward Ramburt. In a slightly louder tone read, "Ship visit in Norfolk, Virginia, in the United States of

America. Kruzenshtern will participate in the International Parade of Sails and related Harbourfest activities on June 7th through the 14th!"

Diana entered the room with wet hair and wearing only a shower towel wrapped around her. "What's the commotion?"

Ramburt stiffened and rolled his eyes, which elicited a chuckle from Cole.

"Chill out, director," said Diana.

The color of his face turned a little redder as Ramburt cleared his throat. "Perhaps we should agree on some signals to indicate when it's appropriate to enter a room."

Diana smiled a wide grin then burst out laughing. Cole chuckled with her. After a few moments, Diana said, "Pardon me, gentlemen, while I get dressed, but when I come back, I want to know what's so exciting."

Cole and Ramburt both allowed their gaze to follow her as she left the room.

"She's a handful, Cole," said Ramburt.

"She is that . . . and, I think I'm in love with that woman," replied Cole.

Ramburt turned toward Cole and cocked his head. He wore a thin smile. "I'm not going to say one word."

Cole chuckled. "I know. I've bitten your head off every time the subject of Diana has come up between us."

"Gee, I hadn't noticed."

"I deserved that," replied Cole. "I've been giving it a lot of thought, my brother. When this is over, I'm going to ask the big question."

Ramburt took both of Cole's shoulders in his hands. "It's about time!"

"It was something that Kulakov said to me. He said that everyone should have someone to share a life with." Cole smiled. "He was right."

"You already know that I think you're making the right decision. You two were made for one another."

Diana returned with Oksana in tow. They both wore black yoga pants and loosely fitted T-shirts. "So, I hate to break up this bromance but, what's all the excitement?" asked Diana.

Cole slid the dispatch across the marble countertop toward Diana. "We have the Kruzenshtern's schedule, and it's perfect." Cole turned his gaze toward Oksana. "Pyotr will arrive in Norfolk on the 7th of June to participate in an International Parade of Sails and Festival. This couldn't be any better. Norfolk is where my home is. I am familiar with the Parade of Sails, and I'm familiar with the facilities in Norfolk." He stood, put his arms around Oksana and drew her close to him. "Mark it on your calendar, Oksana. On June 7th, you will be united with Pyotr."

She embraced him tightly.

CHAPTER THIRTY-NINE

Washington, District of Columbia
24th of May

After a long flight from St. Petersburg and a day full of discussions with officers inside the Russian embassy, Colonel Yustitsiya sat on a park bench near the Japanese Pagoda in West Potomac Park. Wearing an open-collared shirt and sports jacket, he was over-dressed for the warm spring day.

It was a cloudless Saturday morning, and the cherry trees were in full bloom. The pink and white flowers partially obscured his view of the Jefferson Memorial on the small peninsula across the tidal basin. This being peak cherry blossom season, the Rock Creek Park Trails were crowded with tourists. Yustitsiya sat with his legs crossed at the knees, and nodded or smiled at the walkers as they ambled past.

At exactly ten o'clock, a young man with shoulder-length brown hair flowing from under a red Washington Nationals baseball cap sidled up to the bench. As he gazed toward the Jefferson Monument, he asked, "Have you been to Jefferson's home in Monticello?"

Yustitsiya scrutinized the young man. *Skinny, but strong forearms and hands. A laborer, probably.* Then he responded, "Yes, I was struck by the gardens." *He should now tell me there are one hundred and seventy varieties of fruit there.*

The young man sat next to Yustitsiya. With his gaze on the tidal basin, he said, "Did you know there are one hundred and seventy varieties of fruit?"

Yustitsiya inflated his cheeks and expelled the air slowly. "You are not who I was expecting."

"Comrade Pukalova probably told you to expect a he-she. That's been my cover whenever I meet with him."

"Perhaps you haven't heard, we are not communists. Mr. Pukalova is a citizen. The use of the term comrade is quaint and somewhat frivolous."

"Your English is very good."

"I was educated at Eton," replied Yustitsiya. "My father was a diplomat as well." He shifted his position on the bench and re-crossed his legs.

A family with two toddlers strolled past them on the park trail. The boy ran ahead while the father carried his daughter on his shoulders. Yustitsiya and the young man he knew of as The Mole both nodded and smiled.

"Okay, citizen that was educated at Eton," said the young man as he waved his fingers to show air quotes. "We should go somewhere else. My car is parked not far from here. We can talk freely there."

Yustitsiya nodded and stood. "Do you have a name?" he asked as they started walking.

"Jon. Just call me Jon."

They walked across the grassy field between two baseball fields. The crack of a bat was followed by shouts and cheers from a game in progress. Along the way, the young man explained, "I know what Pukalova told you about me. That man is so old school. He probably hasn't had sex in a decade." The mole called Jon glanced sideways at Yustitsiya. He laughed then added, "Just so ya know, I'm all man. The cover is needed so I can't be identified when I meet with the old man."

Yustitsiya drew a deep breath and twisted his head toward him.

Jon kept walking. "My car is right over here." He opened the door of a new model black Toyota Camry.

Jon started the engine. Yustitsiya sat in the passenger seat. As he eased into traffic and headed northeast on Ohio Drive toward the Arlington Memorial Bridge, the mole asked, "The woman that you're interested in, what is this about?"

"I must verify her identity."

"And then what?"

Yustitsiya gazed out the window at the long row of live oak trees that lined the road ahead of them and contemplated his answer.

Jon slowed, and as he approached a turn Yustitsiya turned his head toward him. "If she is who I suspect, then I will ask her to return to Russia with me."

"And if she says no?"

"Then I must resort to force."

Jon pulled over and stopped on the side of the road near a walkway to the Martin Luther King Memorial. He placed the car in park and turned to face Yustitsiya. His hands gripped the gear shift on the console. "And what are you prepared to do?"

"I just told you."

"No. I mean, what are you prepared to do to get access to this woman?"

Yustitsiya crossed his arms and leaned his back against the seat. "I'll do whatever I must do."

* * *

Cole folded two pairs of jeans, some casual shirts and stuffed them into an overnight backpack.

"I'll bet Lieutenant Choesler was a little surprised when you told him that you had another job for him," said Diana.

Cole turned toward the sound of her voice. She stood in the doorway of the bedroom, her back against the door jamb. She wore her hair in a ponytail and had on high rise yoga shorts and a black halter top. "Wow. You could turn heads in that outfit."

She turned into the hallway and spoke over her shoulder, "I just did."

Cole chuckled as he zipped up his backpack and threw it over his shoulder. He followed Diana down that hall and into the kitchen where he placed his backpack on the floor next to the front door.

Diana sat on a bar stool at the granite countered island. Cole opened the refrigerator and withdrew cold cuts for a sandwich.

"So, what did Choesler have to say when you called him?"

"At first, he laughed," Cole placed several slices of black forest ham, a slice of pepperjack cheese and some tomato slices, between two slices of bread. "But when I told him my plan," Cole grinned, "he laughed even harder."

Diana tee-hee'd. "Great! You two will make a great team."

"We *are* a great team, dear. He told me he thought the plan would work." Cole placed his index finger on his chin. "I believe he used words like brilliant, and superior, and glorious." He bit into his sandwich and chewed on it with a wide, closed-mouth grin.

Diana reached across the island and touched the tip of Cole's nose. "You are so full of shit." Her eyes and mouth opened in a smile.

He swallowed. "What's that say about your taste in men?"

"I don't know. I haven't found my man yet."

"Now you're full of shit."

They had a good laugh. Cole lifted Diana off her seat, embraced her, and they shared a long, passionate kiss. They stood locked in each other's arms for several minutes.

They heard Oksana clear her throat, and each turned their gaze towards her. She stood in the doorway to the kitchen. "I am sorry."

Cole stepped back.

Oksana pointed at his backpack on the floor. "You must go?" she asked.

"Yes. I need to go to Norfolk for a couple days. I need to meet with some people that will help me execute the plan to get your husband. Diana will stay here with you."

Fifteen minutes later, Cole stood in the foyer of the safe house with Diana and Oksana. He slung his backpack over his shoulder then gave Oksana a quick hug. He kissed Diana. "This won't take long. I'll be back in two days."

CHAPTER FORTY

Jon, the mole, parked his Camry down the hill from his partner's home on Rosa Drive in a typical middle-class neighborhood of fenced-in yards, neatly mowed lawns, and thirty-year-old oak trees. It was mid-afternoon, the sun burned brightly overhead, and heat waves rose off of the hot concrete.

The mole knew that on weekday afternoons, his partner's wife would leave to pick up their daughter at middle school and take to her swim team practice. This would leave a three-hour window when she would not be in the home.

"What are we doing here?" asked Yustitsiya.

"Let's talk about what you're prepared to do," replied Jon.

"As I said, I am prepared to do whatever is necessary to confirm this woman's identity."

The mole scanned the area ahead and behind him. "The woman that you're looking for, do you have a photograph?"

"Yes, of course." Yustitsiya pulled a photograph from his back pocket that he had retrieved from Captain Kulakov's official biography. He handed it to the mole.

Jon took a quick look at it and handed it back to Yustitsiya.

"This woman is in a safe house in Maryland. It's located in a secluded area with sophisticated security fence and a monitored gate."

"Then I must ask the question again. Why are we here? We should be going there."

"My partner and I are technicians in the employment of the CIA. We perform maintenance on the vehicles, the boats, lawn mowers, and refrigerators. Anything mechanical that is assigned to that safe house, we do it. That includes the HVAC units which are in the basement secure area. That's why I have a top-secret clearance, and that's how I was able to access the files that I gave to Pukalova. That's also why I know that there is a protocol that must be followed if we are going to get access to this safe house."

Yustitsiya turned in his seat to face the mole.

"There is an agent that has stayed with her since she arrived at the safe house. I wouldn't want to tangle with him, but I happen to know that he will be leaving town for a few days. There is another agent there with your girl, and we may need to deal with her if she gets in the way, but she won't be as much trouble. So, the next couple of days are your window of opportunity. A word of caution, though. To do this, we'll have to get past the gate security."

"Yes, and how do we do that?"

"I think the best way is to dress you up like a mechanic. I will say that you are new to the Agency and that you're learning the job. That might get us a jump on them. We'll need to neutralize the guards and then move fast to get inside. That may be your only opportunity to get her and take her back to your embassy. After that, I'm sure you have your ways to secretly send her back to Russia."

"Yes, we do. So, go there now and let's get on with it."

"Not so fast, Pops," replied the mole as he scanned the area around them again. "The brick split-level with the blue siding on the second floor." The mole pointed toward the house. "That's where my partner lives. We need the company van that he keeps in his garage if we are going to get access to the safe house where your girl is."

"Do you have a key to this van?"

"I do not. We will have to get it from my Agency partner, and he will not give it up without a fight."

"What are you waiting for?" he asked. "Let's go get the key."

"Keep your pants on, Pops," replied the mole. "Before I do anything, I need to know what you're going to do for me." Their gazes locked onto one another. "What you're asking me to do is a game changer for me. I won't be able to go back to work at the Agency. In fact, I will become a wanted man. So, before I do what you are asking, I want some assurance from you that I will be properly compensated."

Yustitsiya narrowed his gaze. "What do you want?"

"Ten million dollars should be enough for me to start a new life. In Canada, maybe."

Yustitsiya scrunched up his forehead. "That is a lot of money."

"Look. I don't know who this woman is that you're looking for, but I do know that she's a big deal or you wouldn't be here. So, I think ten mil is a bargain."

Yustitsiya turned his gaze toward the house up the hill. "Very well. I will get you your ten million dollars. Now, let's go get the key."

"When?" asked the mole as he turned his gaze toward his partners home and squinted. "When will I get the money?"

"Tomorrow. I will get you your money tomorrow."

"Good." The mole extended his hand to seal the deal. "Then tomorrow we will come back and get the keys to the van."

CHAPTER FORTY-ONE

Woodbridge, Virginia
27th of May.

The black Escalade rolled to a stop in front of the driveway at the house on Rosa Drive and was parked in front of a blue-and-white Prince William County Police Force crime scene van. Ramburt sat in the back seat and surveyed the scene from behind the black tinted windows. Two more blue-and-white patrol cars, and another black SUV were parked in front of the house. Officers in dark blue uniforms stood in quiet conversation. Yellow tape guarded the front lawn as well as the garage door and the front door to the house. On the red brick doorstep sat a woman and young girl being comforted by four women in casual clothing.

"That must be the wife," said the driver as he nodded toward the scene on the porch step.

Ramburt turned toward the scene. "I hate this part of my job," he replied. "I never know what to say to a grief-stricken wife." He turned back to face his driver. "There are no words to take away the pain."

"Yes, sir," replied the driver.

Ramburt stepped out of the SUV and looked skyward. A grey overcast sky had threatened for most of the day, and the air was damp. *Definitely going to start raining soon,* he surmised. He gazed at the mother and daughter. *God, I hope they have family that they can stay with tonight.* He stepped over the crime scene tape and flashed his CIA credentials in front of one of the officers controlling access.

"Yes, sir," said the officer. "The sergeant is right over there." He pointed toward an overweight officer with close-cut grey hair under a blue police cap. He stood next to a tall, bald man in a grey business suit, in front of the garage. "He's been waiting for you."

Ramburt nodded. As he marched towards them, they broke off their conversation and turned to face him.

The man in the grey suit extended his hand. "No need to introduce yourself, sir. It's an honor to meet you. I only wish that the circumstances were better."

"Thank you, that's kind of you to say that," replied Ramburt. "I assume you are with the FBI and will be handling the investigation."

"We've been going over the details," interjected the sergeant. "The crime is still in Prince William jurisdiction."

Ramburt furrowed his brow. "Right, well I'm not here to argue about jurisdiction. Fill me in," said Ramburt. "Where was the body found and who identified the remains?"

"The deceased was positively identified by his wife, sir," answered the agent from the FBI. "He was found hanging from a ceiling beam in the garage. A pretty grim scene. The wife and daughter came home after the kids' swim practice. She opened the garage door with her remote. As she drove into the garage, there he was, hanging from the ceiling."

Ramburt flinched. "Oh, god." He lowered his gaze toward the concrete driveway and shook his head. The creaking sound of a garage door opening caused him to turn toward the sound. Two men wearing green hospital scrubs rolled a gurney carrying the covered remains. The man that had been identified as one of his agents rolled past them towards the blue and white forensics van.

"Have you interviewed neighbors? Anybody see anything?"

"Yes sir," answered the FBI agent. "One of the ladies comforting the wife said she saw someone drive away in the deceased's work van about two hours ago. She also stated that two men in a black car were parked in front of her house for more than an hour yesterday. She didn't think anything of it then, but with what has happened, she now thinks they may have staked out the house then, and they came back here today to steal the van. Unfortunately, she didn't think to get a plate number on the black car."

"Damn," cursed Ramburt. "That van is registered to the Agency. There may be more going on here than first appearances."

"Why would someone do that?" asked the sergeant.

Ramburt gazed at him quizzically.

"Why would someone hang himself in a place where his young daughter would find him? That poor girl will have nightmares about this for the rest of her life."

"There's no good answer to that, sergeant, but perhaps we should let the investigation run its course before you label this a suicide," Ramburt replied.

"I've been on this job over thirty years. I know a suicide when I see one."

Ramburt turned a silent glare toward the sergeant.

"Would you like to have a word with the deceased wife, sir?" asked the FBI agent. "I'll introduce you."

Ramburt exhaled through his nostrils. "Yes, but I need to make an urgent call first."

***

Traffic was lighter than usual on U.S. highway 50 East headed toward Annapolis. Cole was returning from the short duration two-day trip to Norfolk. Able to maintain a steady 45-50 mph, the Porsche's flat six-cylinder engine hummed softly, and the active suspension management and dynamic chassis control systems flooded his senses with information about the surface, the tires, and the available grip. *Man, this machine is a pleasure to drive.*

As he moved into the left lane to pass a slower moving blue-and-yellow furniture store delivery truck, Coles' Bluetooth enabled smartphone rang. He pressed the phone button on the steering wheel to answer the call. "This is Cole."

"Cole." Ramburts voice resonated over the Bose speakers "Are you on your way back to the safe house?"

"Yeah. About thirty minutes out if traffic stays light."

"Pick up the pace," replied Ramburt. "One of the techs assigned to the safe house is dead, and the utility van appears to have been stolen. I can't rule out suicide, but I think it's far more likely that he was murdered. And with the van gone, I'm uncomfortable."

"Shit. What happened?"

"I'll tell you about it later. Right now, just kick it in gear. I might be overreacting, Cole, but I would feel a lot more comfortable if you were with Oksana right now."

"Yeah, me too." Cole eased his foot down on the accelerator and felt the subtle quiver in the engine as revolutions increased. "I'll call you when I get there." Cole disconnected and weaved in and out of the two lanes as he passed between slower moving vehicles.

***

Jon, the mole, drove the discreet white Chevrolet utility van slowly on Crab Creek Lane until they reached the recessed entry to the safe house compound. He turned onto the driveway and stopped, then reached under the seat and retrieved a Glock 19 handgun with a threaded barrel. He reached under the seat again and retrieved a four-inch-long Guardian 9 sound suppressor which he screwed onto the barrel. The mole then turned toward Yustitsiya as he inserted a nine-round clip in the handle. "Let's do this."

Yustitsiya shook his head, then slowly reached and picked up a small black metal case from the floor of the van. He opened the cover.

"I told you before you wired the money, there is no other way," said the mole. "If you're not willing to take out the guards, then we turn back." He paused a moment, then continued, "And I will keep the money."

Yustitsiya nodded. "No. No, there's no turning back." His fingers pinched the bridge of his nose. "You've already killed your partner, which I don't think was necessary." He ran his hand over his mouth. "But I must see this through." He pulled another Glock 19 and sound suppressor from the case. With two fingers, he screwed the suppressor onto the barrel. With a sharp slap of his palm, he inserted an ammunition clip. "I'm ready."

The mole nodded and eased on the accelerator. A foggy mist hung in the air and accumulated on the windshield. He flipped the arm on the steering column to activate the windshield wipers. The paved driveway to the safe house was S-shaped and curved into heavily wooded grounds. A half mile later, he made the final turn. The last hundred yards were straight and ended with a concrete guard house and wrought iron gates at the terminal. The mole knew that the two guards would recognize the van and would, therefore, let their guard down. He slowly approached then inched to a stop in front of the gate. The two men inside the guardhouse waved, and the younger of the two stood, and came outside.

"Go now," said the mole.

Yustitsiya got out of the van. The mole followed as he slipped the Glock into his jeans at his waistline at the small of his back.

"You guys are not on the schedule today. What's up?" asked the guard.

"Normal partner just got a promotion. Need to show the new guy where things are at. Show him the ropes, ya know."

"Jeez, you'd think someone would have let us know." The guard shook his head then faced Yustitsiya. "Well let's get inside where it's dry and we can run your creds against the database."

The guard opened the door and held it open as the mole entered. Yustitsiya followed. Inside, the mole reached behind his back and pulled the silenced Glock from his jeans and turned on the guard. *Fffut, ffut*. The bullets entered the guard's forehead just above his right eye. A cloud of crimson and grey matter splattered on the window behind him as he slumped to the floor.

"What the — —" yelped the second guard as he reached for his service revolver.

The mole spun quickly and took aim before the guard could turn. *Fffut, ffut*. The guard flinched one time as the bullets entered the back crown of his head. He fell forward onto a desk where several camera monitors were located. A deep red puddle formed on the counter.

"Mother of God!" muttered Yustitsiya.

The mole pushed the guard on his roller chair out of the way. He pressed a green icon on the touchscreen console, and the heavy-metal gate began to open.

"We're in. Let's go," barked the mole. He trotted back to the van and opened the driver side door then turned his gaze back to the guardhouse. Yustitsiya stood inside, his hand on his forehead.

"Come on!" shouted the mole. "We don't have much time!"

***

Oksana was seated on a stool at the kitchen island. "Cole will be back soon?" she asked.

"With him, you never know. Sometimes he takes the interstate, and other times, he drives the Virginia state biways so he can feel like he's racing at LeMans" Diana bent over, pulling clean dishes out of the dishwasher. She stood, and as she gazed through the kitchen window, she noticed the white van rapidly approaching up the long driveway. "Move to the back of the house," Diana said brusquely.

Oksana stepped down from the stool, wide-eyed. "What is the matter?"

"There is a van coming toward us, and it's not on the schedule. I don't like it! I need you to move to the back of the house just in case." Diana opened a dinnerware drawer next to the stainless-steel sink, retrieved a SIG Sauer 226 service pistol, and a loaded fifteen round magazine, which she slapped into the handle.

Oksana scurried to the opening of the hallway that ran between the kitchen and the living area at the back of the house. She stopped and turned toward Diana. "Who could it be?"

Diana crouched low and crossed the kitchen to a touch screen intercom station located on the wall next to Oksana. She touched the icon to establish a link to the guardhouse. No response. She grabbed Oksana by the elbow. "Go to the boat! Right now!"

Oksana hurried down the hallway, past two bedrooms and a bathroom, and exited out the sliding patio door to the rear deck.

Diana tried again to raise communication with the guardhouse. "Damnit!" she cursed. "Answer me!"

From the front door, she heard, click, click. She turned toward the door and saw the handle move.

"Shit!" She turned to run toward the rear exit with the SIG Sauer in her hand. She looked over her shoulder at the sound of two cracks and saw the wood splinter around the lock. The door exploded open. She recognized the first man that came through the door just as she exited onto the back deck.

Diana jumped two stairs with each step down the deck and ran toward the dock. She gazed ahead. Oksana was stepping into the boat.

"Stop!" A shout came from behind her.

Still running, Diana twisted her torso and double tapped the trigger. The recoil from the pistol caused her to lose her grip, and she dropped the weapon. "Untie the boat," she hollered toward Oksana as she stretched her legs in a full sprint.

Bullets ripped into the lawn a few feet ahead of her. She did not hear the report from the shots. *Silencers. Of course.* As she reached the pier, Diana was knocked to the ground from behind. Her left shoulder burned. "Damnit!" she cursed as she got on her knees and then tumbled into the boat. More bullets zinged over her head. "Stay down," she said to Oksana. She turned the ignition key and pushed the starter button.

At the distinctive *rat-a-tat-tat* of a 9mm submachine gun on full automatic fire, Diana looked behind her. The security team in the boat was rapidly approaching, one agent steering while the second agent lay down in the bow of the boat firing. A second *rat-a-tat-tat*. She looked back and saw the bullets impacting and splintering of the wood railings on the safe house deck.

"Oh, God, Diana. You've been wounded!" Oksana cried out.

Diana backed the boat out of the dock area. "Yeah, and it hurts like hell."

"Turn to your left," shouted the driver of the security boat. "We'll stay with you and cover your backside."

"Diana has been wounded!" shouted Oksana.

"Oksana, take the wheel," Diana implored.

Oksana nodded. She stepped into the cockpit. "You need to go hospital."

"I need to tell Cole," replied Diana.

***

A hail of bullets pounded into the deck railing directly in front of Yustitsiya. He crouched low to the floor and crawled behind a heavy wrought iron chair. "I thought you said the only security was at the gate!"

"It would appear that I was wrong," shouted the mole. "I thought those guys in the boat were just fishermen. There have always been fishermen in the water out there!"

"Well, you obviously were wrong. Those are *not* fishermen!" More rounds pounded into the wood deck.

"I'm outta here," replied the mole. He low crawled back to the rear door of the safe house, entered, then ran through the house and back to the van.

Yustitsiya followed. He opened the passenger side door, slid into the seat and tossed his Glock in the back of the van. "If they were a secondary security level, you can be damn sure they have radio contact with others. There are probably more agents already closing in on this place. We have to get out of here fast."

"Way ahead of ya, Pops. Buckle up."

The mole accelerated and turned the van onto the lawn, taking the shortest route back to the gate. The van bounced and wheels went temporarily airborne as they rode over the unpaved grounds. The tires screeched as the van reached pavement. The driver increased speed through the open gate.

***

The large pine trees and rustic wood fence posts that bordered Crab Creek Lane were a blur as Cole accelerated after the turn off of Eaton Lane. His iPhone dinged twice to alert him that a message had arrived. *It will have to wait*, he thought. *Concentrate on the road. You're almost to the safe house.* He recognized the white utility van coming toward him as one registered to the Agency and knew the road was too narrow for both vehicles. Cole flashed his headlights to alert the driver to pull over, but the van kept coming. The distance closed uncomfortably fast. *Shit! We're going to hit!* He took his foot off of the accelerator, pulled the parking brake handle and turned the steering wheel hard. The Porsche's rear wheels locked which caused the back-end to swing around and come to a stop horizontal to the road, on the grass. The van sped by.

He took a deep breath then exhaled. *What the fuck?* He turned his gaze down the road toward the entrance to the safe house and saw the gate open. *That's wrong.* "Shit," he cursed. He picked up his iPhone and opened the messages app and read Diana's message; COMPROMISED. ON THE BOAT.

What the hell does that mean? He looked toward the open gate again, then turned his gaze in the direction that the van had fled. *The only thing that I'm sure of right now is that van is part of the problem.* Cole shifted into first gear, turned away from the safe house and accelerated after the van, the wheels kicking dirt and gravel behind him as the tires spun over the road apron.

***

Yustitsiya turned toward the mole and shouted, "How did you not know about a secondary unit?"

The mole's gaze shifted from side view mirror to side view mirror. "That's not our biggest problem right now, Pops. We've picked up a tail. I think it's the sports car that we almost hit back near the estate. And he's gaining fast."

"Can't you go faster?"

"What do you think are the odds of this beat up utility van out running a sports car on these narrow winding roads?"

"Is he an agent?" asked Yustitsiya.

"Very strong chance. I think I recognize the car."

Yustitsiya leaned forward so he could see the silver Porsche in the side view mirror. The distance between them narrowed after every turn and switchback. "Just go as fast as you can. I have an idea." He unbuckled his seat belt. "I'm going in the back."

"You think you're just going to open the back door and shoot him?" asked the mole.

Yustitsiya climbed over the driver's console and shimmied between the front seats as he crawled to the cargo area. He looked over his shoulder. "You have a better idea?"

"No, I don't, but don't be surprised if he shoots back."

"Just keep the car on the road." Yustitsaya reached for the gun he had tossed there. As the van leaned heavily into a sharp left turn, he fell toward that side. Frustrated, he picked up the gun and chambered a round. As the mole steered through a sharp right-hand turn, Yustitsaya was tossed to the other side of the van. He gripped the handle of a tool cabinet that was welded to the bulkhead and peered through the small rectangular window on the right side rear door of the van. The Porsche was now no more than twenty feet behind them. He looked over his shoulder and shouted, "Keep it steady." With the gun in his right hand, he placed his free hand on the door handle.

***

The van's rear door burst open, and Cole made eye contact with the man who raised a handgun. The van swerved right. The gunman lost his balance then steadied himself against the side of the door as the van maneuvered through a sharp right turn.

Cole accelerated and closed the distance to the van. He braked and turned hard to make the sharp right turn then accelerated and got alongside the van where there were no windows in order to take away the shooter's field. "Can't shoot me if ya can't see me," he muttered.

The road straightened out. Cole paralleled the van within inches. He steered slightly closer, until an agonizing metallic screech confirmed the two vehicles were in contact. He steered slightly further as he tried to force it off of the road but, the van resisted.

Cole shifted his gaze between the van and the road ahead and caught a glimpse of the red brick side of a bridge and the convergence of the road as it narrowed toward the bridge. "Shit!" He clutched hard and downshifted. With a firm foot on the brake and a hard yank on the wheel, he steered away from the van. The Porsche fishtailed and the rear quarter clipped into the rear of the van

Poof! The airbags deployed and slammed him in the face with the force of a heavyweight boxer's punch. The force knocked his hands from the steering wheel. He felt weightless as the Porsche went airborne. Metal crunched concrete with a bone-chilling sound. The Porsche rolled. He was upside down. A splash. Then nothing. Everything went dark.

CHAPTER FORTY-TWO

T he back of the emergency medical van was brightly lit and uncomfortably warm. A red strobe flashed every ten seconds and lit up the scene outside the open door of the van where a crowd had assembled to observe as divers attached metal cables to the white van under the water in the river. Cole sat on a stiff bench in front of a glass cabinet stocked with medical supplies and next to a petite Maryland state trooper. The emergency medical technician, a twenty-something with Sinatra blue eyes and short blonde hair sat across from him. She dabbed a liquid to a laceration above his right eye.

"You're using super glue to close my cuts?" Cole asked.

She nodded. "Something like that. It's called Dermabond, and it has some antiseptic qualities, unlike super glue."

Cole moved his hand over his side and grimaced.

She finished the application then sat straight and placed one hand on her hip. "You really should let us take you to a hospital for observation, Mr. Draper." She placed the tube of Dermabond in a white medical kit on the bench next to her. "You may have a concussion, and I would like to be sure there is no other internal damage." She pointed at his side. That pain in your side might be a broken rib."

Cole grimaced again. "No time for that. But I promise if I feel any more symptoms I'll be sure to get to a clinic."

The EMT placed her hands on her knees, shook her head and turned to speak to the Maryland State Trooper seated next to Cole. "Can't you arrest him or something and take him to the hospital?"

"You know the rules, ma'am. He has the right to refuse care."

She turned her serious gaze back toward Cole. "You're being very stupid."

The back of the van dipped slightly as Ramburt stepped onto the heavy metal ledge of the van just under the rear doors. He held his Agency identification badge in the palm of his hand. The three occupants turned toward him. "I'll make sure that he gets whatever medical care is needed."

The EMT acknowledged Ramburt then returned her attention to Cole. "Just don't wait too long. Okay?"

Cole forced a close-lipped smile and nodded as the EMT stood and stepped out of the van. Ramburt took the vacated seat.

"How do you feel, Cole?"

"A little worse than the time Clemson pounded us, forty-two to zip in the conference championship."

Ramburt suppressed a smile. "So, tell me what happened?"

Cole turned toward the state trooper.

"You want me to answer that?" asked the trooper.

Cole rubbed the back of his head and grimaced. "Tell him about the van."

She cleared her throat. "Alright." She paused. "Well, we haven't had time to do a complete reconstruction of the crash, but it appears during a high-speed chase. Mr. Draper, at the wheel of his Porsche, contacted that white van. Upon contact, the driver was unable to maintain control, and the van was launched over the side of the bridge and into the South River."

Ramburt turned toward Cole.

"Director, the van was registered to the CIA, and there were two men in the van," said the trooper. "They both expired as a result, whether from the crash and/or from drowning. We don't know. The ME will have to make that determination."

Ramburt's gaze returned to the trooper. "Have they been identified?"

"Tentatively. Sir, one of them carried a Russian passport. His name is Yustitsiya, Vasily Yustitsiya."

Cole made eye contact with Ramburt and held it for a brief moment.

"Can you give us a moment to talk?" Ramburt asked the trooper.

"Of course."

Ramburt waited for the trooper to step out and walk away from the EMT van. "The safe house was exposed. The Russians probably know about Oksana."

Cole leaned forward, head in his hands, and looked toward the floor. "That's all I've been thinking about since you phoned me earlier."

"There was an exchange of gunfire at the safe house. Diana and Oksana had to escape on the boat."

"Yeah. She texted me."

"There's more, Cole."

Cole lifted his gaze toward Ramburt.

"Diana was wounded."

***

The nearest trauma center was located at the Anne Arundcl Medical Center. With blue lights flashing and the emergency siren blaring from the black Escalade, it took Ramburt's driver twenty-one minutes to arrive there. Streetlights flickered on and off as they entered the hospital campus. The driver was forced to slow as a man pushing an elderly woman in a wheelchair, and two teenage girls hurried to get out of the white striped crosswalk.

The SUV had barely stopped under the large copper canopy of the red brick half-moon shaped exterior of the hospital lobby. Cole opened the rear passenger side door and jumped out, scanning left, then right, looking for the emergency entrance. His attention was drawn to bright lights coming from a doorway on his left.

Ramburt joined him at a trot. They entered the foyer and approached a middle-aged woman who wore green scrubs and a pair of reading glasses hanging from a silver chain across her large chest.

She slowly raised her gaze and asked, "Can I help you?"

"Directions to emergency." Ramburt pulled his Agency badge from his back pocket and placed it on the desk in front of her. "One of my agents was brought in here with a gunshot wound, and I want to see her."

The receptionist stood and pointed. "Yes, sir. If you follow the red tiles on your left, they'll take you to emergency admittance. I'll call the desk and tell them you're on your way."

Cole turned and hastened along the path. Ramburt caught up, and together they rushed down the halls to the emergency trauma center. Cole pushed open the double swinging doors and was met by a tall nurse wearing flowery scrubs, her hair pulled up under a surgical headdress. "Are you here for Ms. Shelby? Front desk called and said she had anxious visitors."

"Yes," answered Cole brusquely. "Where is she?"

"Are you family?"

Cole's heart pounded. He clenched his teeth, closed his eyes and took a deep breath.

"Nurse," said Ramburt as he again showed his Agency badge, "Ms. Shelby is one of my agents. Can you please tell us where she is?"

"Yes, of course." She perused his badge and identification card. She gave Ramburt a tight-lipped smile. "She's just coming out of recovery. I'll take you to her."

"How is she?" asked Cole as they began to walk.

The nurse walked slowly with Cole at her side. "She will be fine. The bullet entered just under her left shoulder blade." She reached over and touched Cole's shoulder to indicate the location, and luckily, the bullet ricocheted up. Had it went down it could have come close to the heart. She's lucky to have only sustained a broken shoulder blade along with the external wound. The doctor repaired her shoulder with a metal screw. With a little physical rehab, she should have a full recovery." She stopped and pushed aside a curtain.

Diana lay reclined in a gurney. She wore a blue surgical gown, her long blonde hair pinned up. Her left arm was extended in a cast that was immobilized by a shiny metal brace. She raised her gaze.

Cole stood . . . speechless. A sharp pain stabbed his side, and he grimaced.

"What the hell happened to you?" asked Diana. "You look like you ran into a cement truck . . . and lost."

CHAPTER FORTY-THREE

Exmore, Eastern Shore of Virginia
30th of May

Cole steered his rental Chevrolet Impala into the parking lot of a national chain of budget hotel suites. Oksana had been transferred there after the incident at the safe house. The smooth hum of the ride over pavement was replaced by the crunching sound of rubber tires rolling over the macadam parking lot. He parked close to the lobby entrance. As he stepped out of the car, the lobby door exploded open.

Oksana came running toward him at full tilt. She threw her arms around Cole and embraced him tightly. "I heard that you were hurt. I was a lot worried!"

Cole patted her back. "Just a few cuts and bruises. I'll be fine."

She disengaged from the hug that almost took Cole's breath away and held his hand as they walked back into the hotel. There was a small room off the lobby with several tables and chairs where a morning continental breakfast had been served. The hotel staff was in the process of cleaning up. Two men in dark suits, close-cropped haircuts, and shades stood at the room's entrance.

"You must be Cole Draper," said the man on the left, who appeared to be a few years older and a little thicker in the waist than the second man. He extended his hand in greeting, and stepped away from the hotel staff where he could speak freely.

"That's correct," replied Cole as they shook hands.

The second man nodded and also shook Cole's hand.

"Our orders were to stay with Mrs. Kulakov and provide protective custody until you arrived. We've been here for four days. Except for a few families with noisy kids, it's been quiet. Truckers and vacationers are all we've seen," the older man reported.

"That was the plan. Hide out in plain sight," replied Cole.

"Well, sir, I don't know what's going on here, and I know enough not to ask, but my orders came directly from Director Ramburt. We followed them to the T, so you can rest assured your mission wasn't compromised."

Cole nodded. "Thank you."

"Unless you need anything else, we'll be taking our leave now."

Cole offered his hand to the older of the two. "I'll take it from here. Thanks again."

As the suits left, Cole turned to Oksana. "We need to wait in your room for Ramburt. When he arrives, we're going to move you to a safer place."

***

The suite was on the second floor overlooking the parking lot. Cole pulled a chair from the kitchenette and sat at the window.

"Cole, how Diana feel?" asked Oksana. She was seated on a large brown cushioned chair on the opposite side of the room.

Cole turned his gaze toward her. She wore tight jeans, a loose, purple, button-down tunic and had kicked off her sandals. *There is no way that I am going to allow anyone to harm you in any way,* he thought. *With everything we have been through together during these last five months, you've become like family to me.*

"Cole, what you think? Why you not answer me?"

He let out a puff of air and shook his head. "Sorry. I was just thinking. This will be over soon, and you'll be reunited with Pyotr. When that happens, we'll never see each other again."

Oksana stood and joined him by the window. "That make me sad." She put her hand on his shoulder. "You and Diana are good friends." She leaned over and gently kissed his lips.

Her hair had a slight citrus fragrance. Her lips were warm and soft and tasted like vanilla. Cole's heart thumped.

"Tell me. Diana will be well?" asked Oksana.

Cole held her hand and said, "You're a very special woman, Oksana. Your husband is very lucky."

Oksana's nose and forehead scrunched up, and her smile widened. "Cole, my friends call me Ana. Why you not call me Ana."

Cole grinned. "Ana is it, then."

"Good. I like that." She added, "Diana will be alright?"

"Yes," answered Cole. "Diana will be well." He touched his shoulder. "Diana's shoulder is broken. It will take several months to heal, but she will be alright." Cole heard the crunching of tires over gravel in the parking lot. He turned his gaze out the window and saw the black Cadillac Escalade arrive.

***

The elevator chimed. Cole opened the door and stood in the hallway as Ramburt and his bodyguard approached.

"You look like hell." Ramburt shook Cole's hand.

"Thanks a lot" Cole led Ramburt into the room, and after the bodyguard took his position next to the door, Cole closed it.

Oksana moved from where she stood by the window and sat on the edge of the bed. She lifted one leg under her and folded her hands in her lap.

"Well, we're all here," Cole said. "What do we know?"

"Mind if I have a seat?" Ramburt sat in the cushioned chair.

Cole pulled the kitchenette chair away from the window and sat opposite of Ramburt.

"The driver of the van that crashed into the river was one of the technicians who maintained the safe house and the equipment there," Ramburt explained. "His partner was found dead earlier that day. His wife found him hanging from a ceiling beam in their garage."

"Huh!" gasped Oksana.

Ramburt's gaze shifted to Oksana. "The second person in the van was definitely Russian. His name was Vasily Yustitsiya. We think that he was a colonel in the FSB."

Oksana placed both hands over her mouth.

Ramburt's gaze returned to Cole. "Conventional wisdom tells us that our technician was on the Russian payroll, that he was the mole in our midst." He turned toward Oksana. "It's probable that he was feeding information to the Russians and that, based on information that he provided, Colonel Yustitsiya was here to confirm if you were here, and perhaps force you to return to Russia."

Cole crossed his arms over his chest.

"What this mean?" asked Oksana.

"I'm afraid what it means is that someone in the FSB suspects that Pyotr may be planning to defect. And if they were able to confirm that you did not die in a plane crash, that you are still alive and living in America, then they would assume that Pyotr intends to join you. That would confirm their suspicion."

Oksana's eyes became glassy.

Ramburt's gaze returned to Cole. "We've asked the press to sit on this. So far, they have. But they won't for much longer." He tapped his finger on the arm of the chair a few times then said, "We haven't informed the Russian Embassy yet. We'll make up some story that it took a long time to retrieve and identify the body. But we're going to have to notify them soon. When we do that, they will claim the body." Ramburt turned toward Oksana again. "I'm afraid when that happens, the FSB will assume that Colonel Yustitsaya was killed because of what he found out, and they will probably arrest your husband."

"No!" she cried and fell back on the bed, sobbing.

"Wait a minute!" Cole interjected. "The situation may not be that dire! When does Kulakov get underway for that diplomacy cruise?" he asked rhetorically. He pulled his iPhone out of his pocket and opened the calendar app and checked. "He gets underway tomorrow."

"What are you thinking?" asked Ramburt.

"Can you get the press to sit on it a few more days? Wait a few more days to notify their embassy?"

"It's been four days already, Cole."

"C'mon, Todd. Let's give Pyotr a chance. The Russians don't have a large naval presence in the Atlantic. If Pyotr can get out to sea and get a couple days head start on their fleet, he might be able to make it."

"Even if he does get to sea, they'll call him back."

"He'll ignore it."

"What if they send a ship after him?"

"Let's give him that chance."

Ramburt rubbed his forehead then raised his gaze toward Cole. "I'll see what I can do."

Cole nodded. "Thanks, Todd." He stood, and then joined Oksana and sat on the bed. She raised and put her arms over Cole's shoulders and continued sobbing. Cole rubbed her back gently and said, "Don't worry. It's going to work out." He lifted his gaze toward Ramburt. "We'll do everything we can to help your husband Mrs.

Kulakov." Ramburt turned toward the door and said, "Everything we can."

"One more thing," Cole said.

Ramburt turned.

"I'm taking Oksana to Norfolk. I can hide her there."

Ramburt nodded. His eyes were half closed, and his shoulders were slightly drooped. "That'll be fine." He left, and closed the door behind him.

Oksana lifted her head and Cole met her gaze. She wiped a tear from her eye. "Thank you, Cole. You are very kind." She leaned toward Cole and kissed him.

Cole closed his eyes and willingly responded. He placed his hands on her shoulders and gently guided her backward onto the bed as he became aroused. *So pretty. So soft.* He kissed her neck.

Oksana lifted her blouse over her head and let it drop to the floor. She took Cole's hand and placed it on her breast. Their breathing intensified.

Images flashed across Cole's mind; A nervous Oksana, standing before him in the aisle of the Yak-40, wearing only her lingerie; Oksana on the couch at the safehouse, laughing uproariously at a show on the television; Pyotr at the helm of his small boat on the Neva River; Diana on the pier at the naval base, and her exhilarating smile when they made eye contact; Diana, lying next to him in his bed wearing only a satisfied smile.

No! Cole pushed back, his arms outstretched, he gazed down on Oksana. She had a sad smile.

"We can't do this," said Cole. He sat up on the edge of the bed.

Oksana sat up next to him and she reached for her blouse. Her eyes watered and she sniffled. "I am sad Cole, and confused." She sobbed. "I am not thinking good." She wiped a tear off her cheek with the back of her hand. "You are hurt. Diana is hurt. So many people killed. Pyotr in danger."

Cole placed his hand on her thigh and faced her. "Everything will work out. I promise."

Oksana leaned into Cole and said, "You have been very good to me." Then she cried.

CHAPTER FORTY-FOUR

B uilt in 1926 in Germany, the Kruzenshtern had been surrendered to Russia as a war reparation in 1946. She was the largest fully operational and traditional sailing vessel afloat. Her sails were furled and stowed as the ship was propelled along, in calm seas, at twelve knots. The two Benz 1,000 bhp eight-cylinder diesel engines caused a gentle vibration throughout the ship as they drove the two twelve foot propellers.

Captain Kulakov stood on the open-air bridge in his wool topcoat and watch cap, and surveyed the horizon. He closed the top button of his coat to ward off the chill of the night. With the dimly lit island of Ronne on his starboard stern and the bright lights of Copenhagen and Denmark dead ahead, Kulakov looked at his nautical chart and triangulated the ship's position. They were in the Danish Straights between the major islands of Zealand and Funen.

It had been a long day for the crew. They had put to sea nine hours earlier from the home port of Kaliningrad. The crew, made up of cadets on their first cruise, a small contingent of reserve officers, and a navigator who also served as the executive officer, who had been assigned courtesy of fleet headquarters, had settled into an at-sea routine. With the exception of necessary watch-standers, most of the reserve crew and cadets were prepared to set down for rest.

"Executive Officer, set the navigation detail," ordered Kulakov.

This was a deviation from previous times he had made this transit. Standard protocol would have been for him to order the ship to anchorage for the night then navigate the challenging channels in the light of day. Tonight, however, Kulakov wanted to put some distance between the Kruzenshtern and the Russian Northern Fleet. *These are not normal circumstances. These deviations are required. I am running from my own fleet.*

Over strenuous dissent from his subordinate for his decision, Captain Kulakov had decided that he would take the ship through Great Belt Channel and into the North Sea as soon as possible, and he would not be deterred.

"But Captain, the crew has been on watch for nine hours already. What you're proposing will take another ten hours, at night, and in crowded waters. Most of the crew are just young boys. This is too dangerous," argued the executive officer.

"My job is to turn these young boys into sailors, Lieutenant. They will start being sailors tonight. Now set the navigation detail."

The executive officer stood before him, stone-faced. "As you wish, sir."

"I will retire to my cabin," Kulakov said. "Tell me when the watch is set and we are ready to run the channels."

Kulakov descended the ladder from the main deck toward his cabin on the first deck.

The crew, wearing coveralls in a variety of colors, grey for engineers, blue for deck personnel and white for cooks and stewards, scurried about and cleaned up after the evening meal or made preparation for the next watch. At this time of the day, a lone radioman was occupied with other duties.

Kulakov turned in the passageway toward the radio room that was located adjacent to the captain's cabin. Alone inside, he located the cryptographic radio, the only means to communicate with naval headquarters in St. Petersburg. He reached around and ran his hand along the side of the radio case until he felt the warm air that discharged from the equipment through a ventilation grid. With the location of the vent identified, he retrieved a spray bottle of water from his coat pocket. Perspiration beaded on his upper lip as he sprayed four squirts into the vent. Sparks and an acrid smell of burning electronics filled the air. He replaced the bottle in his pocket, then hastened to his cabin.

***

"Fire, fire, fire!"

The shouts originated from the passageway outside of Kulakov's cabin. He smirked. *The boy returned to the radio room and panicked. Like I knew he would.* Kulakov stood, opened the door and stood under the elaborately carved header. "What is going on here?" he demanded.

A pulsating alarm blared from the shipboard speakers.

"Sir, there is smoke in the radio room!" replied a freckle-faced boy as he reached for the door handle.

"Stop!" shouted Kulakov. He quickly pulled a red fire extinguisher from the bulkhead, tore the seal from the handle and kicked open the door. An eddy of acrid smelling smoke curled around the cryptographic radio. popping sounds emanated from within. Kulakov aimed the flexible hose and the nozzle toward the radio vents and unleashed a solid stream of white carbon dioxide. He waited five seconds then unleashed a second stream of the white spray toward the electronic mail server that sat next to the radio.

Five more crew members wearing heavy yellow Nomex fire-fighting bunker kits appeared at the radio room doorway. Kulakov turned to face them. "You may stand down. This was a simple electrical fire. Post a watch in case of flare up."

The first of the firefighters removed his face mask and nodded. "Aye, sir."

"Now, where is that young man that shouted 'fire' in my hallway?"

The freckle-faced boy came from behind the five that were decked out in their bunker kits.

"Young man. Do you know why I stopped you from touching that door handle?"

The young man lowered his gaze toward the floor. "No, sir," he replied.

"Look at me, young man," ordered Kulakov.

The boy raised his gaze.

"If there had been a fire blazing in that room and you had touched that metal handle, you would have burned your hand very badly. Possibly causing permanent damage."

The boy looked at the door handle.

"Do you understand what I am saying?" asked Kulakov.

"Y-yes, sir."

"Good." Kulakov addressed the group of cadets that had assembled behind the firefighters. "Let that be a lesson to all of you."

The ship's executive officer pushed his way through the group and stood before Kulakov. He looked at the destroyed radio equipment and surveyed the rest of the room. "Captain, our ship to shore radio is destroyed. Both voice and electronic mail."

"Yes," replied Kulakov. "It would appear so."

"Then we must return to Kaliningrad and make repairs."

Kulakov raised his hand to his chin and made a show of contemplation. Then shook his head. "No, Lieutenant, we will continue our journey."

"But Captain!" replied the exasperated officer. We won't — —"

"What would you have me do, Lieutenant?" Kulakov asked. "There will be ships from dozens of nations in the American Parade of Sails. Would you have me fail to arrive on time? Would you allow the Americans to gloat over our failure to arrive on time?" Kulakov narrowed his eyes. "We will have bridge-to-bridge radio communication which will provide the ability to communicate with other vessels. This will be sufficient to navigate across the Atlantic. I have made my decision, Lieutenant."

"Yes, sir." The lieutenant crossed his arms tightly over his chest.

"Very well. Should I assume the navigation watch is set?" asked Kulakov.

"Yes, sir."

"Good. Then let us commence our navigation through these channels."

CHAPTER FORTY-FIVE

A dmiral Kletsov sat in a black leather swivel chair at his large, four-hundred-year-old, ornately carved desk that had once belonged to Peter the Great. A fine line of white smoke rose from the cigarette in his hand that he held over the silver ashtray already full with ashes. He rested his head in his other hand and focused on the paper message on the desk in front of him. "I do not believe this message. Pyotr would not betray Russia."

"We should stay positive Admiral. The message only implies that Captain Kulakov may be entertaining the thought of treason," replied the admiral's chief of staff seated on an overstuffed royal blue sofa. "They only want to question him."

"Don't be a fool. This message is from the director of the FSB. Pyotr will be invited for an unpleasant stay in Lubyanka where they have a way of hearing only what they want to hear." Kletsov snuffed out his cigarette then opened a brass case on his desk, picked up another and lit it with a well-worn brass lighter. "This case against him is weak."

"Sir, two or possibly three FSB officers have died pursuing this case."

Kletsov raised his voice, "But there is no connection to Pyotr. Only speculation!"

"Yes, sir," replied the chief of staff.

"Kletsov stood and walked to his floor to ceiling office window that overlooked the Neva River. Cigarette in hand, he gazed at the reflection of the sun off of the blue-green water. "This Colonel Yustitsiya," he turned to face his chief of staff, "he went to America because he had reason to believe that Pyotr's late wife Oksana was, in fact, alive and living in Washington."

"Yes, sir. That is correct."

"What did he find? Did he find the ghost of Oksana?"

"No, sir. Nobody knows what he found there. In fact, nobody knows if he found anything. Admiral, he is dead."

"Yes, he is dead. The Americans said it was an accident."

"But sir, the Americans — —"

"The Americans said he was driving too fast and crashed his vehicle. I am aware of this." He took a pull on his cigarette. "Yustitsiya went to America to find Oksana, and to prove that Pyotr was going to meet her there and defect. He wanted to prove that Pytor was a traitor. But there is no evidence that Yustitsiya found Oksana."

"Yes sir, but, Yustitsiya was only following the evidence that was presented earlier," replied the chief of staff. "And the circumstances of his accident were suspicious enough for the Ambassador to file a protest with the American Secretary of State."

"Bah!" Kletsov marched over to his desk and picked up the printed message. "The case that was presented by Major Ogorodnik. Perhaps you remember that impertinent fool. He had the audacity to come to my headquarters and accuse Pytor."

"And he died after he confronted Captain Kulakov."

Kletsov raised his voice, "What are you saying? Are you accusing Pytor of murdering that major?"

"Sir, I don't — —"

"If I recall, that major drowned. There is no connection to Pytor. Even Colonel Yustitsiya determined that Ogorodnik probably committed suicide because he was despondent that the young agent he was secretly in love with was killed by that American young man."

"And she was also working on this case that is linked to Pyotr."

Kletsov returned behind his desk and sat with a heavy thud. "All circumstantial and speculation. There is nothing in this message that positively proves that Pyotr is a traitor."

Kletsov spun his swivel chair toward the window and gazed outside. "Has Pyotr's executive officer informed you of any suspicious behavior?"

"No, sir."

"Hmmph," Kletsov grunted.

After a few moments of silence, his chief of staff said, "The message states that the FSB chief encourages you to order Captain Kulakov to return the Kruzenshtern to Kaliningrad."

Kletsov turned a hard gaze toward his chief of staff.

A few seconds passed before the chief of staff prodded, "Admiral?"

"Damn!" Kletsov cursed and slammed his open hand on the desk. "Make it so."

***

A reading lamp on his desk was the only illumination in Kletsov's large office. The sun had set several hours earlier, and he was now in near darkness. He sat with his head in his hands. A computerized printout was spread across his desk. It showed repeated failed attempts to establish contact with the Kruzenshtern, one every hour over the last six hours. He heard a knock on his heavy door and raised his head. "Come," he growled.

The chief of staff opened the door and entered.

"Well," asked Kletsov.

"I am afraid there is still no contact, sir."

"There was no distress call," observed Kletsov. "There are no storms on their track toward America. This does not make sense. Pytor would have followed procedures if his ship had run into difficulty."

"The chief of the FSB would like to know if it's possible to send a destroyer after the Kruzenshtern and force Captain Kulakov to return."

"He assumes that Pytor has simply chosen to ignore our communications."

"I'm afraid the chief of FSB will assume nothing."

Kletsov placed his hand on his forehead. "Do we know where she would be? If she is still afloat."

"I'm afraid she would be halfway across the Atlantic by now, sir," replied the chief of staff. "I've taken the liberty of checking on our ship's locations. The only asset near there is a Vishnya class electronics surveillance vessel."

Kletsov pounded his fist on the table. "Send her to look for the Kruzenshtern."

"There is one other thing."

"Go on," replied Kletsov.

"The Director of Security Services will take no chances. If the Kruzenshtern is still afloat and she pulls into the port in America, Captain Kulakov will be arrested. They have sent agents there, and they will arrest Pyotr onboard, confine him to his cabin, and prevent him from going ashore."

CHAPTER FORTY-SIX

Cole sat on the left corner of the red oak desk at his home office. He looked thoughtfully out his window at the clear blue sky of a warm summer morning.

Ramburt and Diana were seated comfortably on a chocolate-colored microfiber guest sofa that faced him.

"Hey, Cole," said Ramburt. "You look like you're a thousand miles away from here. Are you on vacation or is something else on your mind?"

Cole turned to face Ramburt. "Hell, I don't know. There are only a hundred things that could go wrong today. What could possibly be on my mind."

Ramburt replied, "You've planned this down to the smallest detail. You worry too much." Ramburt leaned forward, placed his elbows on his knees. "This is a righteous op, Cole. You know that the information on the thumb drive that Kulakov provided to Keenan was eye-watering. In addition to his schedule, it was a treasure trove of strategy documents and work papers. The analysts have been having a field day."

"Yeah, I know." Cole turned and gazed out the window at a young woman walking her dog. "I suppose it's worth the life of a few people."

"Look, Cole, we all know that we're playing catch up with the Russians in the Arctic. With Kulakov's knowledge, maybe we can counter some of their moves and stake our own interests. Trust me, Cole, this is a big deal. The President is paying attention."

Cole stood and walked toward Ramburt, pulled a roller chair over and sat down across from him. "Making them disappear won't be easy."

"Yeah, I know," Ramburt replied. "I'm sure that Kulakov is worried that their security service will come hard after him. The Russian's have not been shy about having his opponents eliminated, even in other countries."

"That's for sure," replied Cole. "He made it pretty clear that he doesn't want to be the next one of the Russian President's ex-patriots poisoned by nerve agents, and who can blame him for that?"

They each sat quietly for a few moments.

Ramburt broke the silence, "We're doing the right thing, Cole."

"Yeah," replied Cole. He turned toward Diana seated next to Ramburt on the couch. Her arm was still in a sling. "By the way, how is Oksana? I haven't seen her at all today."

"Oksana is fine. A little nervous, maybe." She leaned forward a little as she spoke, "But she seems more comfortable when you're around. I guess the two of you bonded pretty well."

"Yeah," Cole replied. He stood, walked around his desk and sat in his chair facing the window to the street outside.

"We may need to talk about that when this is all over," Diana teased.

"I'm not sure what you mean by that," replied Cole brusquely.

"Jeez, Cole. Don't snap my head off. What are you so touchy about?"

He turned again and faced Diana. "Sorry. Guess I'm a little on edge. Do you know where Katie is?"

"She's on the beach watching for Kulakov's ship, like you asked her to."

"And is she — —"

"Yes, Cole," interrupted Diana. "She will pick up the number for the golf cart from the East Beach coordinator, just like you asked her to do."

Cole half smiled. "I hate that I'm using her like this. She has no idea what's really going down."

"She'll be fine, Cole," replied Diana. "You're worrying too much."

Cole turned toward Ramburt. "Did you get things worked out with your British friends?"

"Yeah, I did. It's your lucky day. British Airways has an Airbus A320 that had a hydraulic problem during a trans-Atlantic flight. They landed safely at JFK, but the plane was grounded until it could be repaired. They flew another one over so they could keep their schedule. Now the original aircraft has been repaired and needs to be repositioned. They were planning to fly it empty to Heathrow. I convinced my friends at MI5 to lean on British Airways. Now the plane will fly into Norfolk Naval Station and pick up a couple of passengers before flying on to Heathrow."

"Perfect," Cole replied.

"Yeah, well it cost the CIA a case of eighteen-year-old single malt. That stuff ain't cheap!"

"And the safe house in London?" asked Cole.

"The apartment is clear. The key is in a lockbox under the front steps. The combination is seven, six, zero, seven, zero, four."

Cole laughed. "The six-digits for Independence Day, year, month, day. Brilliant! That's easy enough to remember."

They all turned toward a hard wrap on the door.

"I assume that will be Lieutenant Choesler," stated Cole. He left the room and walked through the reception area to the front office door.

Cole opened the door inward and extended his hand to greet Choesler. "Bobby." Cole gripped Choesler's hand, and they embraced like the brother's in arms they had become. "Good. We're all here now. C'mon in and let's go over the plan."

"Looking forward to it, sir."

Cole returned to the meeting room, stood with his backside resting on his desk, and faced Ramburt and Diana on the couch. Choesler turned the roller chair towards Cole and took a seat in it.

"Okay," started Cole. "Let's get right into the meat. Time is running short."

"Roger," said the lieutenant. "But before you get started, there's an interesting development that I need to make you aware of. One of our destroyers was returning from training ops off the coast. They had a visual sighting that they confirmed was the Kruzenshtern."

"Good," said Cole. "Pretty close to schedule."

"Yeah, well, what's interesting is that it looks like they were being chased by a Russian spy ship."

"Huh?" said Cole.

"I talked to the skipper myself on ship-to-shore radio. He said the spy ship was going about as fast as it could, maybe fifteen knots in what appeared to be a pursuit, but that they stopped before they entered territorial waters."

"He said they were chasing the Kruzenshtern?"

"The captain said it sure looked like it."

"Why in the world . . ." Cole wondered aloud. He looked at Ramburt who shrugged his shoulders.

"There's something else," said Ramburt. "An official from the Russian embassy in Washington showed up this morning with three newspeople." He raised his hands and made imaginary quotes with his fingers. "We're pretty sure they're with the FSS, the intelligence arm of their security service. They stated their intent to go on board when the ship gets docked at Waterside. Good public relations, they said."

"Where are they now?" asked Cole.

"Last time I checked, they were in a hotel near Waterside. And they have plenty of company. I have watchers on them around the clock."

CHAPTER FORTY-SEVEN

A bright shimmering sunlit path on the blue-green water of the Chesapeake Bay lay ahead of the Kruzenshtern as it sailed west in the afternoon sun past the Chesapeake Bay Bridge Tunnel toward its designated anchorage. The Virginia harbor pilot had positioned the tug Pathfinder fifty yards off the port bow where it maintained position, ready if needed in case of an emergency.

"Captain, your temporary anchorage is position number twelve," advised the harbor pilot. "Number twelve is marked by the bright orange anchor buoy twenty-five degrees off your port bow at about four thousand meters."

Kulakov stood next to his captain's chair on the elevated forward conning station. He lifted his Russian made Komz binoculars to his eyes and sighted the anchor buoy. Beyond position number twelve, he saw an array of tall ships at anchor flying flags from Brazil, Portugal, Spain, Columbia, Mexico, and Indonesia. Interspersed among the tall ships were several smaller sailing vessels that were replicas of pirate ships and Columbus's famous Santa Maria. They were all there to take part in Norfolk's Harborfest, the largest and oldest maritime festival in America.

Kulakov set his binoculars on a hardwood platform next to his chair, stepped to his left and turned the pelorus on the ship's compass toward the buoy. He placed the anchorage in the crosshairs and noted the direction then spoke to the harbor pilot in English, "Sir, thank you. With your help, I have identified my anchorage," He paused. "Is there anything else I can do for you?" He turned to face forward.

In spite of his intent to defect, he was still an experienced Russian mariner, and he thought there was no need for an American harbor pilot to embark on his ship to assist him and his crew accomplish a simple task like proceeding to anchorage at a designated location. However, he also understood that this was a United States Coast Guard regulation that he had to abide by. But he was under no obligation to make it easy for the pilot. "I will take my ship to anchorage," said Kulakov as he stood facing the bow, back straight in perfect posture with his hands clasped behind his back. "You may go back to your tug now." He smiled wryly and shifted his gaze to look left toward the pilot.

"Uhm, sir," The pilot stepped closer to Kulakov and spoke softly. "Under Coast Guard regulation I am required to stay at the conning station until the ship is anchored."

Kulakov turned to face the harbor pilot. "If you must," he said sternly, then stepped around the pilot, and with his hands still clasped behind his back he shouted toward the Russian deck officers who controlled rudder and engine speed. "Left ten degrees rudder to course three-zero-zero, and make the engines one-third speed."

"Engine speed is one-third, sir," sounded the response from the engineer via the speaker control station after the engines responded.

"Steady on course three-zero-zero," responded the helmsman who stood rigidly at attention behind the ship's wheel, his hands at the ten o'clock and two o'clock positions.

Kukalov mentally calculated the speed and distance. *At one-third speed, it will take six minutes to travel three thousand meters.* He counted down the moments and at exactly six minutes he ordered, "All engines stop."

After a short silence, the control station speaker squawked, "All engines are stopped, sir."

With engines stopped it will take two minutes to drift one thousand meters. Kulakov knew this from experience. He counted the moments silently again. After exactly two minutes Kulakov turned around to face forward, looking past the bow and ordered, "Let go the anchor and shift flag position to indicate the ship is no longer underway."

***

Dozens of curious onlookers, amateur photographers, and photojournalists, including a trio of Russian-speaking newspersons, watched from the beach as the Kruzenshtern slowly glided across the calm waters of the Chesapeake Bay toward the temporary anchorage area near Norfolk's East Beach. Her gloss black hull was accentuated with a distinctive wide white stripe with black rectangles that gave the illusion of gun ports. Sailors precariously straddled the ship's three main masts to ensure the sails remained furled. Others executed the precisely choreographed operation to drop the anchor.

Seated in her bright yellow beach chair and wearing an equally bright orange bikini that accentuated her dark summer tan, Katie wiped a small amount of perspiration off of her brow then raised the binoculars that Cole had given her. She watched this ship drift to anchorage, just as she had almost a dozen times with the other tall ships that were part of OpSail Virginia. The calm water and slight breeze blowing toward the shore enabled her to hear the deck officer's loud commands to drop anchor, at least she had to assume that was the command since it was spoken in Russian. The command was followed by a loud metallic *rat-tat-tat-tat*. The large anchor fell from its housing and splashed into the Bay water.

A light cool breeze off the water provided temporary relief from the hot summer heat. Katie fished a cold bottle of water out of her small cooler and twisted the cap off.

"Pretty impressive, huh?"

Katie looked up to her right, squinted, and placed her hand above her eyes to shield the bright sunlight. A tan, well-built young man wearing brown-and-grey board shorts and a Virginia Tech ball cap worn backward, stood over her.

She flashed her smile his way and responded, "Yeah, pretty cool."

She lifted the binoculars to her eyes again and watched as the crew lowered and secured a sea ladder while the tugboat Pathfinder maneuvered alongside the port side of the Kruzenshtern to recover the harbor pilot.

"Wow, those are some pretty heavy-duty binocs you got there," said the beach dude. "You in the Army or something?"

"Nah. I borrowed these from my husband," she lied. "He's a Navy SEAL." She looked up at him again and smiled. Her nose curled as she shielded her eyes.

"Oh . . . C-o-o-l," replied the disappointed beach dude.

Katie lifted the binoculars to her eyes again. She felt beach dude's presence move along. A small motorboat with a delegation of two men and one woman that she assumed were OpSail officials made their approach alongside Kruzenshtern. The three got off and walked up the steps of the sea ladder. Katie guessed they were there to meet the officers of the ship, exchange small gift mementos and discuss some of the activities at Harborfest. Based on her previous discussion with Cole, she also knew the trio would extend an invitation to the ships' captain to attend a sail-in meeting at the East Beach Community BayFront Club in the evening.

Katie turned her binoculars towards the opening in the Chesapeake Bay Bridge Tunnel. The distinctive white hull and red stripe of the tall ship USCG Eagle, which was scheduled to be the last of the tall ships to enter, came into focus. The Eagle was scheduled to anchor at position number fourteen. She reached into her beach bag and retrieved her cell phone and dialed Cole's phone number. Cole picked up after two rings.

"Hey, Cole. Your Russian ship, whose name I can't pronounce, just anchored at position number twelve and the Eagle is just entering the anchorage area."

***

"That's great, Katie. You've been a big help." Cole stood in the center of the room in front of his desk and faced the team members in his office as he spoke to Katie.

"No problem, uncle," replied Katie. "I don't mind being cheap labor for ya, but maybe you could buy me a nice dinner to compensate for spending the whole day here baking in the hot sun."

"Katie, it's your summer break. That's what you do all day anyway!"

"Yeah, but that's leisure time. This was work."

Cole heard her snicker through the phone. He grinned.

"Cole, are you ever going to tell me what this is about?"

"Not now, Katie."

"Well okay, but we'll have to talk about a pay raise then," she replied. The call disconnected.

Cole shook his head, turned and walked a few steps to his desk and placed his phone there next to a silver Macbook. "I love that girl, but she sure is a smartass," said Cole as he turned back to face the group.

"Wonder where she picked up that trait?" said Diana sarcastically.

Cole looked at Diana with a smirk then addressed the group. "Okay, according to my lovely niece, all the tall ships have arrived. Most important, the Kruzenshtern is among them and is anchored at position twelve. So, as far as I'm concerned, we're a go for tonight." Cole returned to his place in front of the group and leaned his backside against his desk. "The last thing on the agenda is weather and tide."

"Roger," replied Choesler. "I checked with the Navy meteorologist before coming over here." He moved the roller chair a little more towards the center of the room and turned toward Cole. "It's almost perfect. There will be no more than a quarter moon, and there will be a partial cloud cover. So, it will be dark out on the water."

"Couldn't ask for better conditions," interjected Ramburt.

"And best of all," continued Choesler as he pushed his roller chair back a few feet, "max ebb tide will be at 2224 tonight. So, between 2145 and 2215 tonight is perfect timing."

"Excellent," said Cole. He slapped his thighs and stood. "All we have to do now is execute."

CHAPTER FORTY-EIGHT

K ulakov returned to his onboard captain's cabin just below the main deck starboard at the aft end. He stood by the window and faced astern, which provided a view of the seventeen-mile-long Chesapeake Bay Bridge Tunnel and the USCG Eagle as it gracefully closed to position number fourteen and dropped anchor. He heard a polite knock on his door, turned to face it and called out, "Yes, who's there?"

The executive officer opened the door partway and stood, half-in and half-out of the captain's cabin. "Sir, there is a delegation from the OpSail committee here. They would like to meet you."

Ugh. The trivial, meaningless things the captain must do. Kulakov rolled his eyes. "Yes, of course. See them in."

After welcoming handshakes and a customary shot of Russian vodka, the delegation presented a gift of two bottles of wine from the Williamsburg Winery, one white and one red, as well as a glass mermaid on a brass stand with the inscription *Norfolk OpSail Welcomes the Kruzenshtern* on the base. "We like to say that Norfolk is The City of Mermaids," said the head of the delegation.

In return, Kulakov presented the head of the delegation with a silver plate engraved with the Kruzenshtern in full sail heading forward through rough seas.

A brief indoctrination meeting was held. Kulakov was invited to attend the captain's sail-in meeting that would be held ashore at the East Beach BayFront Club at eight o'clock that evening. Kulakov was asked to have his ship's small boat bring him to the transient dock at the BayPoint Marina located in the Little Creek Harbor on the opposite side of the peninsula from East Beach. From there, volunteers from the East Beach neighborhood would use their private golf carts to shuttle the captains from the dock to the BayFront Club. Each cart would be labeled with a number corresponding to the ship's temporary anchor position.

Following the meeting, the delegation took a brief tour of the ship. Thirty minutes later, Kulakov happily escorted the delegation to the gangplank and before he bid them farewell asked, "Gentlemen, there is one thing. We had an unfortunate accident during our transit here. A small electrical short in our radio room damaged our ship-to-shore radio and our electronic mail server. Can I impose upon you to help arrange a repair?"

"Of course. We will see to it," replied the head of the delegation.

***

Katie showered and put on a pair of white shorts, blue islander top and pulled her hair in a ponytail through the back of her Old Dominion University ball cap. She drove Cole's golf cart, which she referred to as The Guacamobile because of its olive-green color. At the Bay Front Club, she met with the East Beach volunteer coordinator, and picked up the plastic number that needed to be affixed to the golf cart so the captains could identify which golf cart had been assigned as their shuttle. She had received an e-mail that indicated the coordinator would arrive there at five o'clock to hand out the numbers, and that she would appreciate promptness because she had other Opsail events to prepare for.

Katie arrived a few minutes early, because Cole asked her to ensure she was assigned the number twelve to correspond with the Kruzenshtern. She spotted the coordinator seated at a desk near the gate that led to the small neighborhood swimming pool. She pulled the golf cart into a parking space in front of the club, slid out of the cart and hopped up the three steps to the deck.

"Hi Katie," said the cheery, middle-aged coordinator. "Thanks for being so prompt!"

"This is so cool!" replied Katie. "Having all these ships here and then tonight, all these captains from all over the world will be here at the club." Katie beamed. "This will be so-o-o much fun!"

"Yeah, we're pretty fortunate to be able to have this event take place here." The coordinator looked up at Katie. "And, by being a shuttle driver, you'll have an opportunity to talk to one the captains while you drive him around. You'll probably find him interested in learning about Norfolk and our culture here." The coordinator reached down and picked up a ten-inch diameter, white circular sign with a black number painted on it. "You're the first person here so why don't we just give you, number one."

Katie grimaced. "I was hoping I could have my lucky number." She looked at the coordinator with a pleading expression.

The coordinator chuckled. "That can be arranged. And that number is?"

"Twelve!"

The coordinator set aside the sign with the number one, reached down and picked up the pack of signs, rifled to the back and pulled out number twelve. "Here it is." She handed the sign to Katie and looked at a list on her desk. "Number twelve is the Russian ship Kruzenshtern, and the captain's name is Kulakov."

"Cool!" Katie exclaimed. "Thanks a mil." She took the sign, marched away, hopped down the steps and jumped into The Guacamobile. "See ya tonight." She waved as she drove away.

CHAPTER FORTY-NINE

At the designated pick up time of half-past seven, Cole parked The Guacamobile, in the lot of the Marina next to the transient dock. In addition to the other golf carts and their drivers, there were at least three dozen neighbors with children and dogs who wanted to see the ship's captains as they arrived ashore.

"Hi, Cole," called out one of his neighbors as she walked past, pushing a baby stroller. "I'm surprised to see you doing this. I thought that Katie was going to be a shuttle driver." She narrowed her eyes. "Did she get you into this?"

"Of course she did," Cole replied. "She went to grab a bite to eat and asked me if I would fill in. She said I need to do my part for international diplomacy." *A little fib doesn't hurt.* Cole slid from the driver's side of the cart to the passenger side so he could better interact with his neighbors. *If only you knew what was really going to happen.*

The procession of small boats began to arrive. The first was the commanding officer of the USCG Eagle. The small boats arrival and disembarkation of the captain was executed with military precision. The remaining small boats arrived and departed at short intervals, and the parade of captain's strutted down the dock, each wearing the dress uniform of their respective navy.

Kulakov was the sixth to arrive. He disembarked from the small boat and walked down the pier toward the parking lot and gaggle of golf carts parked there. When he was about ten feet away from Cole, Kulakov momentarily stopped.

Cole nodded and slid back to the driver's side. Kulakov hopped into the golf cart next to him. He sat with his uniform cap on his lap staring straight ahead.

Cole quickly put the cart in gear and drove off before either of them had a chance to speak where others would be able to overhear what was said.

"It is good to see you, Pyotr," Cole said in Russian.

Kulakov turned to face Cole and spoke in English. "I was hoping that I would see you today."

"I trust your transit here was uneventful," said Cole.

"Yes, overall it was uneventful. We did have a small fire that degraded our ship-to-shore communication. We have been unable to talk to our fleet headquarters for six days."

Cole chuckled. "An accident, no doubt."

"An accident. Yes."

"Were you aware that a Russian ship attempted to intercept you?"

"I assumed that Admiral Kletsov would send ships to intercept us, but our fleet has few fast ships in the Atlantic. We were fortunate that we made good speed."

Cole faced forward as he drove. "Pyotr, your new life will start tonight. You and Oksana will have new identities, passports, a place to live and a new career. It has all been arranged."

He drove quickly and turned left out of the parking lot. They drove west on a two-lane road, named Pretty Lake Avenue which was three blocks south of, and parallel to the beach. When he saw that he was safely out of voice range to the other golf carts, he slowed to more-or-less match the speed of the other carts.

Most of the carts ferrying the other captains turned right on 29th Bay Street and headed north toward the beach on the Chesapeake Bay where the BayFront Club was located. Cole continued for three more blocks before turning, to ensure he was out of hearing range from the others.

"Captain." Cole slowed the cart, and turned to face Kulakov. "In a few minutes, I'm going to drop you off for your meeting. I need you to proceed at that meeting just like you would any other group planning meeting."

Kulakov nodded.

"However, there is one small, but very important, thing I would like you to do differently, something you would not normally do at a sail-in meeting. But it fits with the subterfuge of our entire plan." Cole waited for further confirmation that Kulakov was paying attention.

"Yes. What is it?" Kulakov looked at Cole quizzically. He sat, palms up, still holding his cap.

"I need you to drink a little more wine tonight than you might normally drink during an affair like this."

Kulakov's brow furrowed.

"I need you to drink enough alcohol that you will appear to be drunk when the meeting ends."

Kulakov shook his head, "I don't understand —— "

"I don't have time to explain but, I need you to trust me. Can you do this?"

"Yes. Of course." He smiled wryly. "I have recently had the opportunity to perfect that act."

Cole looked back over his right shoulder to ensure that traffic was clear then made a right turn, and headed toward the BayFront Club. They both faced forward and watched the road ahead.

"When you come out of the meeting, walk directly to this cart. Make sure it is this cart. I will not be the driver." Cole turned to face Kulakov, but gazed out the corner of his eye at the road ahead. "Your driver will be a pretty young woman. Her name is Diana. Be very nice to her." He paused. "She's the woman I intend to marry."

Kulakov faced him, and he wore a genuine smile. "I am very happy for you."

"Yes," Cole smiled. "Thanks. This may surprise you, but something you said to me a while ago, made me think I was blowing an opportunity to be happy. You once told that everyone should have a special partner to share a life with." Cole smiled. "Diana is my special partner."

Kulakovs' smile grew wider.

"She doesn't know yet that I'm going to ask her to get married. So, when you see her, just get in the cart like nothing is unusual."

Kulakov chuckled.

"She will whisk you away from the others quickly." He turned his head forward to see the road ahead again. "That's all you need to do."

"I understand."

Cole slowed as they approached the clubhouse. "It's been a long road to get to this point, Pyotr. It's been a pleasure."

Kulakov stepped out of the cart then turned back toward Cole and leaned into the cart. "I will not see you again."

"You will not see me again," replied Cole.

Kulakov offered a handshake that Cole accepted. "Thank you."
Cole returned a tight-lipped smile, nodded, then drove away.

CHAPTER FIFTY

The events room of the BayFront Club was arranged for an informal meeting with the OpSail committee and all the participating ships' captains. Kulakov entered through a side door from a wood deck. Three beige cushioned chairs were placed in a U-shape around a glass cocktail table in front of a large fireplace. Across the room were six hightop tables with white tablecloths and a different flower centerpiece on each one. A small tabletop bar where beer and wine were served was located in the far corner. Two rows of armless chairs were set in front of a large, wall-hung, flat-screen television. On it was a slideshow presentation of photos taken at previous OpSail events and Harborfest activities.

Kulakov walked directly to the bar and ordered a glass of merlot wine, then he walked to one of the hightops where captains from Portugal, Spain, and Mexico had gathered. "Good evening, gentlemen." He spoke in English. "May I join you?"

"Of course," the captains from Portugal and Spain said in unison. They shifted positions to allow Kulakov to step up to the table.

A young woman with braided red hair approached the table. She carried a tray of finger sandwiches and egg rolls. They each took a small plate.

A cool evening breeze through the open bayside windows kept the temperature in the room comfortable.

The captains talked about their journeys to Norfolk, where they had been and where they were headed next. For forty-five minutes, they talked a little about the weather and the sea. Others joined the conversation while some broke off and joined conversations at other tables.

Kulakov was on his second glass of wine when the host of OpSail, the Mayor of Norfolk, asked them all to be seated in front of the flat screen for a briefing from the local Coast Guard Commandant regarding the group sail into Norfolk scheduled for the next morning.

The Coast Guard admiral, in a blue dress uniform with one wide and one narrow gold stripe on his sleeve and six rows of award ribbons on his chest, stepped up to the podium. "Gentlemen, I am Rear Admiral David Morrison, Commander of the Fifth Coast Guard District. It is my privilege to welcome you to this year's Parade of Sail. This is going to be quite a magnificent event."

The captains responded with a polite round of applause.

Morrison spent five minutes reviewing the safety procedures that would be implemented in case of an engineering breakdown during the parade that would require an immediate anchorage or a tugboat assist. He identified the point at which all the ships were required to furl the sails and shift to engine power to ensure safe mooring dockside.

"Gentlemen, the weather report for tomorrow calls for a moderate breeze so it should be a beautiful day for a sail in." Morrison faced the group, and placed both hands on the lectern. "With that said, the first ship in the Parade of Sails will be the representative from the host nation, USCG Eagle." The commandant pointed at a list displayed on the screen. "After that, the order of the procession will go by size. Captain Kulakov, your ship, the Kruzenshtern will be the second in the parade." He pointed his laser pointer at the list on the screen to indicate Kruzenshtern's position.

Kulakov raised his glass to acknowledge.

The brief continued for another thirty minutes, and the designated mooring positions alongside the dock at Harborside were identified as well as a schedule for ship tours for the general public. During the brief, Kulakov stood and walked awkwardly to the bar to retrieve another glass of merlot. Many of the captains exchanged uncomfortable glances as he took his seat.

***

In his office, Cole changed his clothes. He put on the uniform of a Russian Captain, First Rank, and a synthetic wig that matched the exact length and color as Kulakov's. After one last glance in a mirror, he turned toward Diana. "This is it. Time to go."

She stood facing him. "Not bad. You look like Captain Kulakov." She reached out and straightened his shoulder boards. "Not bad at all."

Cole grinned. "You have a thing for Russian Captains?"

"Only the impersonators," she replied.

Cole embraced Diana in a long hug. "Time to get this show on the road."

Holding hands, Cole and Diana walked the short hallway and entered the garage from the back wall of his office. Ramburt was leaning his backside against a wooden workbench along the wall. Oksana was seated in a folding chair next to the door. They both turned their gaze toward Cole.

Cole gave them a reassuring smile. He faced Oksana and held out his hands. She stood and placed her hands in his. "How do I look?" asked Cole.

"Like Pyotr." She narrowed her eyes and smiled. "But not as handsome."

Cole chuckled. "Ana, I'm very glad that I met you."

Oksana's eyes watered.

"In less than thirty minutes, Pyotr will be here, and you will be together again. If things go as planned tonight, you will be taken to a destination where you and Pyotr will start a new life together. When you get there, you will be introduced to another agent who will ensure your transition is a smooth one. I wish a wonderful life for you."

"I will not see you again?"

"No, Ana. We will never see each other again."

Oksana fell into Cole's arms. They embraced. "Thank you. I will miss you, Cole," she whispered.

***

At a quarter after nine, the OpSail meeting adjourned. While the other captains briefly mingled in place, Kulakov headed back to the bar for one last glass of wine before the East Beach volunteers were scheduled to arrive in their golf carts to shuttle the captains back to the Marina.

With his drink in hand, he walked outside and spotted the green golf cart with the number twelve affixed to the front of the cart. Diana, the woman that Cole intended to marry was in the cart talking on a cellphone held in a hand encumbered by an arm cast. He set his drink down on a small table on the outside deck area. He deliberately stumbled as he walked toward Diana's cart, parked in front an elevated boulevard and park area.

As he approached the cart, he overheard the driver say to whoever was on the other end of the cellphone, "We're on our way."

He leaned into the cart. "You are Diana?" he asked.

"Yes."

"Are they watching?" he asked.

She looked over his shoulder to the club deck where a gaggle of captains and residents mingled. "Yes. They sure are," answered Diana.

"Good."

Kulakov slid into the cart next to her. She pulled out of the parking spot and bolted, as fast as the golf cart would go. He held on tight with one hand on the handle under the cart top as Diana drove down the narrow road.

"Mr. Draper is a good man. I'm very happy for both of you."

Diana looked quizzically at Kulakov as she turned abruptly into an alley. She turned hard left into a garage. The cart screeched to a stop. She leaned forward and pulled the magnetic number twelve from the front of the cart and tossed it to Cole, who was in the passenger seat of a second golf cart, also the color of The Guacamole. It faced in the opposite direction. He leaned forward and placed the sign on the front of the cart.

Diana snatched Kulakov's hat from his lap and tossed it to Cole. She quickly jumped out of The Guacamobile and into the driver's side of the second cart. They sped off in the opposite direction.

Standing with her back to the wall in front of Kulakov was Oksana. Tears welled up in her eyes as she raised her trembling hands to her mouth.

Ramburt pressed the remote to close the garage door. He walked to the passenger side of the cart and, as he extended a handshake, he said, "Welcome to America, Captain Kulakov."

***

Cole held on as Diana used her good arm to steer. She drove the golf cart as fast it as would go.

"Let the games begin," said Cole as he turned his head to face her, his left hand on the seat and his right hand raised above his head holding the handle.

Diana drove southwest on 25th Bay Street, skidded through a left turn onto Pretty Lake ahead of the other carts, and headed toward the marina.

"By the way." Cole put his hand on Diana's forearm. "When this is over, let's have that long overdue talk about our future together."

Her head tilted slightly to her left side and she burst out laughing. Over her laughter, she shouted, "You're such an ass. This is how you tell me you want to get married?"

Cole's demeanor dissolved into laughter. "Yeah. I guess it is. Not very romantic, huh?"

"Jeez, I pick 'em'," replied Diana.

They arrived at the receiving dock twenty-five meters ahead of the next cart. As Cole slid out of the cart he turned back toward Diana, he reached in and touched her hand then gazed over the top of the cart. He saw a line of carts approaching. "Love you." He turned and staggered like a drunk down the dock to the Kruzenshtern's waiting small boat. Before he reached the boat, Cole turned and saw Diana mouth the words, "I love you." She blew a kiss his way.

Cole placed Kulakov's hat on his head and walked up to the boat. The coxswain jumped to attention as Cole stepped in.

"Welcome back, Captain," said the coxswain.

Cole walked forward in the boat without saying a word and sat with his back to the coxswain. He raised his right arm in a lazy, drunken movement, and motioned the coxswain to take him back to the ship. He removed his hat and held it in his lap just as Kulakov had done earlier.

The coxswain backed away from the dock and turned forward into the channel, followed lighted buoys, green on the right and red on the left, toward the Bay. They made a left turn out of the channel and headed straight toward Kruzenshtern. It was dark on the water. At best, there was a quarter moon. A forty percent cloud cover had rolled in. The lights of all the tall ships at anchor reflected off the water, flickering like diamonds as the small waves changed the reflective angles. Cole remained with his back to the coxswain for the entire ride.

As they approached the Kruzeshtern, the officer of the deck onboard shouted, "The captain is returning."

The coxswain slowed the small boat as it approached the gangplank that had been lowered to water level.

The night air on the water was cool. Still, Cole felt beads of perspiration on his forehead. *For the love of god, I must have lost my mind,* Thought Cole. *If Choesler ain't there, I'm a dead man.*

The small boat was about three meters from the platform at the bottom of the gangplank when Cole saw two ships' officers descending the ladder to greet him.

Easy . . . Easy . . . Focus. Just execute the plan.

As the small boat drifted slowly toward the platform, Cole stood. A sharp pain in his side caused him to grimace, and he placed his hand there. He put Kulakovs' cap on his head and stepped forward. At one meter out, Cole pretended to lose his balance and fell forward. As he did so, he dipped his head so the hat would fall into the small boat. He slapped his hand hard against the gangplank platform to make it sound like he'd hit his head.

Splash. In the water, Cole immediately swam downward and toward the back of the ship.

***

Choesler loitered at a depth of twenty feet near the large rudder of the Kruzenshtern for about ten minutes. He had left the restricted area at Joint Expeditionary Base Little Creek forty minutes earlier and was seated in a prototype SEAL torpedo underwater delivery vehicle. The vehicle was battery powered and could accommodate one additional swimmer and equipment in the open area behind the pilot.

He wore a Draeger rebreather to ensure that no air bubbles would rise to the surface that could indicate the presence of divers in the water during the operation. The Dreager was a closed-circuit breather system. The diver's breath was recycled and filtered through carbon dioxide and reused as breathable air.

To compensate for the near total darkness below the surface, Choesler also wore a diver night vision system that allowed him to see objects as far away as twenty meters with a forty-degree field of view.

Choesler saw Cole as soon as he entered the water. He piloted the vehicle down to the bottom depth of thirty-five feet, in the direction of Cole. He deposited the vehicle on the sandy bottom directly below the keel, and attached a velcro strap around his ankle at the end of a rope tether. He unstrapped a second Draeger from where it was loaded in the passenger area, threw it over his shoulder and swam toward Cole, who had dived to a depth twenty feet above him near the keel.

***

Cole held his breath after he hit the water. Although it was pitch darkness, he stroked and dove deeper. Each stroke felt like a punch in his already sore ribs. He knew from his experience as a certified diver, that with each stroke he took he was burning oxygen. Without air, and with each stroke, carbon dioxide was accumulating in his blood. His body began to react to the absence of oxygen, and he fought the instinctual urge to inhale.

His lungs burned as he fought the powerful urge to breathe. *Do not breathe!* The pain from his bruised ribs was exacerbated by an excruciating chest pain caused by lack of oxygen. He would soon reach the point when he could hold his breath no longer. He stopped swimming downward and flipped around so his legs were now below him and his arms outstretched as he frantically swung his head from side to side looking for some sign that Choesler was nearby. He saw nothing. *Shit! I have to surface!*

Just as Cole began to kick his legs upward, a powerful grip took hold of his left ankle and pulled him down. Cole looked down and saw the dim green light of Choesler's night vision device get closer and then felt the SEAL's hand grab him behind his neck and place a breathing tube against his lips. Cole grabbed the mouthpiece with both hands, placed it in his mouth just as he exhaled and made room in his lungs for the much-needed oxygen. The pain in his chest subsided.

With Choesler pulling and guiding him deeper, Cole pulled the Draeger over his chest. Choesler helped him strap it on. They reached the vehicle on the bottom, and Choesler handed Cole a diver facemask which he placed over his face and secured the straps on the back of his head while Choesler guided him into his seat behind the cockpit.

Cole attempted to clear the mask of water but was unable to keep an airtight seal because of the synthetic wig he wore to impersonate

Kulakovs hair color and cut. His eyes burned from the salt water. He undid the mask straps, removed the wig and placed it in his pocket before he replaced the mask and attached the Draeger to it. This allowed him to breathe normally, inhale through the mouthpiece and exhale through his nose. Choesler secured the passenger seat straps. Cole looked up and saw narrow light beams searching the surface. He knew it would only be a matter of minutes before rescue swimmers entered the water. *Gotta go, gotta go!*

Cole was about to signal the urgency to Choesler when he saw him quickly and effortlessly slide into the cockpit and immediately Cole felt the forward surge of the vehicle as Choesler turned the control to full throttle. He made an immediate right turn and headed away from the anchorage, staying close to the bottom. As they cruised away at seven knots, Cole turned to look back toward the anchorage. He saw only darkness. *We did it.*

CHAPTER FIFTY-ONE

Naval Air Station, Norfolk, Virginia
7th of June

Ramburt's black Escalade had black tinted side and rear windows. It was met at Norfolk Naval Station Gate Four by a Naval Police escort vehicle one hour before midnight. After a brief conversation and identification check with the officer, they drove down Air Cargo Road along the outer perimeter of the naval air station. With the police vehicle in the lead, they passed through runway security and stopped at a British Airways Airbus A320 parked on the apron in front of the Air Mobility Command passenger terminal.

The vehicle sat at the base of the staircase for several minutes with the engine running until the pilot of the aircraft stepped onto the top platform of the staircase. He wore an impeccable white shirt with captain's epaulets on the shoulders and gold wings on his chest.

Ramburt turned to face his passengers in the rear seat. "Okay, there's the pilot. You guys stay put. I'll go talk with him and make sure he understands what's happening here."

Both passengers nodded. Ramburt turned toward the driver and ordered, "Kill the interior lights. I don't want them to flash on when I open the door. You never know who's watching."

The driver turned the interior light switch off. "Done boss."

Ramburt opened the passenger side door, stepped out and slipped on his grey sports coat, which adequately hid his shoulder holster and Glock 42 sidearm. He walked toward the staircase. The door to the police escort vehicle opened and an officer, tall and lean, with biceps the size of an average man's thigh, walked over to him.

As he approached, in a deep voice the officer said, "I don't even want to know who your passengers are, Mr. Director." He looked around the concrete apron. "But this *is* highly unusual."

Ramburt nodded without comment.

"If you like though, I'll stay here in case you need anything else."

"Thanks." Ramburt looked at the officer's large chest and noted his nametag on the charcoal grey uniform. "Officer Coolidge, I'm sure I won't need anything else, but I'd appreciate it if you did stick around."

"I'll be right here next to the car, sir." The officer tapped his forefinger on the bill of his grey cap and stepped back to his vehicle.

Ramburt climbed the stairs to meet the pilot who still stood at the top platform.

"I assume you must be Director Ramburt," said the pilot.

"That's correct."

The pilot nodded. They shook hands. "This is quite unusual, Director, but I have been asked to cooperate with you if at all possible. I understand you have two passengers that need to go to London."

"Yes, that's correct." Ramburt assessed the pilot's demeanor. He seemed wary. "Sir," Ramburt continued, "this has been approved by both of our governments. I assure you there will be no negative consequences for your help tonight." He stepped closer to the pilot and guided him back toward the entrance of the aircraft. "As I'm sure you have ascertained, there is a good deal of secrecy in this affair. But we will not ask you to do anything illegal or unethical. We just need to quietly slip these passengers into London."

The pilot's eyes were riveted on Ramburt. "Director, as I said, I have been told to cooperate with you fully, and I intend to do so."

"Excellent," replied Ramburt. The two of them stopped just inside the aircraft and faced one another.

"Director," the pilot said, "I am sorry that I have to ask this, but will the passengers be able to legally pass through our customs and passport control at Heathrow?"

"Yes, yes, of course. As I said. Everything is perfectly legal. Just a little under the radar."

"I see. Well, we only have a minimal flight crew onboard, Director," advised the pilot, "but we'll do our best to see to your passenger's comfort. We've had some box lunches prepared, but that's about all we can offer."

"That won't be a problem. If they can just make some coffee, they'll be fine." Ramburt turned and exited the aircraft. He stood on the platform and gave the thumbs up signal to his driver.

The doors to the Escalade opened. A man and woman stepped out. They each wore jeans and a black hoodie that covered their heads. The driver stepped around to the back of the Escalade and opened the rear liftgate. He reached in and handed each of them a large suitcase. The two climbed the staircase and met Ramburt at the top. He escorted them into the aircraft.

"Welcome to British Airways flight . . . whatever," commented the pilot. "Please make yourselves comfortable. We'll fire up the engines and be on our way."

The two passengers stowed their luggage between seats in the first-class cabin and fell into a pair of seats on the starboard side.

The passengers had slits for eyes. "It's been a long day," Ramburt commented. "You two need some rest." He turned and walked to the cockpit and stuck his head inside. "Captain, The United States of America thanks you." Ramburt tapped his fingers on his forehead in a quick salute. "Have a safe flight, gentlemen." He turned and walked out of the aircraft onto the platform. The co-pilot closed and secured the cabin door.

***

Oastes Creek was located off the end of runway 10 on Naval Air Station Norfolk. On the east side of the creek was an established middle-class neighborhood with two-story homes, large yards, boat docks and a mature tree line that bordered the edge of the creek. One home was situated on a cul-de-sac. For twenty-two years, it had been occupied by an elderly couple who, according to neighbors, kept to themselves.

The couple sat side-by-side on a wooden deck bench. The man held a set of Russian-made Baigish long range binoculars up to his eyes that provided sharp definition optics to distances in excess of two miles in darkness. His wife had a tablet computer on her lap.

The man lit a citronella candle to help with the mosquito-infested evening. Toads croaked and large bass slapped their fins on the water as they fed on the abundant bug population.

"They have buttoned up the airplane. It is taxiing to the runway," said the old man.

"Are those two mysterious people still onboard?" asked the wife.

"Yes, they are."

The aircraft began its takeoff roll down the runway.

The man dictated to his wife. She tapped his words on the tablet. "The unusual arrival of a large British Airways jetliner in the late afternoon on June 7th, was followed by five hours of inactivity. The following observation was of interest. The terminal area was darkened at 2230, followed by the arrival of a police-escorted vehicle. Two persons, one male and one female, embarked on the aircraft of interest. Unable to provide further information on passengers."

"This is most unusual," said the woman.

"Yes, it is. Why would a large commercial airplane from Great Britain land here and only pick up two passengers? This will interest the directorate in Moscow."

"I will prepare a coded message."

"Yes." The man yawned. "Then we should sleep. It has been a very long day. Look, it is after midnight."

CHAPTER FIFTY-TWO

New London, Connecticut
15th of July

Leaders from the United States, Russia, Canada, and other Arctic nations met for a three-day conference at the U.S. Coast Guard Academy to discuss safety and environmental cooperation in the Arctic. On the final day of the meeting, Secretary Perry and Russian Foreign Minister Sergie Alekseyev had a private breakfast.

Secretary Perry and Minister Alekseyev were seated near a window overlooking the parade field. A mess specialist first class had just placed a silver pot containing fresh coffee on the table. He stepped away while a second petty officer cleared some empty plates from the table. Secretary Perry was spreading strawberry jam on a piece of toast. Minister Alekseyev placed his napkin on the table.

Secretary Perry looked up over his spectacles. Alekseyev was looking at the coffee pot on the table. He wore a frown, and his eyes were half closed.

"Mr. Secretary," said Alekseyev, "thank you for this meeting. I must admit that I was pleasantly surprised that your positions on the subject of the Arctic waters had considered many of concerns of my Security Council. You're understanding of my nations' positions was somewhat of a surprise. I am pleased that we have covered many important subjects, and I believe the Arctic will be a safer place because of the agreements that we have made these past few days."

Perry smiled and nodded. The Russian had opened the door for a discussion filled with falsehoods and half-truths. Neither would admit to any wrong-doings, and no accusations would be leveled. These two were diplomats, and they were both fluent in the language of lies.

Alekseyev brought his hand to his chin. "But there are unresolved circumstances that I am compelled to mention."

Perry stopped spreading the jam. "I'm listening."

"The disappearance of Captain First Rank Kulakov and his wife." His brow furrowed, and deep lines on his forehead were pronounced.

"Minister Alekseyev," replied Perry irritably. "We have discussed this already. You have our Coast Guard report on the accident. He was intoxicated. He fell overboard and drowned."

"Yes. But the remains have never been found."

Perry put the knife and toast on a plate and leaned forward with both elbows on the table to match Alekseyev's stance. "Sergei, it's all in the report. The Coast Guard searched for ninety-six hours, with divers and helicopters, yet found no trace of Captain Kulakov. As the report states, the ebb current was strong that night. The most likely scenario is that he was carried out to sea by the current."

He sat back in his chair. "And as far as his wife is concerned . . ." he paused briefly before continuing. "Really Sergei? That accident happened in Siberia. What is it that you think we would know about that?"

Alekseyev sat silent and turned to look out the window. After a brief pause, he turned back to face Perry and spoke tersely. "A crash site has never been located." He tapped the palm of his hand on the table. "And through sources, we have learned of a British airliner that landed at your Norfolk Naval Air Station on the same evening that Captain Kulakov went missing."

Perry sat stone-faced and resisted the urge to protest that his counterpart had just admitted to spying on naval base activity. He leaned forward on one elbow, his jaw clenched. "Minister, I don't see the connection to this conversation."

"Our source informed us that this airliner stayed on the ground only a few hours and departed, presumably for London, with only two passengers. A man and a woman. This is unusual, is it not?"

Perry angrily tossed his napkin down on the table. Alekseyev glared angrily back at him. "Minister Alekseyev, if that happened, and I emphasize *if*, I might agree that it is unusual for a civilian aircraft to land at a military facility but it is by no means unprecedented. There are times when a diplomat travels that commercial airports cannot provide adequate security." Perry paused, his stare fixed angrily at

Alekseyev. "Sir, you are treading very close to making an accusation against the United States of America."

Alekseyev began to speak, but was interrupted by Perry. "Captain Kulakov is dead. I don't know anything about what happened to Mrs. Kulakov other than what I have read, and what you have shared with me previously. You told me there had been a loss of cabin pressure, and all onboard succumbed to hypoxia. By your own admittance, this was confirmed by your own fighter jets that were scrambled to investigate when the flight veered off course. So, tell me Sergie, what is it you believe we would know about that?"

"Mr. Secretary, I do not presume to accuse the United States of any crime." Alekseyev stood and pushed his chair away from the table. "It is simply the circumstances of the *disappearance* of Captain Kulakov and his wife," he said sarcastically, "have raised some suspicion that they may have survived their ordeals and are alive and quite possibly are living within the large Russian ex-patriot community in London. If that is the case, they will eventually be discovered. Well," he said smugly, "Mr. Secretary, that might lead to some embarrassing questions for the governments of Britain and the United States. I would simply like to give you the opportunity to avoid such circumstances."

Perry also stood, towering a head taller than Alekseyev. "That, sir, is a circumstance that I will not lose any sleep over because it cannot happen." Perry stepped away from the table and stood, facing Alekseyev. "Might I suggest, Minister, that you send the same Russian television news crew that you sent to Norfolk to *greet* Captain Kulakov on his arrival to London and charge them to seek out the captain and his wife."

Alekseyev narrowed his eyes.

"Did you think that the CIA was not aware that those men were FSB operatives?"

"Mr. Secretary, I assure you —— —"

"Thank you, Minister Alekseyev, for joining me for breakfast." Perry stepped around the table. "Now, I believe this meeting is over. I'll see you out."

"That is not necessary, sir. I will see myself out. Thank you for inviting me." He turned to face the petty officers. "My compliments to the chef and the staff."

Alekseyev walked to the suite door that led to the hallway outside. As he placed his hand on the doorknob, he turned to face Perry.

"Sergei," said Perry as he seated himself at the table again, "you're chasing ghosts."

"Perhaps you're right," replied Alekseyev. He smiled and nodded his head. "Good day, sir." He opened the door and left, closing it softly behind him.

Perry picked up the toast and jam and took a bite as he poured another cup of coffee from the silver pot. *So, he believes they are alive and living in London.* Perry turned toward the window and noticed the smile in his reflection off of the glass.

EPILOGUE

Pyotr and Oksana Kulakov walked hand in hand on the La Jolla beach just before sunset.

Oksana put her head on his shoulder and spoke in Russian, "Do you think we will ever see Cole and Diana again?"

"I doubt that. I would think that would be very dangerous for us."

"That makes me sad."

They walked for a few minutes without speaking then Oksana broke the quiet. "I love our evening walks, Pyotr. They are so peaceful."

"Mrs. Postojna. Mrs. Anica Postojna," he replied softly in English. "You must stop calling me Pyotr. The Americans have given us these new identities and a new way of life." He stopped and looked her in the eyes. "Pyotr Kulakov no longer exists. I am now Doctor Gregor Postojna. I am an immigrant from Slovenia and a professor of European history at the University."

They both turned to look at the sunset.

"Yes. You are right. But, it will be hard to forget the past." With her head still on his shoulder she looked up and into his eyes. "Let's just sit here and watch."

Doctor Gregor Postojna and his wife Anica spread a blanket on the beach, sat down and opened a bottle of cabernet sauvignon from a California winery.

"It's so beautiful when the sun drops into the Pacific, and the sky turns orange," said Anica.

***

CIA Headquarters

Langley, Virginia
17th of July

Ramburt sat at his desk with his morning cup of coffee and reviewed emails on his classified network. He then opened his unclassified email account, and the third one that he read was from Cole Draper.

Hey Todd,
London is great! Please thank your uncle Samuel for allowing us to use his flat in Kensington. It's a great neighborhood and a great location. Quiet, good restaurants, a short walk to the tube station. Wish it didn't have to end, but oh well, all good things must. I've attached a few pictures of Diana and I enjoying the sights. And I thought that you might want to see this photo of Diana's new manicure.

- Cole and Diana in front of Buckingham Palace Change of the Guard.
- Cole and Diana by the lagoon in Hyde Park.
- Cole and Diana with Big Ben in the background.
- A photograph of Diana's hand with a modest engagement ring.

See you soon,
Cole

Ramburt laughed out loud.

Acknowledgements

To Candy and Brandon.

It also needs to be said that this story never would have been written without the guidance, support, and enthusiasm of my friends and members of the East Beach Writer's Guild. Special thanks to Sally Parrott (writes as Jayne Ormerod) and Mike Owens for their steadfast encouragement and mentorship.

Also by PATRICK CLARK

The Monroe Decision (July 31, 2017)

When US covert operative Aaron Monroe is given the assignment to eliminate two high profile ISIS leaders, he discovers dozens of children locked in rooms in the basement of a European villa. He enlists the help of Sarah, his socialite girlfriend, and together they uncover a pipeline that supplies child brides and terrorist recruits to ISIS. Just when he is about to close the case, Monroe is betrayed. No one is above suspicion, not even members of his own agency. Filled with action and intrigue across the globe, the Monroe Decision is a thrill ride that could come from tomorrow's news.

By the Bay 2; More East Beach Stories (April 28, 2017)

Fourteen fictional tales written by members of the East Beach Writer's Guild, about life along the Chesapeake Bay. The neighborhood of East Beach in Norfolk, Virginia is the setting for these vignettes of family, friendship, mystery, history, adventure, love, and light-hearted fun. Join the characters as they walk the tree-lined streets, stroll the sandy shores, or relax on a rocking chair on one of the deep front porches that define this community. By the Bay 2: More East Beach Stories is the perfect beach read, whether you've got your toes in the sand or simply wished you did. Patrick's short stories; *Boneyard*, and *The Town Hall Incident*, are included in this anthology.

By the Bay (July 23, 2015)

By the Bay, East Beach Stories is a collection of twelve fictional tales written by members of the east Beach Writer's Guild, about life along the Chesapeake Bay. They range from murderous to romantic, from humorous to dramatic, from gritty noir to political thriller to the sweet and the spiritual. The thread that ties them together is their connection to a 100-acre peninsula in Norfolk, Virginia. East Beach is nestled on the shores of the southernmost point of the Chesapeake Bay. Patrick's short story, *Dead Drop*, is included in this anthology.

Visit PATRICK CLARK'S website at www.patrick-clark.com or on Facebook @patrickclarkauthor

www.ingramcontent.com/pod-product-compliance
Lightning Source LLC
Chambersburg PA
CBHW071515110726

47908CB00003B/850